"I'm not a female who will cling and ask favors of a man.

"I'll do my duty by your children and your house. That's what you told me you expected of me."

His eyes narrowed. "I think we'll come to an understanding eventually, ma'am. In the meantime, we'll just have to work it out as we go."

She was a magnificent specimen of womanhood, he decided. Standing tall, as if her spine were made of finest steel, yet only reaching his shoulder in height. She was a strong woman, carrying a graceful figure, with hair not quite golden, but rather, streaked and honey-colored. Her eyes were the true blue of her ancestors, her slender body well-proportioned. And then he allowed his gaze to scan the length of her.

Her cheeks had turned more than rosy with his scrutiny, and she pursed her mouth. "Do I pass muster, sir?"

Dear Reader,

This month we're celebrating love "against all odds" with these four powerful romances!

Carolyn Davidson's voice has a warmth to it that always assures a happily-ever-after for her characters, even during moments of great adversity. Set in Minnesota, *The Midwife* is the poignant story of Leah Gunderson, a young "spinster" fleeing from her past as a midwife, and Garlan Lundstrom, the taciturn farmer who presses Leah into helping care for his newborn after his wife dies in labor. Leah has secretly admired Garlan from afar, which makes it all the more complicated when he proposes a marriage in name only….

Lady of the Knight by rising star Tori Phillips tells the tale of a courtly knight who buys a "soiled dove" and wagers that he can pass her off as a noble lady in ten days' time. The more difficult charade, though, lies in ignoring their feelings for one another! Catherine Archer returns with *Winter's Bride,* a medieval novel about a noble lady, long thought dead, whose past and present collide when she is reunited with her beloved and overcomes her amnesia.

Rounding out the month is Barbara Leigh's *The Surrogate Wife,* set in the Carolinas in the late 1700s. In this story of forbidden love, the heroine is wrongly convicted of murdering the hero's wife, and is sentenced to life as his indentured servant….

Whatever your tastes in reading, you'll be sure to find a romantic journey back to the past between the covers of a Harlequin Historicals® novel.

Sincerely,

Tracy Farrell
Senior Editor

Please address questions and book requests to:
Harlequin Reader Service
U.S.: 3010 Walden Ave., P.O. Box 1325, Buffalo, NY 14269
Canadian: P.O. Box 609, Fort Erie, Ont. L2A 5X3

Carolyn Davidson

THE MIDWIFE

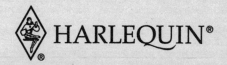

HARLEQUIN®

TORONTO • NEW YORK • LONDON
AMSTERDAM • PARIS • SYDNEY • HAMBURG
STOCKHOLM • ATHENS • TOKYO • MILAN • MADRID
PRAGUE • WARSAW • BUDAPEST • AUCKLAND

ISBN 0-373-29075-6

THE MIDWIFE

Copyright © 1999 by Carolyn Davidson

This edition published by arrangement with Harlequin Books S.A.

® and TM are trademarks of the publisher. Trademarks indicated with
® are registered in the United States Patent and Trademark Office, the
Canadian Trade Marks Office and in other countries.

Visit us at www.romance.net

Printed in U.S.A.

CAROLYN DAVIDSON

Reading and writing have always been major interests in Carolyn Davidson's life. Even during the years of raising children and working a full-time job, she found time to read voraciously. However, her writing consisted of letters and an occasional piece of poetry. Now that the nest is empty, except for three grandchildren, she has turned to writing as an occupation.

Her family, friends and church blend to make a most fulfilling existence for this South Carolina author. And most important is her husband of many years, the man who gives her total support and an abundance of love to draw on for inspiration. A charter member of the Lowcountry Romance Writers of America, she has found a community of soul mates who share her love of books, and whose support is invaluable.

Watch for her next Harlequin Historical novel, *The Bachelor Tax,* coming in January. She enjoys hearing from her readers at P.O. Box 2757, Goose Creek, SC 29445-2757, and promises to answer your letter.

The Midwife came into being because of my granddaughter, Rachel, a wonderful young lady who aspires to that profession. When she asked me to write a book about a midwife, I agreed to consider it, and was surprised and delighted when she sent me a brief outline of a story. Although I chugged down a different road and steered in different directions than she, and even though I added characters I thought were important to my book, this is basically Rachel's midwife story. To her I dedicate the total effort, with all good wishes that her dream will one day be fulfilled.

And as always, to Mr. Ed, who loves me.

Chapter One

Kirby Falls, Minnesota
January 1892

"It's a pity that such a handsome man should always look so forbidding." Bonnie Nielsen's eyes cast a longing look at the man she spoke of.

"He's married, Bonnie." Leah mentally calculated her purchases and searched through her purse for coins, spending barely a glance in the direction of the man in question. He stood on the outskirts of a group of menfolk who clustered around the stove in one corner of the general store. His arms were crossed, his mouth formed in a thin line, and he did indeed glower, Leah decided as she favored him with a second look.

Bonnie's cheeks flushed a becoming pink and she looked up at her customer through a pale fringe of lashes. "All the good-looking ones are. More's the pity!" Her hands were making quick work of Leah's sparse selections, and she tied the package deftly as she spoke.

"Don't you even look at the men, Leah?" Bonnie

pushed the paper-wrapped bundle across the counter and accepted Leah's coins in return.

"It's enough that I wash their clothes. Why should I look at the men who wear them?" Leah picked up her foodstuffs, then made a liar out of herself as she allowed her gaze to pass over the group of men who were laughing at some private joke as they warmed themselves.

As always, her eyes hesitated, just for the smallest second, on the somber man, the tallest of the group. The one who said little, who seemed drawn to the noisy, friendly men, even though he appeared not to belong in their midst.

Gar Lundstrom. He did look forbidding. Bonnie had it right on the money. And yes, he was handsome, with pale hair that never darkened in the winter, as did her own. His eyes were striking, pale blue beneath dark brows, another puzzle. He should have been fair, right down to his eyebrows. Perhaps the hair on his chest…

Leah closed her eyes, aghast at the thought she had allowed to enter her mind. She'd been too long indoors, spent too many evenings alone, talked to herself too many hours on end.

And always, she kept the vision of Gar Lundstrom from her mind. Only when she caught sight of the man did she allow her thoughts to stray in his direction. But to what purpose? The man was someone's husband. Hulda Lundstrom was the woman he'd chosen to wed: a small, nondescript woman who seldom came to town, and whose son always remained close at hand when she did venture into the general store.

Lundstrom was no doubt on his way home now, Leah decided, taking care to turn aside as he said terse good-byes and made his way from the store. The talk resumed around the stove and Leah walked to the door, aware of eyes that watched her progress, her own gaze straight ahead, lest she mesh glances with one of the men who gathered on these winter mornings.

Most of them were married, but there were always, in their midst, one or two bachelors. Several had approached her, the elusive widow, hoping to strike a bargain of some sort.

She closed the door behind her and walked down the wooden sidewalk, her package dangling by the string with which it was tied. Tea, a bit of sugar, and a small piece of bacon weighed little, and cost less, but it had taken most of her cash. If the menfolk didn't pick up their bundles of laundry today, she would be hard-pressed to find money for the rent this month.

Her feet turned up the path to the small house she called home, and she stepped onto the porch, reaching for the doorknob.

"Yoo-hoo! Mrs. Gunderson!" From next door, a fragile voice called her name and Leah halted, one foot already past the threshold.

"Yes, Mrs. Thorwald," she answered, pulling the door closed, lest the heat escape. "Are you all right?"

"I believe I have a touch of the quinsy, dear," the old woman answered, barely visible behind the windowpanes, bending low to speak through the narrow opening she'd allowed above the sill.

"I put some soup bones on the stove to cook before I went to the store. I have to find some vegetables to put in with them, and then I'll bring you a bowl of soup when it's ready," Leah promised, knowing that, more than soup, the widow lady wanted companionship. She waved a hand as she opened her door again and stepped into the warmth of her parlor.

The heat from the kitchen cookstove permeated the

whole house, each room opening up into another. She could walk in a circle and visit each room within seconds. Leah hung her cloak by the front door and placed her boots on a mat beneath. Then she donned her knitted slippers.

Her skillet awaited, warming on the back of the shiny black stove. She unwrapped the bacon quickly, her mouth watering at the prospect of such a luxury this noontime. She sliced it, then placed the thick pieces in the pan, inhaling the scent as the edges began to sizzle.

A knock at the door halted her while she was pouring water from her teakettle into her favorite flowered cup.

"I'm coming," she called, her slippered feet silent as she crossed the parlor.

"It's Hobart Dunbar, Mrs. Gunderson," the man said loudly, as if he would allay any concern a man at her door might bring.

The owner of the only hotel in Kirby Falls was most circumspect, always careful to remain on her porch while she brought him the big bundle of tablecloths and aprons she washed and ironed with such care. Bleach and starch were commodities he paid extra for, and gladly, since, as he'd told Leah upon their first encounter, his wife refused to spend half a day over a scrub board twice a week.

"Do come in, Mr. Dunbar," Leah said cordially, waving her hand to usher him in.

As always, he shook his head. "No, no. I'll just wait right here, ma'am. Close the door. Don't waste your heat." And all the while, he stamped his feet and shrugged his ears down into the collar of his heavy coat, until the brim of his hat met with it.

Leah hastened to the room she used as her laundry and snatched up the washing she'd completed late last evening. Wrapped in a stained sheet, the bundle contained sparkling white, heavily starched linens. Even the caps that Mr. Dunbar's three waitresses wore when they served tables had been ironed and creased, ready to be buttoned at the back when the wearers donned them.

The three women also cleaned the hotel rooms and lobby daily, in between mealtimes, a sign of Hobart Dunbar's frugality. Even his wife took her turn, standing behind the walnut desk, her lacy handkerchief attached to the front of her dress, her hair curled and pinned, her eyes ever watchful.

Mr. Dunbar accepted his laundry and pressed his money into Leah's hand with a nod. "Thank you, Mrs. Gunderson. I'll send the boy over tomorrow night with another batch." He backed from her door and Leah closed it quickly, her fingers closing over the coins that were cold against her palm.

Through the glass that centered her front door, she watched as another gentleman passed through her gate, pausing to speak with the hotel owner. Quickly she hurried to find the appropriate bundle of laundry for Brian Havelock, knowing only too well that he would more than welcome an offer to enter her parlor.

Leah was breathless from her hasty movements when she opened the door for him, her smile barely moving her lips. "I thought I saw you coming through the gate," she said brightly.

Brian peered past her into the house. "Are you all alone, Leah? Can I join you for a cup of tea, perhaps?"

She shook her head. "No, I'm about to step over to visit with Mrs. Thorwald. She's not feeling well."

His disappointment was visible, and his gaze swept the length of her body, from the crown of her head to where her slippers peeked from beneath the hem of her dress. "I'd really enjoy spending time with you, you know." His words were wistful, and he smiled with beguiling charm.

Leah sighed. "I know what you want, Mr. Havelock. At the risk of being too bold, I must tell you that I am not available for such a thing."

"My intentions are otherwise, Leah," he said quickly, a blush climbing his cheeks, turning them even more rosy than the wind had done.

She blinked, mouth open and mind wiped clean as he denied her accusation. "Otherwise?" she said after a moment.

He nodded, edging closer to her. "I'd like to come calling on you, ma'am."

"I thought you were courting Kirsten Andersen," Leah said bluntly. Her hand waved distractedly. "No matter. I'm entirely too old for you, Mr. Havelock, and too busy to waste either my time or yours."

"Will you at least dance with me Saturday night?" he asked hopefully.

She nodded quickly, willing to promise that small boon, if only he would leave her house with his clean underwear and work clothes.

He smiled eagerly, counting out the money he owed her, managing to squeeze her fingers as he placed the coins in her palm. "I'll plan on it, Leah."

She shut the door behind him and leaned back against its cold surface. Now if he were only taller, with wide shoulders and the hands of a... She shook her head. The image in her mind was forbidden to her, the features of Gar Lundstrom taking form behind her closed eyes.

Never in her almost thirty years had she found herself in such little control of the thoughts and desires she lived with daily. Garlan Lundstrom had done nothing, said nothing, to insinuate himself into her mind. And yet he dwelt there.

She bent her head. From the very first time, over a year ago when she'd seen him in church, she'd felt a yearning for the man and scolded herself all during the long walk home. He was married.

And she was Leah Gunderson, wash lady to most of the bachelors in town. Not that that was anything to be ashamed of. On top of that, she was fairly skilled in the art of healing, enough so that she had been called upon to sew up cuts and set broken bones.

Her skills as a midwife were not known to the townspeople, and never would be, she had decided from the first. The doctor who tended the new mothers was old and beyond his prime, content to let the widow lady on the back side of town care for the odds and ends of healing that came her way.

Yet Leah mourned for the disuse of those abilities she had learned in her young years. She'd visited women in all stages of labor with her mother, Minna Polk. She'd helped with birthings from the time she was sixteen. And then called herself a widow in order to set up her own practice.

A single woman could not deliver children. There was a stigma against it that forbade such contact. Young girls were supposed to be innocent.

Innocence. Sometimes Leah could not remember the meaning of the word.

Laundry came first, as always, and the soup kettle was moved to the back of the stove so Leah could heat wash water in the copper boiler. She scrubbed on her board in between cutting up her store of vegetables for the kettle on the stove. The day was waning by the time she reached the bottom of Orville Hunsicker's laundry basket, and Leah hurried now to complete her mission to the neighbor who depended on her kindness.

The soup was a bit thin, but Mrs. Thorwald was most appreciative in any case, tasting each spoonful with appropriate murmurs.

"You are such a joy to have right next door," she said sweetly, her spoon scraping at the bottom of her bowl. "You'll never know how much I appreciate your company, dear."

Leah smiled, ashamed of her impatience, as she watched the old lady enjoy her soup. "I'm happy to help out," she said, pleasantly enough. Her mind raced ahead to the pile of washing she had yet to hang in her kitchen tonight. It would be dry by morning, and she would iron it before noon.

"Do you have any more of that salve you gave me to rub on my chest, dear?" Peering up at Leah, the wizened old woman's eyes were rheumy and her mouth trembled.

A pang of guilt struck Leah. "Of course, I have. I'll just run home and bring it back to you, Mrs. Thorwald." She rose and eyed her soup kettle. "Why don't you just keep the rest of the soup, and I'll take the kettle home to wash."

Mrs. Thorwald's eyes brightened, and the widow nodded eagerly. "It'll be just the thing for my quinsy, won't it, dear?"

Leah donned her boots and coat and let herself out the front door, walking on the path to the gate to her own yard. The sun had gone down, and dusk had settled while she sat in the widow's kitchen. Beneath her feet, the snow was too deep to attempt crossing the yards.

"I feel I've adopted a grandmother," Leah muttered

to herself, stomping up the stairs to her house. And that wasn't all bad, she admitted silently. It was just that some day, she yearned—

"Mrs. Gunderson."

The voice was dark, deep and richly resonant. It halted her in her tracks, one foot on the porch, the other on the top step. From the shadows beneath the steep roof, a tall figure stepped forward, and Leah watched as one long arm reached up to scoop the wide-brimmed hat from his head.

"Ma'am?" That single word held the power to set her heart beating almost double time, and Leah pressed her palm against her chest.

"I'm sorry, ma'am. I didn't mean to frighten you."

Leah made her way slowly, carefully, to her door, her legs trembling as she turned to face Gar Lundstrom. "You only startled me, Mr. Lundstrom. I was thinking about my neighbor. About her quinsy, actually." She peered up at him. "What can I do for you?"

"I'm not sure, ma'am. I was told you might be able to help, since the doctor is…indisposed," he said carefully.

She leaned forward. "Are you hurt? Have you sustained a wound?"

He shook his head. "No, it's not me, ma'am." He stepped closer and she caught sight of his face, strained and anxious in the twilight.

"What, then? Your boy?"

"My wife. She is about to give birth, and she needs help. The women in the store have told me you are learned in the art of healing, and I thought—"

"I don't deliver babies, Mr. Lundstrom," Leah interjected forcefully. "I can sew up a cut or give herbs for some ailments, but babies are the business of the doctor.''

''He's—''

''Yes, you said. Not available.''

He stepped closer, and his dark eyes burned with an intensity that stopped Leah's breath in her throat. ''I've driven my team hard to come back to town, ma'am. I fear to leave my wife alone longer.'' He reached to grip Leah's arm. ''I need you to come with me. Surely you know about birthing babies. There is no one else to ask.''

''Doesn't your wife have any women friends?'' Leah asked, her voice hopeful.

He shook his head. ''She doesn't leave the farm much. Only to church, when she's able, and to the store.''

''I haven't seen her for quite some time.'' Leah tried to remember the last occasion.

''She's been in bed most of the time. For months,'' Gar Lundstrom said tightly. ''She's not been well.''

''I can't do it,'' Leah told him, tilting her chin and gritting her teeth as she faced him.

His eyes narrowed as he looked at her. ''You must. There is no one else. My wife needs your help.''

She shook her head even as her heart raced in response. How could she turn this man away, knowing that, as they spoke, his wife was probably in the throes of labor, alone in a farmhouse, miles outside of town.

Gar Lundstrom's big hand slid up her forearm and gripped her elbow more firmly. ''You must come with me. Do you need a warmer coat?''

He hesitated only a moment as she stared up at him. ''Come then,'' he said tightly, tugging her to the steps.

Leah closed her eyes. It was too much. How could

she deny the woman what small help she could give? Either she would deliver a healthy baby or she wouldn't. "I'll get my bag," she whispered, snatching her arm from his grip.

He followed her into the house, and she fumbled for the lamp, striking a match and lighting it quickly.

"Wait here," she said, striding purposefully through the doorway into her bedroom. Falling to her knees before the big chest she kept beneath the window, she opened it wide. Under her summer dresses was a leather bag, and she gripped the handles, feeling them warm in her palm.

She rose to her feet and drew a deep breath. It was happening again. She could feel the hopelessness grip her as she turned to face the man who had followed her into her bedroom. As if he were afraid she would disappear, he stood in the doorway, eyes alert and scanning the simple contents of her room.

"You needn't follow me, Mr. Lundstrom. I said I'd come with you."

He nodded his head. "Yes, you did." His eyes were bold as he surveyed her. "Are you stronger than you look, Mrs. Gunderson?" He waited for a moment and nodded again. "Yes, I think you are. You may need to be, ma'am."

He turned and she followed him, her gaze filled with the broad back, the slight hitch in his gait and the glow of his golden hair in the lamplight.

She blew out the lamp and they walked out onto the porch. "I need to tell my neighbor where I'm going, and I promised her some salve for her quinsy," she said, suddenly remembering Mrs. Thorwald. "Pick me up by her gate."

She hurried down the path, aware of his big sleigh

sitting in the street. It was a wonder she had not noticed it earlier.

Mrs. Thorwald accepted the jar of salve with thanks, then clucked her tongue knowingly as she heard Leah's words of explanation. "That one will keep you up all night, I'll warrant. She's what they call a hard delivery, Leah. Perhaps she's lucky the doctor's not available. He hasn't done her much good in the past."

With those words ringing cryptically in her ears, Leah made her way to the sleigh, where a gloved hand reached down to her. She hesitated for only a second, then placed her palm in that of Gar Lundstrom. He pulled her with little effort into his sleigh.

A fur robe was tucked over her lap, and Gar cast her one searching glance before he picked up the reins. Leah felt the heat of his body beside her, yet shivered as if an icy blast had cut through her covering.

"Sit closer," he said bluntly. "You need to stay warm." His big hand circled her shoulder, and he moved her across the seat until their thighs were brushing.

Leah swallowed words of protest that begged to be spoken. He was too big, too warm, too close; yet, for just a moment, she relished the warmth, the size and the nearness of the man. For just this short time, she allowed her mind to be blank of all else, to dwell only on the presence of Gar Lundstrom beside her.

The woman who labored on the big bed was as pitiful a sight as Leah had ever been exposed to. Hulda Lundstrom's dry lips were drawn back over clenched teeth and her hair hung lank with sweat. She groaned unceasingly.

In less than a second, Leah cast a glance around the

bedroom, tossed her cloak aside and placed her bag on a chair. "I need water to wash with, good hot water."

"Right away." Gar Lundstrom's voice was gruff with emotion as he left the room, Leah's cloak over his arm.

"How long have you been like this?" Leah asked Hulda Lundstrom, who panted harshly as her body convulsed with the pain of a violent contraction.

"Not long...a couple of hours maybe." Her voice was raw, weakened by her pain, and Hulda opened her eyes to reveal a dull acceptance of her state. "It's no worse than the other times." She rested, taking deep breaths as the pain left her, her body seeming to sink into the depths of the mattress.

"How many other times have there been?" Leah asked, looking up as the door opened and Gar backed into the bedroom, his hands cradling a basin of steaming water.

"Two. No, three. But one was only three months gone and it was nothing." Hulda's gaze fastened on her husband. "You don't need to be here, Gar. Go be with Kristofer," she whispered. "It will be a long time yet."

Leah turned to the man, anger rising in her throat. "You didn't tell me your wife was having a difficult labor. I think you need to go back to town and find the doctor. If she has lost several babies already, we need to use every precaution this time."

The wash water was deposited on the dressing table with care, lest it slosh over the edges. The tall man straightened to his full height, turning to face the bed.

"He won't come." There was a finality to his words that sent a chill down Leah's spine.

"He told her the last time that she would not be able to deliver a live child, that her organs were damaged from the other times. He said he would not be responsible for encouraging her in her foolish efforts.''

"Foolish efforts." Leah repeated the words without emotion, though her heart was pounding within her, and her anger rose even higher.

"I want to give my husband another child. Is that so bad?" Hulda's eyes filled with tears as she turned her head to look at Leah. And even as she spoke, she stiffened, groaning as another contraction knotted her belly. Her hands spread wide over the mound, and her head tipped back against the pillow as the pain ravaged her.

Leah stepped to the side of the bed and sat next to the woman who labored now in silence before her audience. "Wring out a cloth in the warm water," Leah said, glancing only momentarily at Gar, who watched from across the room.

He took a clean flannel square from atop a pile and wrung it out in the basin, then brought it to the bed. "Let me do this while you wash," he said quietly.

Leah rose, giving way to him, and walked across the room, rolling up her sleeves as she went. Immutable sadness enveloped her as she scrubbed at her hands with the carbolic soap she carried in her bag. The chances of a live birth seemed small, given Hulda Lundstrom's history. And yet, Leah must do all she could to birth a live child for this small, needy woman.

"Pull back the sheet," she told Gar, returning to the bed. "Then put a clean sheet or blanket beneath her."

"I don't…" Hulda gasped for a breath, her face contorting as she allowed a groan to escape her lips. "Leave, Gar. Go…I don't…"

"He can leave when he's done as I asked," Leah told her softly. "Let him lift you, Hulda. I want you to have clean bedding beneath you."

A nod signified Hulda's agreement, and Gar did as
Leah had requested. His big hands were gentle as he
slid them beneath his wife's limbs to spread a clean,
folded sheet under her lower body. He stood erect and
looked at Leah, awaiting further instructions, and she
was struck by the hopelessness in his eyes.

No longer the possessor of the dark, arrogant glare
of a strong man, he cast her only a pleading, anxious
look that begged mercy at her hands. "I'll be in the
kitchen if you want me."

Leah nodded and took his place on the side of the
bed. "Pull up your gown, Hulda," she said quietly. "I
want to feel the child."

Hulda's fingers twisted in the white flannel cloth, and
she tugged it high over her stomach, exposing the swollen mound that contained her child. As Leah watched,
it rippled, the muscles still strong as the womb fought
to expel its contents. She placed her hand against the
hard surface, closing her eyes as she felt for the body
parts within.

Nothing nudged her hand, no trace of movement,
only the pulsing rhythm of the pain that would not cease
until the child was delivered.

"Has the baby moved since you began laboring?"
she asked once the spasm had passed.

Hulda shook her head, her eyes closed. "For a bit,
then not so much." A sob escaped, and she spoke between gritted teeth. "This time he must live. I cannot
do this again."

For the first time, a cry passed through the lips of the
woman who suffered, and Leah called out for Gar, pulling Hulda's gown down over her writhing belly.

"Look in my bag and find the containers of dried
roots. I need the ones marked baneberry and wild yam.

Brew one piece of each, please, and make a cup of strong tea with it," she ordered, not ever looking up as he awaited her orders near the doorway. "It will ease her pain."

Gar hastened to do as she asked, and Leah heard the rattle of a kettle in the kitchen. In less than ten minutes, he was back.

"Here." He placed the cup on the bedside table and hovered for a moment. "There is more when this is gone. Can I do anything else?"

Her tone was sharp as Leah glanced up at him, rebuffing his offer. "You've done enough already."

His eyes narrowed as he caught her meaning and he retreated, shoulders stiff, as if he would deflect any further insult. The door closed behind him, and Leah picked up the cup and stirred the brew.

She filled the spoon, blowing a bit on its contents, then lifted it to Hulda's lips. "Here, open your mouth for me, Hulda," she said quietly.

Hulda obeyed, allowing the warm liquid to enter her mouth, and swallowed. Leah repeated the movements until the tea was half-gone. Then she swirled it in the cup, deeming it cool enough to drink.

"I want you to lift up, just a bit, and drink this down," she said, careful that the woman did not choke on the liquid as she drank.

There was no cessation of the labor, but as the tea began to work its magic, Leah whispered a prayer of thanksgiving. She lifted Hulda's gown again, easing her hands beneath, spreading them wide on the distended belly as another contraction made itself known. Then, as it reached its peak, Leah bent to watch for the sight of a baby's head, hoping fervently that the hours of labor had begun to reap some results.

There was no sign of imminent birth, only a steady leaking of bloody fluid. The skin beneath her hand was stretched and taut as Hulda's body tried to complete this process.

It was not going well. Leah shook her head. She needed to know what was going on inside, there where the mouth of the womb held its prisoner. It must be done, she thought grimly, readying her hand with a coating of oil. She slid it within the straining woman's body and sought the opening of Hulda's womb. There, instead of the rounded head she prayed to come in contact with, she found twin globes—the buttocks of a baby. Too large to be born in this manner, the child was slowly tearing his mother asunder.

Leah withdrew her hand and sighed. "Is he dead?" Hulda whispered in a faint, hopeless voice. She had begun to perspire from every pore, it seemed, drenching her nightgown and the bed beneath her.

"No, he's alive," Leah said quietly. "It's a breech birth, Hulda. Our only chance is for me to turn the baby around."

"Then do what you must," the woman said, each word punctuated by a moan. "If I cannot give Garlan another son, I don't want to live."

"Your life is worth more to your husband than another child," Leah whispered fiercely.

Hulda shook her head in a hopeless gesture. "Nay, not so. But if I give him another live child, another son, perhaps he will love me."

Leah's eyes filled with useless tears, and she brushed at them with her forearm. "You will not die," she vowed. "You will not."

Chapter Two

Gar Lundstrom's face was pale and twisted with anguish, his eyes sunk deep from lack of sleep. His fists hung at his sides, and he swayed in place. As if he gathered energy from some unknown source, he lifted both hands beseechingly, then twisted them together as he glared at the woman who faced him.

"Why?" The single word seared the air, and Leah felt its lash, bracing herself against the scorn of the man before her.

"I'm not a doctor, Mr. Lundstrom. I'm a woman who knows a little about healing." Leah drew a deep breath, unable to absolve herself, even in her own mind, let alone free herself from the taint of guilt cast upon her by Gar Lundstrom.

"Have you ever delivered a child before, Mrs. Gunderson? Or was this the first time you've butchered a woman?" His voice rasped the accusation, his shoulders hunching as if he bore a great burden.

Leah was reluctant to answer, and yet she knew she must defend herself against the blame he cast on her. "I did not ask to come here, Mr. Lundstrom." She drew in a deep breath, as if to calm herself in the face of his accusations. "Yes, I have delivered other babies. But none whose mother presented such problems as your wife."

"She survived three times being brought to childbed before this. What could have caused..." He waved his hand as he groped for words to express the horror so vividly written on his face.

Leah shook her head wearily. "She was a small woman, delivering a breech baby." She raised her head and glared at him, determined not to let him brand her as careless. "I tried to turn the child, but it was not possible. You were here. You saw the bleeding. The birth was more than she could stand this time, Mr. Lundstrom."

Between them, Hulda lay beneath a clean sheet, her face serene in death. She was a slender bit of a woman, who, to Leah's mind, should not have been subjected to such an ordeal. An ordeal that had killed her.

Leah closed her eyes, as if she would erase the vision before her, as if death could be evaded so easily. "You'd better go into town and let the undertaker know, Mr. Lundstrom. See if there is anyone who can nurse the child for you."

From the depths of a small cradle in the far corner of the bedroom, a thin, fretful wail caught Leah's attention. "She sounds hungry now," she said quietly, then turned to answer the infant's cry.

Gar's glance followed Leah as she went to the child. "I will take my boy and make arrangements for my wife. There is milk in the washroom from this morning."

Leah looked from the window onto a freshly fallen snow. Sometime during the long night, several inches had created a pristine landscape. Now, beneath the

newly risen sun, it glistened and shimmered, offering a
clean slate on which to begin this day.

The fourteenth day of January. The birthdate of
Hulda Lundstrom's daughter.

Leah picked up the child, cuddling the slight form
against her breast, rocking back and forth to soothe her
cries. "There, there…" she whispered, breathing in the
newborn scent that never failed to touch a chord deep
within her.

"What will you call her?" she asked, sensing Gar's
lingering presence behind her.

"Hulda could not decide between Linnea or Karen."

"Karen is a good, strong name," Leah said. "She
can always take another name when she makes her first
communion."

Gar nodded and Leah watched as the tiny babe pursed
her lips and made a suckling movement. "So soon they
learn," she murmured.

Gar stood by the door, his head bent, his whole body
seeming to have shrunk during the long, stressful hours
of the night. "I'll go to the church and speak to the
pastor first. He is more likely to be up than the doctor."

"Where is your boy?" Leah asked. She'd heard the
soft murmuring of their voices, then the muted crying
of a child in the kitchen only minutes past. "Is he all
right?"

Gar cast her a scornful look. "His mother is dead.
He will never be 'all right' again." Turning abruptly,
he left the bedroom. Leah followed slowly, unwilling
to embarrass the grieving child by coming upon him
without warning.

She waited in the doorway as Gar led the boy from
the house and firmly closed the door behind them. On
weary legs, she made her way to the window, watching

as father and son walked through the snow to the barn, where Gar must have already harnessed the team to the sleigh.

Within moments he led the rig through the wide double doors, the young boy ensconced in the front seat with the fur lap robe warm about his small body. Gar joined his son on the carved seat and picked up the reins. With barely a glance back at the house, he set his team into motion and turned his sleigh toward town.

The milk warmed quickly on the stove. She poured a small amount into a saltshaker and tied a double layer of tightly woven flannel over the top. Holding the baby in her left arm, she allowed the milk to drip slowly into the child's mouth.

"A nipple would work much better," she whispered aloud, her little finger rubbing the babe's lips, coaxing her to open them enough for the milk to enter. "Maybe the doctor will think to send one back for you, little girl."

The baby twisted her head toward Leah's breast, opening her lips in a timeless gesture. "I cannot help you, sweetheart," Leah crooned, coaxing the tiny lips with a slow drip, drip, drip of skimmed milk. "This is the best I can offer for now."

It was a frustrating task, but Leah knew it well and she worked patiently with the baby for almost an hour, until both infant and woman were well nigh exhausted from their efforts. At least an ounce or so of the milk had gone down the baby's throat, Leah guessed, the rest of it dampening the blanket she was wrapped in.

"I must bathe you, little girl," she sang in a tuneless fashion. "But not until you've had time to sleep a bit and gain some strength from your nourishment." A pillow provided a sleeping place for the baby, and Leah anchored it on two chairs, near the stove.

A ham bone with large bits of meat still attached sat on the kitchen bureau, covered by a dish towel, as if Hulda had planned for its use today, probably for soup. Making soup was the least she could do for the small family, Leah decided, transferring it to a kettle.

She cut up an onion, which she plucked from a string of them hanging from a ceiling beam, and added it to the kettle of water. A visit to the pantry, just off the kitchen, produced a quart of tomatoes, and she added that too, along with a measure of dry beans.

From the looks of it, Hulda had planned well for the winter. Her pantry shelves were filled with the harvest from her garden. Leah's fingers rested on the jar she had just emptied, as if she might sense some lingering trace of the woman who had spent hours in this kitchen, providing for her family.

Her heart was heavy with a guilt she knew she didn't deserve yet must bear. Gar Lundstrom had been more at fault than she, with his need for more sons to work his farm. And for his efforts, he had gained a puny girl child. There seemed a sense of rightness about that, she thought.

The boy…she wrinkled her forehead as she considered him—Kristofer, Hulda had called him, who was now in the midst of plans for his mother's funeral. How would he survive such a loss? It was almost easier for the babe. She would never have known a mother's love, and so could not miss it.

As for herself, her own life must be put to rights after the events of the past night. The laundry she'd left in a basket would need to be hung, for there would be at least two gentlemen banging on her door, looking for their clean clothes. And here she was, ten miles out in the country, tending a newborn baby.

For now, she would do what she could to help while she waited for Gar Lundstrom to come home. Sweeping the floors and dusting the furniture took but thirty minutes. And all during her efforts, she stayed far from the bedroom on the second floor, where Hulda Lundstrom lay beneath a white sheet.

Leah warmed a fresh bit of milk and spent another half hour feeding the baby, then washed the infant with tender care before rocking her in the big oak chair in the parlor.

The ham was falling off the bone by the time the sleigh traveled past the kitchen window. Close behind it came the black, covered vehicle that Joseph Landers drove when the occasion called for it. Leah went to the door, shivering from the cold draft of air as the menfolk came in.

"Kristofer, stand near the stove and warm yourself," Gar said abruptly to his son, and Leah watched as the boy obeyed. His thin hands were red from the cold, and his nose and ears were the same rosy hue. His eyelids barely lifted as he passed Leah, the skin swollen around each eye as if he had spent the whole time aboard the sleigh crying.

And so he probably had, she thought, shaking her head as she watched the boy. He rubbed his hands together, then wiped his nose on his shirtsleeve. Leah pulled the square of cotton from her own pocket and pressed it into his hand.

"Thank you, ma'am." His child's voice was rough with the tears he had shed, and Leah felt a pang as her heart ached for his loss. This was a house of sorrow, and it weighed heavily on her.

She watched the men proceed to the second floor, heard their footsteps as they entered the bedroom over her head, and listened to the soft murmur of voices through the vent in the kitchen ceiling.

"Kristofer?" Leah tasted his name upon her tongue, liking the sound of it. Had his mother chosen it? Likely so. Gar would probably have preferred Lars or Igor or some such harsh-sounding name. Kristofer was a name a mother would choose for her tow-haired son.

"Ma'am?" The boy looked up, his vivid blue eyes bloodshot with the hours of weeping he had done.

"Are you hungry, Kristofer?" she asked kindly. "I made you some beans and ham. You should try to eat something."

His gaze flickered toward the kettle on the stove and he licked his lips. "Yes, ma'am. I didn't have any breakfast."

Leah snatched the opportunity to perform a task, bustling about the kitchen, her movements masking the sounds from overhead. "Come to the sink and wash," she said, her keen hearing aware of the men on the stairway.

She stood behind the boy, her body a shield as the wrapped, frail body of his mother was carried through the kitchen. Then, as the back door closed behind the two men and their burden, she placed her hand on the boy's slender shoulder.

"Come, eat now. I'll slice you some bread to go with it," she offered, steering him to the table and pulling out the chair for him. He obeyed listlessly, only his trembling fingers revealing his hunger as he picked up the spoon she provided.

Leah busied herself on his behalf, slicing bread, searching out the butter and jam. Each trip past the window revealed to her the progress outdoors. She noticed a man opening the boxy black undertaker's wagon back door, where a rough, wooden coffin was slid from within as Gar held his wife's body in his arms. Gar closed the black door and the two men stood talking, Gar's head bent low as he watched the toe of his boot kicking at the wheel of the wagon.

Before long, Leah heard the sound of a harness jingling in the yard, and moments later Gar came in the door. "You need to eat something, Mr. Lundstrom," Leah said. "I've made some soup with beans. I hope you don't mind."

His shrug spoke an answer. *What does it matter?* he seemed to say in silence. Then on a sigh, he admitted his frailty. "Yes, please, if you would. I'm hungry."

While she dished up a generous helping, he washed at the sink, then paused beside his son as he stepped back to the table. "Kristofer." As if he had only needed the comfort of the boy's name on his tongue, he closed his eyes.

"I'm here, Pa." Mumbled through a mouthful of food, the answer seemed to satisfy the man, and he sat down next to the boy.

"What will you do with the baby? Did you see the doctor in town?" Leah asked quietly, pouring fresh coffee for the man who gazed into the bowl of meat and beans. As if he had no notion of what to do next, he lifted his head and focused on her.

She fished a spoon from the glass container and placed it next to his bowl. "Go on. Eat," she said briskly, aware that his mind was not on the food before him.

"Yes." He spooned sugar into his coffee and stirred it, then lifted the cup to his mouth, glaring down at it after a moment. "There is no cream in it," he said accusingly.

"I'll get you some," she offered, snatching the small pitcher from the dresser. The cream was rich, yellow and thick, and she poured the china container full to brimming.

"Thank you," Gar said, his voice more subdued, watching her intently through narrowed eyes as she added a dollop to the black coffee, where it swirled and changed color.

He picked up the soupspoon she had provided and ate with automatic movements, chewing and swallowing in silence. Leah watched from across the room, nursing her own cup of coffee.

And then the baby stirred, snuffling softly. In seconds the faint sounds became a wail, and Leah put her coffee cup down to hasten to the makeshift bed beside the stove. She bent to pick up the small bundle and held it against her shoulder, murmuring soft words of comfort.

"Give her to me." Gar's face was a mask, a forbidding frown furrowing his brow, his mouth taut. His arms outstretched for his daughter, he repeated his demand. "Give her to me."

Kristofer gaped at his father, his glance sliding to Leah and then back.

"Go to the barn, son, and help Benny feed the stock," Gar told him. "I did not do it well this morning."

The boy nodded, donning his coat and leaving the house quickly.

"I will take my child now, Mrs. Gunderson." Before she could voice any words of agreement, he lifted the baby from Leah's arms and stepped back. "I watched my wife bleed to death, right before my eyes. I cannot find it in myself to excuse what you did.''

Leah's legs trembled as she heard his accusation and she sat down in the chair across the table from where he stood.

"I told you when I came here that I was not a doctor. I did the best I could, sir. The doctor had told you and your wife that she should not have any more babies. Her organs were damaged so badly that the child could not have been born had I not drawn her out forcibly.''

The vision of gushing blood and mucus flowing onto Hulda's bed was still vivid in Leah's mind, and she closed her eyes against the horror. "Hulda could not have lived through the birth, no matter who attended her.''

She looked up, her mouth trembling, her eyes wet with unshed tears. "You are the one who must take the blame for this, Gar Lundstrom. You got her with child, after the doctor told you she should not bear another baby. Don't lay your guilt at my feet.''

His skin changed from the ruddy complexion of an outdoorsman to the ashen gray of a man with a grave illness. "I know what guilt I must bear,'' he said harshly.

"Be ready to leave in ten minutes,'' Gar told her. Then, snatching up a quilt to bundle around the tiny infant, he left the house.

Where he took the child, she did not know. His steps were purposeful as he went toward the barn, then on to a small house at the edge of the meadow. When she could bear to watch no longer, she turned from the window.

He took her home, both riding atop the wagon in silence, as if they could not abide each other's company.

He drove his team to the front of her house, and waited only long enough for her to slide from the seat before heading on his way.

"My bag! You have my bag, Mr. Lundstrom!" she cried, running behind the wagon.

He bent to lift it from the floor near his feet and tossed it in her direction, his eyes filled with an anger and a depth of despair she knew only too well. It had been her companion for many a long night.

The wet clothing was hung, draped over lines that crisscrossed the kitchen. Her task finally completed, Leah ducked beneath Orville Hunsicker's second-best white shirt as she escaped from the sea of laundry. The house closed up for the night, she left the kitchen for her bedroom.

She was bone weary and though she had thought sleep would not come, the pillow was barely beneath her head when she sank deeply into oblivion.

The woman suffered without sound, her dark eyes holding only hatred for the child she bore. Then, in a twinkling, that sweet, healthy infant, suddenly unmoving, lay beside his mother, his neck at an awkward, unnatural angle.

Shrieking, the mother pointed at Leah, her accusation resounding in the eerie light. "Murderer! Murderer!" Waving angry fists, the vengeful father roared his fury and Leah backed from the room, then turned to run; fleeing, always fleeing.

She breathed harshly, running blindly through a maze, only to enter another room, where Hulda Lundstrom rose up in the midst of a bloody bed to point her finger accusingly, her voice hoarse. "Murderer! Murderer!"

Leah awoke to a dark room, gasping for breath, as if she had been running for a very long time and her accusers were fast on her heels. The window held a full moon within its grasp, and it was there she focused her sight.

Beyond the white curtains she caught a glimpse of the hotel on the town's main street. Next to it the grocery store and the bank lined up neatly, their rooftops visible from her viewpoint. No longer was she running through the streets of Chicago, escaping the vengeance of a distraught father.

Leah bowed her head into her hands. How long? For how many years would she be haunted by the memory of that tiny baby boy, by the cold eyes of the mother who wanted nothing of the man she had married, least of all his child?

And now, as if that were not enough, she was to be tormented by the death of Hulda, who had sought only to please the man she had married.

The week passed more slowly than any she could remember, each day longer than the last. She walked to the store once, but the gossip was rife, with word of Hulda Lundstrom's death on every tongue. Leah was relieved to receive sympathetic glances and words of encouragement from the ladies who knew her best.

Yet even that was not salve enough for the wounds she bore within her soul. The thought that she must do something for the tragic little family struggling alone without a wife and mother in their midst filled her mind.

And yet at the end of that long, dreary week, when

Gar Lundstrom appeared on her doorstep with a tiny bundle in his arms, her kind thoughts disappeared as he glared at her through her screen door.

"I have brought you my child," he said bluntly, his fingers gripping the door handle, forcing her to step aside as he entered her small parlor.

"Whatever for, Mr. Lundstrom?" she said, her gaze intent on the wiggling form of the child he carried.

"I have found that it is not possible for me to care for the baby at the farm. I left her with Ruth Warshem, my Benny's wife, but she had to bring her back to me at night. I cannot do my work when I am up with a crying baby for all hours."

"And you want me to take care of her?" Leah was flabbergasted. The very nerve of the man, to intrude in such a way, with his demands.

"I can do it no more. I have stock to tend to and chores to keep me from the house all day, and I am weary at night. It is all I can do to keep Kristofer with me and care for him."

"What makes you think I'm the one to take on the job?" Leah asked, anger vying with astonishment at his edict.

His head tilted at an imperious angle. "There is no one else."

Leah laughed, the sound harsh and grating. "Well, you can forget it, Mr. Lundstrom. I am not available."

His mouth tightened and his eyes snapped with an icy flame, the pale blue depths piercing her. "I will pay you well," he growled, a penitent without a scrap of humility in his bones.

Leah's mouth opened and words of denial begged to be spoken, yet in her mind fluttered a small flag of caution. She could salvage her pride while lending a helping hand to this family if she accepted a token amount and gave the man a respite from his overwhelming responsibility.

"Perhaps, for a short while, I could do it," she said slowly, her eyes drawn again to the bundle he carried, which was emitting small cries of distress.

"Here, let me take her," she said, her hands itching to touch the infant form.

He handed over his burden, his hands reluctantly releasing the baby, as if it were not his choice but a dire necessity that had brought him to this.

Leah opened the blanket, where round blue eyes blinked at her and a small mouth opened in an *O* of surprise. Then those rosy lips yawned widely, squeezing the blue eyes into tiny slits. Leah touched the soft cheek with her fingertips.

"What have you been feeding her?" she asked, turning away as she felt unwelcome tears mist her vision.

"Milk from the cows, but it must be heated to almost boiling first. Then Ruth said to cool it. I got nipples at the store and bottles to use."

"Ruth cannot do this twenty-four hours a day?" Leah asked, wondering privately how the woman could have given up this precious package so easily.

"No." Gar shook his head. "She has a sister who needs her, and she never knows when she must go there. There has been sickness in the family, and now the sister is going to have a child."

"It would mean being available night and day. Babies require a lot of care, Mr. Lundstrom. I would need fresh milk daily for her."

"I will bring you a cow." His words fell like stones against her wall of objections.

"I don't know how to milk a cow," Leah snapped,

moving the baby to her shoulder and bouncing her lightly.

His look of exasperation touched her face and moved to the child she held. "Then I will teach you."

"For how long?" she asked, unwilling to look away although uneasy beneath the burning scrutiny of his gaze, fearing the return of the tears she had fought to subdue.

"For as long as it takes you to learn," he said impatiently.

Her teeth clenched and she sighed with an equal amount of aggravation. "You know what I mean. How long do you expect me to keep her?"

"As long as need be."

And wasn't that a dandy way to leave open her term of responsibility for a newborn child? Leah inhaled sharply and lifted her chin. "I've never had a child. How do you know I will provide for her well?"

His eyes traveled her length as if he gauged her ability, and his words were firm and final. "I know."

"But why me?"

"You owe me." He leaned forward, his nostrils flaring, his teeth bared, and for a moment Leah caught the broadside of a fury she could not fathom. "I know what guilt I must bear," he said. "As for you, perhaps you can ease your conscience and earn a respite from whatever blame you feel."

Had she not wondered earlier what she could do? And now, for all his male arrogance and stubborn Swedish pride, he had given her a chance to help. Her arms were full with the soft movements of a newborn, and her heart was touched by anticipation of the joy inherent in tending the child.

"All right, I will keep her. For six months. Perhaps

by then you can find a woman to live in your home and care for both children. In six months you will be past the sowing of crops and the first cutting of hay.''

Gar stood beside her and she focused on his boots, heavy and work worn, laced up the front, with his trousers tucked in them. They shuffled on the floor, as if he sought words to speak.

''Well?'' The warmth of the child Leah held was welcome against her cool flesh, as were the infant's small, awkward movements. The pattern of its breathing soaked into her almost as if it were her own.

''Yes, for six months,'' he agreed. ''I will pay you two dollars a week, and I will bring the cow and some more clothes for the baby tomorrow.''

She came near to refusing his offer, her mouth opening as she watched him take two coins from his small leather purse, placing them on the table before the window. It was too much. Two dollars was more than she had expected. And yet, the thought of buying what foodstuffs she pleased and perhaps putting a small sum away every week was tantalizing.

''I have a basket with some of her things in it, out in the wagon. Enough to get by with for a day or so. Ruth is washing up her diapers today and I will bring them back with me.''

He stepped through the door, across the porch and down the path to his wagon. His arms hugged a basket when he returned and he placed it on the floor near the door.

''I think we are agreed, then?'' he asked.

She nodded and he focused on the baby she held, one hand reaching to touch the downy head. With his long index finger he brushed the fine, pale hair.

And then he was gone.

* * *

Leah had slept fitfully, aware of the living presence next to her, then wakened at some small noise. Beside her, warm in her cocoon of pillows, the child she had taken into her home made her presence known. She fussed, whimpering for only a few seconds as she turned her head from side to side. As if she sought the warmth of a mother's breast, she nuzzled against her own hand; then, with a howl of displeasure, she announced her hunger.

Leah watched the baby in the moonlight streaming through her window, smiling as she recognized the healthy cry of need, a need she could supply in minutes.

She rose from the bed, donning her robe and slippers, then gathered the baby girl into her arms. For a few seconds the cries abated, and the child gazed up at her with wide eyes.

In the kitchen, she heated the bottle she had prepared, placing it in a warm pan of water and moving the pan to the hottest part of the stove. It was snowing again, flakes spitting past the window. But in the kitchen it was warm, and Leah dragged her rocking chair closer to the stove.

The baby fussed as her blankets were opened in order to change the wet diaper, and Leah clucked her tongue and whispered soft endearments as she worked. "There, there, wee one. We'll soon have you warm and dry. There, there, little bird."

The cries rapidly grew in intensity and only the fitting of the rubber nipple in the baby's mouth brought about peace and quiet. Leah rocked back and forth in the chair, her arms and hands busy with the feeding and the burping and the comforting. The presence of the child warmed her, erased the horrid dream from her mind, bringing her peace.

This child, whose destiny was forever changed from what it might have been. Leah felt a sadness for the woman who had been buried just days ago, who now lay beneath the snow-covered ground while her babe was cared for by another.

She felt a moment's guilt that she should reap the reward of pleasure in the tending of this infant, that, from another's pain, she should find such comfort in the middle of the night. Yet, she knew a sense of satisfaction that her arms held this precious being and provided it nourishment.

And almost, she felt like a mother.

Chapter Three

Kirby Falls, Minnesota
May 1892

"Miss Leah!" Against her screen door, a nose pushed the wire as eager eyes gazed into the parlor. On the porch, Kristofer Lundstrom waited impatiently for Leah's response, his hand on the spool handle, only good manners keeping him from stepping inside.

"Come in, Kristofer," she called, her feet moving quickly across the kitchen floor. He was late today. School had been dismissed for almost a half hour already and Leah had been listening for his voice for nearly twenty minutes.

She could set her clock by the boy. His feet clattered up her steps and across the small porch every afternoon, his intentions clear. Always there was the traditional greeting, a nod of his head as he spoke Leah's name. And then his eyes searched for the small form of his sister, seeking her out as if she drew him like a lodestone.

Even at six years of age, he was the picture of his

father, his hair golden in the sunlight, his eyes a pale blue beneath dark brows. He was tall for six, straight and sturdy, somehow seeming stronger now that he must stand alone, without the hovering presence of his mother.

Leah touched his head with her fingertips, ruffling the hair just a bit. "Did you stay after school, Kris?"

He shook his head. "No, ma'am. I saw Pa at the store and he had me to wait for a few minutes while he bought something for Karen."

Leah looked down at the package the boy carried. "For the baby? What is it?" She reached for the paper-wrapped parcel and Kris placed it in her hands.

"He thought you might need to make her something for summer. You know, not such heavy stuff like she wears now."

Leah's fingers were quick as she untied the string and sought the contents of the package. A piece of light-weight cotton, batiste, she suspected, met her gaze. It was covered in a delicate print of pink flowers, with pale green leaves forming a vine upon which the blooms and buds trailed.

"Oh, so pretty," she whispered, already envisioning the dress she would create from it. Tiny puffed sleeves and a high bodice, with a long skirt that would cover bare baby toes in the warm summer days.

"Tell your father I'll make it up before Sunday, so he can see it," she said with a smile.

From the kitchen, the baby squealed her opinion of being neglected even for so short a time, and Kristofer headed toward her door, intent on seeing his sister. Leah heard his murmurs of welcome, her smile widening as the baby greeted her visitor with cooing sounds signifying her pleasure.

"She gets bigger every day, don't she, Miss Leah?" the boy asked, bending low to place a kiss on the infant's downy head. He hastened to the sink, with backward glances as he went. "I'll wash up quick, so I can hold her, all right?"

Leah nodded. "She's been waiting for you, Kris. It's almost time for her to have a bottle. Would you like to feed her?"

Kristofer smiled, showing a gap where two front teeth were missing. "Yes, ma'am, I surely would."

That his hands were still damp was a small matter, Leah decided as he held out eager arms, and she nodded at the rocking chair, gathering up the four-month-old infant from the clothes basket where she spent most of her daytime hours.

With a pillow beneath his elbow, Kristofer held the baby tightly, offering the bottle to her eager mouth. Tiny hands groped for a hold on the glass, and the boy chuckled as he shared his grip with his sister's slender fingers.

"Look, Miss Leah! She's holding it, too. Before long, she won't need me to help her. She'll be eating all by herself."

Leah shook her head. "We'll still hold her, Kris. It's important that we cuddle her while she eats. It's what happens when a mama nurses her baby and holds her tight. Just because Karen has to drink from a bottle doesn't mean she has to do without the cuddling."

His small face was stricken. "I didn't think about that. She's sure lucky she has you, isn't she?" He bent his head to look with longing eyes at the babe he held. "I wish we could have her at home where I could see her all the time. I'll bet my pa wishes he could see her, too."

"He comes on Sunday afternoons," Leah reminded him. And those visits were the highlight of Leah's week, she admitted to herself. The sight of Garlan Lundstrom on her porch after church on Sunday was welcome—and not only for the eggs he brought to her, emptying his small blue-speckled enamel bucket into her egg bowl on the dresser with care.

His next task was to transfer two dollars into her keeping, placing it on her kitchen table. Then he inquired about the health of his daughter, watching as Leah brought the baby from her basket to the rocking chair where he settled himself. He managed to look at home there, his big body filling it, his feet flat on the floor, his arms surrounding the bundle that was his daughter.

Leah had found it easier to leave him there alone with the child rather than watch as he spoke in halting words and sentences, his voice soft and almost too tender to bear. Gar Lundstrom was a good father, a kind man. And yet, he wore a harshness about him that spoke of long, lonely days and nights.

Only when he held the baby or spoke to his son did that veil of austerity part. His eyes, when he looked into Leah's, were icy. His hands, when he took the babe from her arms, were hard and callused. His mouth, when he said his greetings and farewells, was firm and thin lipped.

He did not allow her to share the warmth of the spirit he spent so generously upon his children, and that was a pain Leah bore in silence. Gar Lundstrom looked at her with eyes that still held chill accusation. Even as he spoke words of thanks for her care of the babe, he was reticent. His only generosity was in the money he provided for that care.

She picked up the dainty fabric Kris had brought, her fingers smoothing it as she folded it neatly. ''I'll make up Karen's dress tomorrow,'' she told the boy.

He nodded absently, caught in the wonder of the baby's blue eyes and the plump body that filled his arms. ''I'll be glad when summer comes and we take her home with us, Miss Leah.''

''Did your father find someone to keep house, Kris?'' she asked quietly, holding her breath lest his answer shatter her heart. The presence of a baby had filled this small house to overflowing with warmth, and she had played the game for four months already, with herself as not only nursemaid but mother to the child.

Kris shook his head. ''Naw. Mrs. Andersen said she has to keep house for Lester. My pa said Lester was old enough to be on his own, but his ma doesn't think so.''

Leah smothered a laugh. Lester Andersen was a big strapping man of twenty-two, working at the lumber mill at the north end of town. If his mother didn't spoil him so thoroughly, he might make a good husband for some woman, or so the ladies at the store said beneath their breaths.

Where Gar Lundstrom would find his housekeeper and child minder was a problem he would have to solve on his own, Leah decided with a sigh. And if he didn't come up with an answer when the six months' time was up, she would continue to accept his two dollars every week and bank half of it gladly. Her dresser drawer held a tidy sum besides, hidden in a wooden box beneath her extra nightgown. Her laundry service was prospering, with seven clients every week.

''Miss Leah?'' Kristofer's small face held a frown. ''I have to go home now. Pa will be waiting for me at the store. I told him I'd ride home on the wagon with him.''

Leah nodded, rising from her chair to take the baby from the boy's embrace. "I'll see you again,'' she said lightly.

"Tomorrow. I'll be here tomorrow. My pa says I mustn't get in your way or be a bother, Miss Leah. You must let me know if it's not conven...'' He hesitated, as if he sought the word his father had used.

"Convenient? It's always convenient for you to stop by, Kris,'' she said easily, following him to the front door. Her hand rested on his shoulder for just a second as she stood beside him. He hesitated there, his face soft with yearning as he stood on tiptoe to press his lips against the brow of the baby Leah held.

And then he was gone, the door slamming behind him as he jumped from the porch, ignoring the steps, and ran to the gate. He half turned, lifting a hand in farewell as he opened the gate and crossed the street to make his way toward the grocery store.

Leah watched as he picked up a stone, examined it and stuck it in his pocket. She smiled, then walked back across the parlor and into her kitchen, bouncing the baby as she walked.

"He'll be back tomorrow, Karen. And on Sunday, your papa will be here to see you.'' It would be three days until Sunday. Three long days.

The spring was unusually warm for Minnesota. All the farmers predicted an early cutting of hay. By the end of May the crops were coming up in the fields, and the cows and horses in the pastures were accompanied by their own yield of calves and colts. The farmers' wives tended clutches of newly hatched chicks, gathering them into the henhouses at night lest the cool air should creep beneath their mothers' hovering wings and kill the youngsters.

Leah stepped into the hubbub of activity in the general store on a Monday morning in early June, Karen Lundstrom on her shoulder. Around her, the local ladies were catching up on gossip, most of them repeating stories heard at Sunday church.

"Ah, Mrs. Gunderson, here with the little one this morning," Hazel Nielsen called out. "Bonnie, come see your friend," she said, moving aside the curtain that led to the storeroom.

Eyes swung in Leah's direction, and she found a smile for the eager ladies who hovered around her like bees surrounding a hive.

"How is the baby doing?" Lula Dunbar asked, her forefinger nudging at a dimpled elbow. "Look how blue her eyes are, just like her mama's were." She dropped her voice in deference to the dead mother. "Not pure ice like her pa's, thank the good Lord. He's a cold man, that one."

Leah swallowed a retort and turned to listen to Eva Landers, the town's postmistress, who had left her desk in the corner of the store, where she had been sorting the day's mail.

"Let me see that little girl. What a darling she is!" Eva's long, slender fingers threaded through Karen's hair with a gentle touch, and Leah halted her progress through the store. "Don't pay any mind to Lula Dunbar," Eva whispered next to Leah's ear. "She hasn't said anything nice about a man since the day she married Hobart."

Leah smothered a laugh. Eva was a kindly woman, married to the undertaker, who doubled as the town's

cabinetmaker. It was handy, being accomplished at
woodworking, when you were the one in charge of providing caskets for the occasional burial in town. Joseph
was a sturdy man, solemn, as befitted his occupation,
and Leah had often wondered how he managed to catch
a joyous woman like Eva.

"I'll stop by for tea, if I may, later this afternoon,"
Eva suggested brightly.

Leah nodded eagerly. Visitors were frequent but usually bearing some cut needing stitching or seeking a
poultice or remedy for the ills of another. Her practice
had expanded since the winter months, ever since the
Lundstrom baby had been hers to care for. As if every
woman in town wanted a peek at the child, Leah had
been inundated with requests for cough syrup or chest
rub.

"Leah! It's good to see you." Bonnie Nielsen came
from the stockroom, brushing at dust on her sleeve as
she passed her mother behind the counter. "What can
I get for you today?"

Leah groped in her dress pocket for the list she'd
made up at breakfast this morning. "Not too much,
Bonnie. Are there any early peas, yet?"

Bonnie nodded. "Old Mrs. Havelock planted some
next to the house where they get the morning sun, and
she covered them at night so they wouldn't freeze last
month. She brought me a peck of them this morning."

"I'll take a pound, if you can spare them," Leah said
quickly, aware of the treat she'd been offered. "How
are the potatoes?"

"Pretty much shriveled up, I'm afraid," Bonnie answered. "I'll see what I can find for you."

"If you need potatoes, you need only ask, Mrs. Gunderson," a male voice said from behind her. A hush fell

over the store as Gar Lundstrom stated his offer, and Leah pasted a smile on her face before she turned to face him.

"I didn't see you in the store, Mr. Lundstrom," she said brightly.

"I just came in. Just in time to hear you ask about potatoes. I have plenty left in the dugout. I'll bring you some tomorrow."

She shook her head quickly. "Oh, you mustn't bother. Just bring them to me on Sunday when you come to see the baby." Leah felt a flush climb her cheeks as she became aware of the hush within the store as the women moved closer, the better to hear the words she spoke.

Garlan Lundstrom shifted uncomfortably, as if he had only now become aware of the several women who surrounded him. "Well, maybe I can hang a bag over my boy's horse when he rides to school tomorrow. He can bring them to you."

Leah nodded. "That would be wonderful. I'll pay you for them when I see you next."

His brow furrowed and his eyes narrowed at her words. "You will feed my child with them, no?"

Leah swallowed, unwilling to get into a confrontation in the middle of the store. "Yes, certainly," she agreed.

"Then you don't need to pay me." His gaze scanned her, softening only when he smiled at his daughter. "Give the child to me," he ordered gruffly, holding out his arms. "I'll carry her to your house and wait for you there."

Leah gave over the child, nodding her thanks as Gar turned from her to leave the store. Karen was growing by leaps and bounds, her small, round body weighing heavily after a time in Leah's arms.

The store buzzed with half a dozen voices as the tall Swede left, the door closing with a bang behind him. "He's a stern one," Lula Dunbar said with a sniff, peering at Leah over her glasses. "You'll do well to be rid of him once he finds someone to live out there and tend those children and his house for him. Though I don't know where he's going to look next. I declare he's asked every old maid and widow in the county."

Leah shrugged. "I'm in no hurry to have him take the baby. She's good company."

Bonnie called her name, and Leah turned gladly to heed her questions. "Do you want green tea today? We just got in a new shipment. And how about fresh baking powder? We've been out for almost a week, and I remember you asked for a tin last Friday."

"Yes and yes," Leah said with a smile. "Green tea is good for the stomach, and after today—" she nodded surreptitiously at the black-clad figure of Lula Dunbar "—I'll need something soothing to drink, I believe."

Bonnie nodded, then spoke in an undertone. "Everyone's thinking the only way Gar Lundstrom will find help out there will be to marry someone." Her voice was wistful.

Leah blinked. "Marry? You think he's going to get married?" she whispered. "It's only been five months since..." She still had trouble speaking the words.

"Mourning is a privilege reserved for those who can afford it," Bonnie said sagely. "Around here, a man's lucky if he can find somebody willing to take over a family if he loses his wife. Of course, a handsome man like Garlan might not be so hard put to talk some lady into it." Bonnie's eyes grew soft, as if she yearned in that direction, and Leah nodded.

"You like him, don't you, Bonnie?"

"Yes, for all the good it does me. He looks right through me. Always has, always will, I suspect. I'm not pretty enough for a man to take a second look at."

Leah privately concluded the same, but her tender heart prompted her to disagree. "One of these days, the right man will come by and snap you up like a bolt of lightning, Bonnie. You just watch."

Without Karen to carry, Leah added ten pounds of flour to her order, then pondered over a piece of yard goods for a dress. Her bundle was large, and she carried it in both hands as she made her way to the small house where Gar Lundstrom waited for her.

He sat on the porch, leaning against the upright post, his long legs propped on the second step. Karen was across his thighs, and her feet pushed at his waist as he lifted her to stand on his lap. She swayed, holding his index fingers, cooing and gurgling her delight at the man who held her.

"She enjoys seeing you," Leah said, watching from the bottom step.

Gar looked at her, his gaze stern as always. "She is growing before my eyes. I miss much, only spending time with her on Sunday afternoons."

Leah smiled brightly. "Well, as soon as you find a housekeeper, you can take her back, Mr. Lundstrom. I only agreed to keep her for six months." Any longer than that would be a mistake, Leah had already decided. As it was, giving up the baby would be heart wrenching.

"I wonder if I have been looking in the wrong places, Mrs. Gunderson." His eyes met hers, and Leah was stunned by the calculation she sensed in their depths. He allowed his gaze to sweep over her length, pausing almost imperceptibly on her narrow waist and the flare of her bosom above it.

"I think I need more than a housekeeper, Mrs. Gunderson," he said quietly, his eyes once more touching her face with pale concentration. "I'm in town today to speak with you about a matter of interest to both of us."

Leah's heart bumped, halted and quivered in her chest. Surely not, she thought. The man didn't even like her, even though his hatred had waned over the past months. Surely he couldn't be thinking of making her an offer?

"Shall we go inside?" she asked, drawing in a breath lest her voice break and reveal her uncertainty. She stepped past his seated figure and opened her door, holding it ajar as he stood and carried the baby into the parlor.

He watched while Leah carried her bundle into the kitchen, and her mind raced. Perhaps it would be better to speak with the man in the parlor, where the atmosphere was not so homey, where she might sit on the horsehair sofa and listen to his offer. For, sure as the world was turning, an offer was what she was about to hear. She'd be willing to bet her bank account on it.

"Mrs. Gunderson. Leah." He'd followed her into the kitchen, speaking her given name, as if what he was about to say was too personal to merit formality.

"Yes?" Leah turned to face him, the table between them, her fingers working at the string that tied her purchases.

His hand waved at her efforts. "Leave that alone for a moment and sit down. Please." He drew a chair from the table, waited until she had obeyed his order and then sat down, facing her.

Leah bit at her lip, nervous as she anticipated the words he was about to speak. If he should offer to hire her as housekeeper, she would refuse, for the gossip would not allow her a reputation worth having.

Her eyes lifted to meet his gaze and she tilted her chin, as if she dared him to suggest such a thing. Again his eyes made a survey, this time touching the honey-colored braids she wore as a coronet atop her head, then focusing on the set of her jaw and the tight pursing of her lips, before he returned to meet her gaze.

"I would like to ask you to marry me, Leah Gunderson."

His voice was solemn, his words slow and ponderous, as if he had thought long and hard before he made his offer. "I need someone to live at my place and care for my children. I want my daughter where she belongs, and my house shows neglect."

Well, that was about the most honest proposal a woman had ever received, Leah decided. He hadn't minced any words, just spelled it out and let it lay.

"I'm being offered a dirty house and two needy children. Am I right?" she asked quietly.

He shrugged, his wide shoulders moving almost imperceptibly as he lifted an eyebrow in response. "Perhaps I'm also making a way for you to clear your conscience, Mrs. Gunderson."

"I bear no guilt, sir," she said firmly, her mouth quivering as the pain of his words vibrated within her. She'd spent too many hours going over the events of that night to accept blame for the death of Hulda Lundstrom. "I did the best I could for your wife."

"No matter," he said, dismissing her words. "If you will come to my farm and be Leah Lundstrom, I will give you a place to live for the rest of your life. I will treat you well and never lay a hand on you in anger."

"Well, that's some offer," she said smartly. "It's not

really what I had my heart set on, though.'' Her voice mocked him, and she felt a pang of remorse as he dropped his gaze.

"It's all I can propose,'' he said after a moment. His hand lifted and swept the circumference of the room. "It will be better than this.''

"Once it gets cleaned up, perhaps.''

"It shouldn't take you any time at all, as strong and healthy as you are, ma'am. You will even find a supply of potatoes in my dugout, ready for your use.'' His mouth twitched as he reminded her of her need.

The sun from the window over her sink glinted on golden strands of hair as Garlan rose to his feet. It formed a nimbus around him, causing his hair to shine, as if the sun had taken up residence within each lock. Like a warrior from the olden days, he stood before her, long legs spread, wide shoulders and long arms husky with muscled strength.

Only the dainty form of his daughter lent a note of disparity to the picture. Her round face peered from his shoulder as she twisted to view Leah, unwilling to allow her to disappear from sight. And perhaps it was that smiling visage that turned the tables in Garlan Lundstrom's favor.

"I thought you might ask me to be your housekeeper, Mr. Lundstrom,'' Leah ventured. "I didn't have in mind marriage at this late date. I will be thirty years old in a month.''

He shook his head. "I don't think that should be a barrier, Leah. Thirty is not so old these days. I am thirty-four myself.''

"It's different for a man,'' she argued. "I'm too old to begin having children.''

His eyes grew chilled, the pale blue orbs turning to

ice. "I did not ask for that. I have two children. I have had a woman in my bed. I did not find it rewarding to bring her to the childbed and watch her die. I'll not take that risk again."

So it was to be that way, Leah thought. She would not know the touch of a man's hands on her body in the act of loving. Her virgin flesh would know no ease from its aching need.

"You have been married, Leah. Can you honestly say you desire that attachment again?" he asked quietly. "It has been my experience that women do not seek out a bedding, but only endure such a thing in order to have children."

She shook her head, not even aware of what she agreed or disagreed with. She'd never been wed, had only taken her mother's maiden name and made it her own, so that she would not be despised as a maiden lady doing the work of a midwife. And now this man was telling her that she would not have the knowledge of his body atop her own, that he would not use her to create more children of his loins.

"Let me think about it, Mr. Lundstrom," she said, proud of the steady quality of her words.

He turned to place Karen in her basket, his hands reluctant as he slipped them from her body. Then he faced Leah and offered her his hand, waiting till she met it with her own.

His palm was broad, warm and strong. His fingers enclosed hers in a firm grip. Not a handshake as men exchanged, but rather a clasping of hands, as if they sealed a bargain between them. Leah felt her fingers soak up the warmth of his, felt the pulsing of his heartbeat as her middle finger touched his wrist. The heat of his flesh encompassed her palm, spreading to her forearm and up to her shoulder. It met the frantic beat of her heart, and she knew a moment's panic as that organ seemed to swell within her breast.

"I will call on you tomorrow, Leah," he said, his words almost harsh in their intensity. She met his gaze as her hand slipped from his grasp, and she noted a flicker of emotion there. As surely as her name was Leah Gunderson, she knew that Garlan Lundstrom held something from her. He was not so forbidding suddenly, not so reserved.

"Bring the potatoes then," she said pertly, and was not surprised when the flicker became a flame and his eyes warmed for a moment.

"Yes, I'll do that." His mouth was firm, his lips thinning as though he forbade them to speak further. He then turned from her and walked to the front door.

"I will come for my answer tomorrow afternoon." With a nod of his head, which caused a lock of golden hair to brush against his forehead, he was gone.

Leah's fingers itched to brush that errant lock back into place and she stifled the urge, clenching her hands at her waist as he turned back to look at her from the bottom of the porch steps.

"He doesn't want a wife," she muttered to herself. "He wants a housekeeper and someone to watch his children." Her skirts swished around her ankles as she spun in place and marched back into the kitchen.

From the laundry basket, a squeal of delight greeted her, and Karen's pudgy fingers waved a distracted welcome as she clutched a string of thread spools in one hand. As always, Leah's heart melted at the sight, and she moved across the floor and knelt by the wicker basket.

"You are so tempting, sweet one," she said, twining

her fingers in the silky locks of hair that covered the baby's head. "Between you and your brother, you are enough to steal my heart."

The baby gurgled a response, and Leah bent to kiss the crown of her head. She rose, stepping to the sink to wash her hands before she got out her teapot for the promised visit from Eva Landers. The sun was almost blinding, brilliant in a vibrantly blue sky, and she blinked, shaking her head against the vision that rose in her mind.

He was there, as vivid as if he stood before her. Gar Lundstrom, tall and golden haired, a man of the earth, solid and dependable. A man who still despised her.

A man who could steal not only her heart, but her soul as well.

Chapter Four

"I will marry you, Garlan Lundstrom." Leah spoke the words to her mirror and watched as a pink flush rose from her exposed throat to cover her cheeks. She peered closely into the looking glass, willing away the trembling of her hands as her fingers worked the top button of her dress into its buttonhole.

"I'll marry you, Gar." There, that was better. More casually spoken, more sincere. Her eyelids fluttered, and she leaned closer to seek the blue depths, groaning at the sparkle within. The man would think her dotty! This was to be a business arrangement, if she had heard him right. And now she blushed and simpered like a schoolgirl.

A sharp rap at the screen door broke her concentration, and she turned from the oval mirror that hung over her chest of drawers. At least he would not marry an ugly woman, she decided, and then chastised herself for vanity's sake. Her skin was decent, her eyes a clear blue and her nose was only a trifle too long. Her mother had told her that her stubborn chin was troublesome, but then, that doggedness had stood her in good stead more than once.

The rapping increased, and Karen's squeals of joy signified the sighting of her father through the mesh screening. "Leah! Are you there?" Gar Lundstrom's voice was strident, and without awaiting her reply, he opened the door and entered her parlor.

She hurried to greet him. "I'm here," she said, her breathing restricted by the rapid beating of her heart.

He looked up at her from his daughter's side. Karen was clutching the edge of the basket, leaning toward her father, and Leah was struck by the babe's fickle streak. Once Gar Lundstrom walked in that door, the rest of Karen's world ceased to exist. Her lashes fluttered, her mouth cooed soft phrases that might sound like so much babbling to another, but to the man who watched her so dotingly, she was obviously sheer perfection. And in her innocence, she returned his regard a hundredfold.

Now he squatted beside her, one hand touching the crown of gold that curled in a silken cap over her perfect head. "I thought I heard you speaking, Leah. Is there someone here with you?"

She shook her head. "No, I'm alone. I find myself talking to Karen when I'm out of the room. It pleases her." She held back a smile. Practicing her acceptance of his proposal would certainly please Garlan Lundstrom should he know. It would give him an edge she could not afford to allow. Better that she hold an upper hand in this.

He rose easily to his feet, and Karen let forth a blast of sound that brought a wide grin to his mouth. "Such lungs, little girl. You put your brother to shame!" He leaned over her and extended his hand. "Hush now. I must speak to your friend, Mrs. Gunderson."

As if she understood, Karen sniffed and rubbed one tight fist against her eye, then smiled with delight.

"She's flirting with you," Leah said softly, totally taken with the child.

"And you?" he asked. "Do I get a smile from the Widow Gunderson today? Am I to hear an answer this morning?"

Such levity was almost unknown from the man who stood before her, and Leah's tongue searched for a reply as she scanned his handsome features. Her head nodded after a moment and she shoved her hands into the deep pockets of her apron.

"Yes, I've thought about your offer, Mr. Lundstrom. I'm willing to marry you. It would be beneficial for me."

"And for me," he conceded. His gaze fell to the baby in the basket at his feet. "Not to mention my daughter. Kristofer, by the way, is waiting outside to hear your answer. He's very anxious, Leah. You've quite a champion in my son." The smile flashed again. "He likes your cookies."

"He's a wonderful boy." Such inane words they shared, she thought. Speaking of children and a beneficial relationship, when all she wanted to hear was that she would finally be appreciated as a woman. And now she hadn't even put to use all the posturing she had practiced before her mirror.

"Saturday next would work well for me. Do you have any objection?" Gar asked, his gaze firm on Leah's face.

She nodded. "I can be ready by then. I'll let my bachelors know. Mr. Dunbar will have to make other arrangements for the hotel linens, unless he wants to

bring them out to your farm, and I doubt he'd be willing
to do that.''

Gar shook his head. "You will find plenty to do
there. Don't even think about washing for the hotel.
You've done your last laundry for the town bachelors,
too, Leah.'' His words were firm, decisive and not altogether welcome to her ears. Not that she craved the
scrub board, but it was a decision she would have preferred to make on her own.

Her chin tilted and she almost smiled, recognizing
the stubborn stance she was about to take. "I'll let my
clients know, but I have time enough and to spare for
the rest of this week and next to earn the extra money,
Mr. Lundstrom.''

He set his gaze on her, and the look was that of a
stormy sea, his blue eyes turning almost gray as his
mouth made a thin line across his face. "I will not argue
with you over this, Leah. We are not married yet. But
mark it well, once you promise to live with me and be
my wife, you will listen when I tell you my wishes.''

She gritted her teeth against the words that begged to
spew forth, settling for a more docile attitude than was
her wont. "I expect to do as you wish in most things,
Mr. Lundstrom. However, you're not marrying a young,
green girl. I'm a woman who has lived on her own for
a number of years. I'm not a female who will cling and
ask favors of a man. I'll do my duty by your children
and your house. And unless my memory is flawed,
that's what you told me you expected of me.''

His eyes narrowed on her. "I think we'll come to an
understanding eventually, ma'am. In the meantime,
we'll just have to work it out as we go.''

She was a magnificent specimen of womanhood, he
decided. Standing tall, as if her spine were made of

finest steel, yet only reaching his shoulder in height. She was a strong woman, carrying a graceful figure, with hair not quite golden, but, rather, streaked and honey colored. Her eyes were the true blue of her ancestors, her slender body well proportioned. And with that, he allowed his gaze to scan the length of her.

Her cheeks had turned more than rosy with his scrutiny and she pursed her mouth. "Do I pass muster, sir?"

His reply was slow in coming. So intent was he on the woman herself, he barely heard her sharp words of inquiry.

She held herself well, he decided, her breasts generous within the bodice of her dress. It fit her nicely, snug against the graceful line of her waist, then flaring gently over her hips.

"Mr. Lundstrom? Will I do?" Blue eyes flashed with irritation and her skirts flounced as she turned from him to walk across the room. His gaze was drawn by the serviceable boots that nudged the hem of her dress. She would do well with softer shoes for the house, he decided. He would have her fitted at the store before...

He watched her soberly now, his mind fixed on the time, only ten days hence, when they would marry. Perhaps she needed other things, new dresses maybe. With that thought in mind, he stepped closer to where she stood. "Will you go with me to Nielsen's store next week, before the wedding?" he asked. "Whatever you need...I'll pay for it."

Her eyes widened at his words, and he watched as her chin tipped upward. A stubborn woman, if he knew anything about it. She would not take well to his ways, perhaps. There would have to be a time of building bridges between them.

"I don't think so." Her full, lush lips separated,

opening as she spoke her denial of his offer. And then, from within, her tongue appeared, touching lightly against her top lip as he watched. The sight fascinated him, that tiny bit of flesh leaving a speck of moisture on her lip, then retreating within her mouth.

The urge to step closer to her assailed him and he fisted his hands at his sides, aware of a heated response deep within his belly. Such foolishness! She was a good woman with a clean reputation, and surely that was what he sought.

"I will provide my own necessities," she said primly, jarring him from his contemplation.

"I would be pleased to buy you a dress for our wedding, Leah," he said quietly. "And shoes, and whatever else you need."

She shook her head. "No. I have money in the bank. I'll not come to your house a pauper, Mr. Lundstrom. I only need a bedroom with a chest of drawers for my belongings and hooks on the wall for my dresses."

He nodded, strangely pleased by her prideful behavior. She would serve him well. "I'll be here on Sunday," he said, his eyes scanning her again. She'd stepped back from him, and now her hands were clasped at her waist, and she looked the very picture of docile, dutiful womanhood.

Somehow, he doubted the veracity of that impression.

"But if you marry that Lundstrom fella, who will do my washing?" Brian Havelock stood at Leah's door, bundle of laundry in his hands, and uttered his query with unknowing appeal. To Leah's eye, he was a boy still. Had she been ten years younger, she might have bent forward and planted a kiss on his rosy cheek. Or ten years older, she amended.

"You know I depend on you, Leah," he said piteously, his blue eyes sad beneath lowered brows.

"I'm sure Mrs. Pringle will be happy to take you on as a customer, Brian," she said briskly, holding her fingers closed around the coins he had pressed into her palm.

"You're wasting yourself on that man, Leah," he told her firmly, stepping closer. "I'd make you a good husband. I have a steady job at the sawmill, and my house is almost built."

Leah stepped back from him, easing inside the door into her parlor. Her voice was firm as she dashed his hopes although a twinge of pity nudged her tender heart. "I'm sorry, Brian. I told you last winter, I'm too old for you."

He opened his mouth to speak and she waved him to silence. "Never mind! I'm set on the matter. I will marry Mr. Lundstrom on Saturday next. I'll do your shirts on Monday, and that's the last time."

Her would-be suitor stepped backward, nearly falling from the porch as he nodded his agreement. "Yes, I understand." Turning from her, he trudged up the path to her gate and she watched him go.

He would make a fine man for the right woman someday, she thought. Young and still wet behind the ears, he was like a puppy, all rosy cheeked and almost panting in his eagerness to please. Kirsten Andersen had missed a good bet when she married that man from the next county.

Swooping down to Karen's basket, Leah lifted the baby high in the air, turning in a slow circle as she parodied a waltz across the floor. "You will live with your papa soon, little bird," she sang tunelessly.

"And you, too," came a clear, youthful reply from outside the screen door.

Leah whirled to face the newcomer. "Ah, Kristofer! You startled me. I didn't see you coming."

The boy swung the door wide and faced Leah from across the parlor. "Are you glad you're coming to live with us?" he asked hopefully.

"Oh, yes," she reassured him readily. "We'll have a good time, Kristofer. You and Karen and I. We'll pick flowers in the meadow, and you can help me carry in the milk from the barn and sort out the eggs for market."

"Don't you like to go hunting?" the boy asked, his mouth pursing as if he scorned the choices he'd been offered.

Leah shook her head. "I could never find it in me to kill a living thing," she admitted.

"Hunting is different," Kristofer said patiently. "You only kill what you're going to eat, my pa says. Unless it's rats or rattlers."

Leah shivered. "Do you have a lot of those on your farm?"

He shrugged. "Once in a while."

Leah hugged the baby to her and then offered her to the boy who had come on such a transparent mission. "Did you want to see Karen?"

His eyes lit with a pale glow, silvery yet blue, like his father's. Leah handed him the baby, still holding the infant's weight as Kris made his way to the rocking chair.

"Sit, now," she said quietly, knowing that the two would speak their own language for several minutes. Kristofer whispered words Leah could not understand

and the baby smiled and chortled her delight at the brother who doted on her.

"Leah?" From the porch, her third visitor in ten minutes begged admission. "Are you busy?"

"Come in, Eva. I'm just ready to put my supper in the oven." Leah smiled at the woman who hurried through the door, then cast an admonishing look at Kristofer. "Watch that Karen doesn't get away from you."

"No, ma'am, she won't," he answered patiently, flashing her a smile.

"You got a letter," Eva said quietly. "The first one you've had since you've been here, Leah. I hope it isn't anything bad."

Pulling the envelope from her pocket, Eva offered it to her friend and watched worriedly as Leah inspected the writing, then the stamp, then the back of the envelope, with care. Leah's long, slender fingers shaped the rectangle, brushing the edges as she straightened out a wrinkle in one corner.

"Aren't you going to open it?" Eva's curiosity was evident, but Leah forgave it without thinking, knowing that the woman's concern was foremost.

"Yes, I suppose I am," she announced, as if a momentous decision had been made. Her fingers edged beneath the flap carefully and she lifted it to expose the letter within. Written on onionskin paper, it was filled from top to bottom with a scrawling, ink-blotted message.

Leah turned it in her hand, glancing down at the bottom of the page, to first identify the sender, before reading the script. "Anna Powell," she whispered, her voice tinged with something akin to fear. Her eyes flew to the top of the page and she devoured the words, unaware of the breath she held within her lungs. Not until her head swam and spots appeared before her eyes did she release thc soft puffs of air she had held within her. Her hand reached for a kitchen chair and she settled on it abruptly.

"Leah! Are you all right?" Eva knelt before her, eyes filled with concern, her hands gripping Leah's wrists.

"Yes...yes, of course." Leah smoothed her tongue over lips gone dry and attempted a smile. "It's just a letter from a woman I knew, back in...back where I come from."

She tipped her head to one side, blinking away the dizziness as she caught her breath. "She says that a friend has been looking for me. I'll have to let her know where I am, won't I?" Her smile was trembling, but she loosened Eva's grip upon her wrists, clasping her friend's fingers tightly.

"You looked so strange there for a minute," Eva said slowly. "Almost as if you'd seen a ghost, though heaven knows I don't believe in such a thing."

"No..." Leah shook her head. "Neither do I." And yet, within the pages of the letter she held, folded in on itself so that another's eyes might not see the words, dwelt a ghost she would give much to be rid of.

The nightmare was back for the first time in months. Perhaps having Karen to love and care for had kept the dream in abeyance. The dark was more friendly these days, holding memories of sweet infant scents and the familiar sound of her rocking chair as it moved against the floor.

For a while, the terror of death had seemed far removed from Kirby Falls, Minnesota. As far away as the streets of Chicago. As far as the ornate house in which Sylvester and Mabelle Taylor lived. That house of hor-

ror where a baby boy had met his fate at the hands of
his evil mother.

His head tilted to one side, his breath forever stilled,
his tiny, perfect body...

Leah drew in a deep breath, closing her eyes against
the vision she saw. Awake or asleep, this night would
hold the memory of death, and she'd as well accept that,
she decided.

Her robe brought warmth to her chilled body as she
donned it, her slippers adding to the comfort. The
banked fire in the stove needed only a bit of kindling
to bring it to life, but Leah added a good-sized chunk
of firewood for extra measure. She ladled water into her
coffeepot and poured beans into her grinder. The pun-
gent odor rose as she turned the handle and inhaled
deeply, comforted by the familiar scent.

She settled into the rocking chair, one foot pushing
at the floor, setting her in motion. In her pocket, the
letter rustled and she drew it forth, the contents already
committed to memory.

Anna Powell, neighbor and friend, the only person
who had knowledge of Leah Gunderson's whereabouts.
Her fervent assurances had rung true. She'd not di-
vulged anything. But she'd been questioned by an im-
pressive-looking man from a detective agency.

Garlan Lundstrom's proposal had come at a perfect
time. How better to cover her tracks than to change her
name, Leah decided. A woman named Gunderson
would no longer exist in Kirby Falls. Instead, on a farm
outside of town, married to a prosperous farmer, a
woman called Leah Lundstrom would live in peace.
With the protection of a husband, perhaps even a man
like Sylvester Taylor would find it difficult to pursue
her and berate her for a sin she refused to own.

As that thought lodged in her mind, Garlan's daughter announced her displeasure—most likely a wet diaper—from the next room. Leah rose quickly, a smile replacing the somber cast of her face, her steps light as she made her way by moonlight to where the baby lay.

Covers kicked aside, plump legs and dimpled fists waving in the air, Karen Lundstrom was a sight to behold. Beneath the window, she was bathed in moonbeams, her rosy cheeks pale in the absence of sunlight. Leah scooped her from the basket and held her against her breast.

"Hush, little bird. Shh, shh, sweet one! Mama has you now." Her whispered words of comfort stilled the babe, and Karen gurgled her delight as Leah carried her back to the kitchen. The lamp on the dresser was lit quickly, and the table served dual purpose as Leah stripped the diaper and replaced it with a fresh one.

A soft lullaby eased the babe into sleep in short order, and yet the rocking chair continued to move in its prescribed motion. Not until the sun was fully risen in the eastern sky did Leah's head tilt against the high back, her eyes closed in slumber.

The farm wagon wore a coat of paint, an unheard-of thing so far as Garlan Lundstrom knew. Red enamel covered the weathered wood, and upon the board seat a leather-covered pad had been nailed into place, providing a comfortable cushion for driver and passenger. More than one pair of eyes followed the wagon's trail as it wended a path down the main street on Saturday morning. Atop the seat, Garlan Lundstrom and his son sat, the boy waving proudly at each passerby.

"Pa, they really like our wagon, don't they?" Kristofer's feet kicked at the front of the wagon, keeping a rhythm with the slow trot of his father's team of horses. A glance of reproof halted the contact of toes against wood, and he grinned cheerfully. "Sorry, Pa. I was just excited about pickin' up Miss Leah and all her stuff today. It sure took a long time for Saturday week to get here, didn't it?"

Gar nodded, his color high as he withstood the knowing glances of the townspeople who watched his progress. Painting the wagon had probably been a foolish gesture on his part, but the old wagon had looked so shabby, and the red paint had been handy, left over from the barn raising last year.

And Kristofer had been adamant.

Gar lifted a ready hand, answering a like salute from Joseph Landers, standing outside his cabinet shop, sawdust apparent against the dark trousers he wore. There was always about the man the fine scent of freshly cut wood. A clean smell, Gar thought.

The sun shone brightly, and the men who sat beneath the wide porch in front of the hotel fanned themselves with pieces of newspaper and an assortment of brightly printed paper fans, red roses vying with the garden of Gethsemane for the preferred design.

The hotel door opened as the wagon passed by, and Lula Dunbar stepped to the sidewalk. Her hand lifted in greeting, then a stunned expression seemed to hold it aloft and suspended, bringing her to a halt. Her mouth half-open, she turned her head to watch as Gar drove past.

"Well, I never…" he heard her say, her words sharp and crisp on the summer air.

"I think Mrs. Dunbar likes our red wagon," Kristofer said cheerfully, wiggling on the seat as if he could barely stand the inactivity.

"Yah...I noticed," his father answered glumly, halting before the general store. He slid to the ground, several seconds after Kristofer's feet had found their way into the store.

"You must paint some flowers on the sides of that wagon," Eric Magnor said from where he stood by the hitching rail. The sawmill owner, a graying, handsome man in his fifties, grinned at Gar's discomfort. "Becoming a bridegroom must have put you in a festive mood, Lundstrom. Perhaps your bride will add the finishing touches for you."

Gar growled a reply, silently cursing the urge he'd followed when Kristofer grumbled about the old wagon. "Miss Leah would like it if we painted it up nice and bright," he'd told Gar. And somehow, it had seemed like a good idea—yesterday.

"Don't pay him any mind, Mr. Lundstrom," Bonnie Nielsen said from the wide doorway. "We think it's downright pretty." Behind her a bevy of women beamed their approval, Kristofer in their midst. "Kris said he talked you into it. I'll just bet Leah will think it's grand," Bonnie said, holding the door open for Gar's entrance.

"What time is the wedding?" Orville Hunsicker asked. "I bought me a new tie for the big event."

"In about an hour," Gar answered, feeling a flush climb his cheeks as he braved the group of womenfolk who stood before him. "I need to pick up a few things, Miss Nielsen," he said to Bonnie, handing her a list. "If you'll get them ready, I'll go on over to Mrs. Gunderson's place and load up her things."

"Shouldn't take long," Bonnie said quietly. "That house was furnished when she rented it. I think the rocking chair was all she bought, besides her bedding and such.''

''Well, the sooner begun, the better,'' Gar said stiffly, only too aware that he was the center of attention. He turned on his heel and went back outside, Kristofer on his heels.

''Are we gettin' Miss Leah now, Pa?'' Kristofer skipped to keep up with his father, squinting at the tall man.

''Yes,'' Garlan answered shortly. ''Right now. Get in the wagon, son.''

Brian Havelock paused on the sidewalk and kicked at a stone, sending it flying into the road. Gar tossed him a glance, noting the sour look on the young man's face.

''He kinda likes Miss Leah, Pa,'' Kris said in a loud whisper. ''I don't think he wants us to marry her. He told Mr. Dunbar he'd be needin' a new laundry lady, too.''

''Well, he can't have ours,'' Gar muttered, aware of young Havelock's continued scrutiny. ''He'll have to look around for his own woman.''

The wagon turned in to a wide alleyway between the newspaper office and the barber shop, and Kris looked back over his shoulder. ''I'll bet everybody will be at the wedding,'' he surmised. ''Those ladies in the store had on their Sunday dresses, Pa.''

Ahead of them, beneath maple trees, a row of five houses sat, each neatly fenced with a gate opening onto the street. From the front steps of the center dwelling, Leah watched as the wagon rolled closer.

Gar brought it to a halt, then stepped down, tying his team to the hitching post near her gate. He followed Kristofer toward the porch.

"Do you like our wagon, Miss Leah?" Kris asked with an eager grin.

"I could paint some flowers on the side panels if you like, Kris," she answered. "Maybe you could help me."

"Eric Magnor had the same idea," Gar told her with a sharp look.

Leah's brow raised in appreciation. "Well, as the most prosperous man in town, he surely must be an authority on such things, I would think. They tell me he has nothing but the best in his house and his stable."

"I suspect he was pulling my leg," Gar muttered, following her inside the house.

"Flowers would be lovely," Leah persisted. "I used to be quite handy with such things when I was young."

A big hand halted her midway across the parlor. "You're still young, Leah. Don't make yourself old before your time."

She turned to face the man she would marry today. "I feel young today, Mr. Lundstrom. Do you like my new dress?" She'd bought it ready-made, with Bonnie's approval. Daisies flourished against a dark blue background, their yellow centers adding a cheerful touch.

Gar nodded his head. "I couldn't have chosen better myself," he said politely.

If he only knew how hard it had been for her to settle for something so sedate it would set him on his ear, Leah thought to herself. She'd yearned for the pale pink dimity with ruffles over the shoulders and around the hem, but she'd turned to the more sensible gingham that would stand her in good stead for a Sunday dress later on.

Her hair gleamed, the color of clover honey, she'd decided in front of the mirror earlier on. Her cheeks were rosy, with no help from pinching fingers, and if her hands trembled just a bit, surely no one would notice.

After all, it was her wedding day. The Widow Gunderson was to be wed in less than an hour, and half the town would be there to celebrate the marriage inside the Lutheran church.

And not a one of them was aware that the Widow Gunderson would be a full-fledged virgin bride.

Chapter Five

She was not to be tucked away in a hidey-hole beneath the eaves, it seemed. The bedroom he led her to was large, with walls nine feet high. A room where a body could look out upon the land from wide windows on two sides. Windows that would catch the rays of the morning sun, allow it to filter through the gauzy white curtains and then hold it close during winter mornings.

Now it lay in shadow, this room that was fit for a bride. The bed was large, topped with a gem of a quilt, and Leah leaned to inspect it, its tiny stitches almost invisible.

"Was it hers?" Her voice held just a hint of censure as she awaited his reply, and Garlan Lundstrom leaned against the doorjamb with indolent ease.

"No. The quilt was my mother's."

"Not the quilt," Leah said. "The bedroom."

He would not make her wonder such a thing. "She never slept here. She hated the windows. When it stormed, Hulda hid in her closet."

No hint of mockery touched his words, only the truth about the woman he had married and brought here as his wife.

Leah turned to face him. "Who slept here, then?" Her face held a trace of...what? Dismay, perhaps? Or fear that she had been given his own room as her own?

No, Gar thought, such an emotion would not escape this woman's thoughts. She would cover it with disdain, or pride or even arrogance. She would not allow fear to give him an edge over her.

"No one. No one has ever slept in this room. It was built for the master of the house and his wife. When Hulda refused it, I moved our things to another, one with a single window. And a large closet," he added, with dark humor.

Leah paced to the dresser, glancing across the room at its matching chest of drawers. "I only asked for a bed and a place to keep my things. This is more than that."

She looked into the mirror, and her gaze found Gar across the room. Blue eyes pierced him, questioning his motives. And then she turned to face him. "Where is your room?"

He shrugged and nodded his head toward the hall-way. "At the other end of the corridor, across the hall. Beyond the room where I put Karen when we came in. In fact, there are two rooms between us," he said, bow-ing his head in a mock gesture of compliance.

Then he met her gaze, and his own was arctic. "I told you I would not expect you to warm my bed. I meant it, Leah."

She nodded. "I believe you, Garlan Lundstrom." Her sigh sounded weary, her eyes losing their luster as she bent to pick up the satchel he'd placed on the rug.

"I'll do that," he said, almost snatching it from her hand. "Where do you want it?"

She waved at the bed and then shook her head almost

immediately. "No, not there. It will soil the quilt." She looked about distractedly. "There, on the window seat."

And there he placed it. Then he looked past its scratched, cracked leather out the window to where one of his hired hands shepherded the cows into the barn, the tricolored, long-haired collie nipping at their placid heels. A surge of pride stiffened his shoulders as he watched his guernsey cattle mill about, waiting their turn to enter the barn, several of them anxious to be rid of their bulging supply of milk.

She was behind him. Gar felt her presence as a cloud of warmth, as he had all this livelong afternoon. She wore no scent that he could name, only the clean, woman smell of her announcing her nearness.

"How many head do you have?" Her words held a note of interest and he seized it, anxious to turn his thoughts elsewhere.

"Twenty-seven all told, only six milkers now. A pasture full of calves, most of them still attached to their mothers. They'll be crying to get inside soon. I have two bulls, but they're kept in a separate shed and let out in a well-fenced corral. In the far pasture, I keep the young steers."

If there was a note of pride in his answer, he would not apologize for it. He'd worked long and hard to build his herd. He'd hired three men to work for him and paid the highest wages in the area for their loyalty and the hard work they gave unstintingly.

"Do you raise horses?" she wanted to know, pressing closer to peer past him at the pastoral scene below. "Are those pigs beyond the barn, there in that pen?"

The afternoon sun was fast falling, and twilight would soon be covering the distinct edges of his buildings, leaving only the lights in the barn to guide the men who worked there.

"Yah, there are two sows and their half-grown litters beyond the barn, where the smell will not reach the kitchen so easily. The horses are in box stalls in a stable next to the cow barn. I have six of them."

"One is mine," said Kristofer from the doorway.

Gar swung about from his position at the window, and Leah stepped back quickly, their clothing brushing, hands almost touching.

"Did you take the wagon to the shed?" Gar asked, his words softened for the boy's benefit.

Kristofer's head nodded. "Yes, Pa. Benny put the team away, and I brought in the rest of the things from the store." He looked at Leah with eager eyes and moved closer, his feet shuffling. "I left everything on the kitchen table. I didn't know where you would want things put."

She bent her head and offered her hand. Kristofer grinned, his face lit from within. He took her fingers in his and tugged. "Come with me and see Karen's room. We'll have to be quiet. Pa laid her down, and she's asleep in my old bed. Me and Pa washed it down, and we found sheets to fit it and everything."

Leah glanced at Gar and her look became more reserved, as if with the child she could open that unseen door within her heart and allow him access, but with the man, she must contain those soft emotions. Her brow lifted in question.

"Go ahead," he said, clearing his throat as the words growled with unintentional harshness. "I'll bring up the rest of your things, Leah. Where do you want your rocking chair?"

She paused in the doorway. "I thought in the kitchen.

There is room by the big window over the porch, I think.''

''Yes.'' He watched as they went, this son of his heart and the woman he had chosen to mother the boy. He had never had a woman cause his heart to swell in his chest. He feared this one might do that very thing.

Poor Hulda had come to him with her bowing and posturing and meek spirit, and he had all but turned from her. He had come to appreciate her housekeeping skills, her cooking and sewing and the care she took of the boy. But there was a lack in their marriage, and he knew that much of the blame could be laid at his feet. He shook off the worrisome thoughts, the regrets that had haunted him over the past months as he'd mourned the woman who had died to give him a child.

A cry split the air as that very tyrant announced her displeasure with something, and Garlan Lundstrom hurried down the hall to join the rest of his family.

''Hush, hush, sweetkins!'' Leah had swung the plump little elf from her new bed and held her closely. Karen's eyes were shiny with tears as she pointed an accusing finger at the wooden crib she'd awakened in only moments before.

''She don't like her bed, Pa,'' Kristofer said with a frown.

''She'll get used to it in no time,'' Leah assured him quickly. ''For now, we'll take her downstairs and let her sit in her basket while I fix something for us to eat.''

''I'll carry her,'' Gar said abruptly as he scooped the babe from Leah's arms. Karen fussed for a moment, but her father found a ticklish spot with his index finger and she subsided, giggling and clutching at his shirt.

''How about some bread and jam and a pot of tea?'' Leah suggested, striking a match to light the lantern that hung over the round kitchen table.

"I think you'll find some cold roast beef and cheese in the cooler," Gar said.

"Cooler?" Leah's eyes were puzzled as she considered his words.

"Beneath the floor of the pantry, I've put steps to a basement. In one wall, there's a door to an underground room, lined in metal. It holds the ground temperature during the summer. For the most part, it keeps the left-over meat well."

Leah hurried to the pantry and found a short set of steps going beneath the first floor into a basement area. A window above the ground shed muted light and she looked around her at the shelves that held even more canned goods and glass canning jars. Against one wall, another door opened into the metal-lined room, the temperature there causing her to shiver. A covered dish was on a table, cheese wrapped in a towel beside it, and she picked them up, backing from the dim interior.

"I could barely see down there," she said, her breathing a bit unsteady as she climbed the eight steps into the pantry proper.

Gar watched her from the doorway. "There are candles in the cooler. Next time you must take down a match or carry a lantern with you."

"Did you build that yourself?" she asked, brushing past him and placing her find on the table.

Gar shrugged his wide shoulders, and she thought she detected a hint of pride in his bearing. "Yah, I did."

She sliced meat quickly, cut the cheese in chunks and found a loaf of fresh bread beneath a dish towel on the cupboard. "Who bakes bread for you?" she asked.

"Benny's wife, Ruth, comes in and does it for us.

She keeps us in bread and an occasional cookie,'' Gar answered, bouncing Karen on his knee.

"She can't bake cookies as good as yours, Miss Leah,'' Kristofer announced quickly.

Leah felt a flush of pleasure color her cheeks at the child's sincere words, and she sent him a smile of thanks. Her hands worked quickly at the familiar tasks, and in less than five minutes the family was assembled around the table, the teapot waiting for the big kettle to boil.

Gar bent his head and uttered a short, stilted thanks for the food, and Kristofer heaved a sigh of relief. "I was really hungry,'' he said as he filled his plate eagerly. His bread was topped by a slice of beef, and he folded it over on itself and took a bite.

"Let me get you some tea, Kris,'' Leah said. "The kettle is probably warm enough for the first cupful.''

As if she could not bear to sit across the table from the big man who watched her so intently, she sprang to her feet and fussed over the teapot. Kris thanked her politely, Gar nodded his own silent thanks, and Karen took a swipe at the china pot, drawn by the roses painted on its round sides.

"Let me take her while you eat,'' Leah said, reaching for the baby. Gar nodded his agreement, and she lifted the child from his lap, returning to her own seat.

It was a short meal, Kristofer and Gar hungry and unwilling to spend their time on small talk, Leah poking at the food she had placed on her plate and offering small crumbs of bread to Karen, much to the delight of the child.

"I need to go out to the barn now,'' Gar said, pushing back from the table. "There are chores to finish up. The men have been good about doing everything today, but I must lend a hand.''

"Yes, all right." Leah watched as he left the house, snatching his hat from a hook by the door as he passed. A straw farmer's hat, not what she'd have thought he would wear. In town, he'd appeared in one that was wide brimmed and made of felt, settling it on his head at an arrogant angle. Now he looked like a farmer, she decided, watching as he tilted the simple straw head-gear.

A tall, handsome farmer, she amended. She watched as he strode across the yard to where his barn windows held a welcoming yellow glow from the lights his hired hands had lit within.

Leah looked around her at the kitchen he'd given into her keeping with such a casual touch. As he had given her the whole house the moment they walked in the door together. For an instant she had held her breath, wishing, oh yes, wishing for just a second or two, that he would sweep her up and carry her over the threshold.

Foolish woman! To even desire such a thing. This was to be a marriage for their mutual benefit. It would be far from a love match. She had known that from the start. Leah would cook and clean and make him a home where there had been only loneliness for six months. He would bring her the food to cook, praise her skills and bask in the warmth she provided.

"Miss Leah?" Kristofer called her name from the doorway, one hand holding the screen door ajar. "Pa tracked in something awful. You better sweep it up before it gets ground into the carpet. Ma always had to get down on her hands and knees to brush it out."

Leah blinked and looked to where the boy stood. Clumps of dried dirt littered the doorway, and beneath the table a layer of the same marred the wooden floor. "Don't you and your father know how to stomp your feet on the porch?" she asked, frowning as she caught sight of the trail across the kitchen, scattered bits of the yard showing the path Gar Lundstrom had taken on his way across the room.

Kristofer grinned. "Ma kept a rug out here, but I guess it got lost. Mrs. Warshem scrubbed the floor for us yesterday, so it would be clean for you, but it won't stay that way for long."

Leah's frown was heartfelt as she sought the broom from the corner of the pantry. The first order of the day tomorrow would be to find a throw rug for the porch. She'd be jiggered if she'd spend her days cleaning up after a man's dirty boots.

The moon was high in the sky as Leah settled Karen in her crib and covered her with a light quilt. She left the window open from the top so that the draft would not blow on the child, and left the door ajar. The hallway was dark and she stepped carefully as she sought her room, a soft glow from beneath its closed door guiding her steps.

The knob turned in her hand and she stepped inside the lovely haven Gar had designated as her own. Leaning back against the paneled door, she surveyed the expanse of her private place. He'd carried up her boxes, stacking them against the far wall, next to the closet door. Now he was in another part of the house, this house with five bedrooms upstairs and four rooms below.

A house such as she had never thought to call home. She blinked, releasing twin tears that slipped down her cheeks. She smiled at her foolishness. To weep when all was so perfect. To feel a sense of emptiness when her life was going to be filled to the brim with work and play and...almost all that being a wife entailed.

"Leah?" From the other side of the door where she leaned, a gruff voice spoke her name, and she straightened, brushing at the errant tears before she turned the knob.

"Yes?" She stepped back, allowing him entry. He paced to the center of the room, then turned to face her.

"I thought we should set up some sort of schedule tonight. There is no sense in waiting until morning to let you know how things will be." His words rang with assuredness, and she watched him with half-shuttered eyes, wondering at his meaning.

"Do you want breakfast before or after you do your chores?" she asked, willing to be pliable.

"Coffee before I go out to milk, then breakfast afterward. I like a big meal, bacon or sausage or even a pork chop when we have them on hand. Eggs, oatmeal, and bread toasted in the oven."

She considered him in the light of the candle on her bedside table. He was dressed in his pale shirt, smoothed inside the waistband of breeches, which were tucked into boots. Suspenders clasped the trousers, holding them tightly to his well-formed body, and she allowed her gaze to slide his length—quickly—lest he think her brazen.

"A big breakfast. All right, I can do that. And when would you like this big breakfast served, Mr. Lundstrom?"

His hand waved with an imperious motion. "When the chores are finished. You can ring the bell on the porch when it is about ready and then hold it in the oven until I come in."

She nodded slowly. "I see. I am to cook a big breakfast, and then, if you don't show up to eat it while it is still hot, I am to keep it edible until you can tear yourself away from your cows long enough to devour it."

He looked at her from beneath lowered brows. "I think you mock me, Mrs. Lundstrom."

Leah swallowed. He'd called her by his name, a name he'd given her only today. She leaned back against the wall, suddenly finding her knees to be made of something other than bone and muscle.

"Yes, I suppose I was," she conceded. She nodded her head and looked at the floor near his feet. Those big feet that wore boots that were shedding bits of dirt wherever he walked.

Perhaps tomorrow would be a better time to pursue that angle, she decided, vowing to place rugs both before the screen door and outside of it.

"My breakfast is not a point of discussion," he said, his chin taking on a stubborn look that Leah was sure more than matched her own.

"I said I would tend to it," she repeated.

"We can discuss the rest of your schedule later. For now you'd best get a good night's sleep. This house is almost too much for one woman to keep up. Perhaps Ruth Warshem could be persuaded to come in and give you a hand."

"Benny's wife?" Leah asked.

"Yes." Gar nodded. "She is a fine woman, a hard worker."

"You've married a hard worker, Mr. Lundstrom," Leah said, just a hint of defensiveness in her tone.

"I know that," he agreed, his hands clasping behind his back as he watched her in the faint glow of the candle. ''I have every confidence in you, Leah. I think you will suit me well.''

She stepped aside as he came toward the door, aware of his gaze on her and unwilling to lift her head to meet his blue eyes, now gone silver in the candle glow. He was her husband, this was her wedding night, and she would sleep alone. Just as she had bargained for.

She hoped, as she shut the door behind him, that his sleep would be unsettled, that he would regret the bargain he had made, and that his long, strong body would ache for the presence of a woman's form beside him in his lonely bed.

She was not a woman to be easily tamed, Gar Lundstrom decided after one short week. She was downright snippy some days, poking at him if he failed to shake the dirt from his feet. She defied his schedule, deigning to place Karen's bath ahead of her housework.

He'd come in the third day to find her awash in a tub of water, up to her elbow in suds, a squealing, unhappy child with soap in her eyes—and not a lick of sympathy for his daughter in the woman who lifted her from the water. Leah had wrapped the squirming babe in a towel and hushed her while she splashed fresh water in her eyes at the sink.

''What did you do to her?'' Gar had demanded from the doorway. ''Why is she crying?''

Leah had turned to him, Karen on her hip, exasperation alive on her expressive features. ''She splashed soapy water in her eyes, then rubbed it in. Now she's unhappy because the bath is at an end. If you will just go away for a few minutes, I'll dry her and dress her and then find time to speak to you.''

He'd watched silently, unwilling to leave the sight of

Leah's damp dress clinging to her full breasts, aware only of the shape of that lush, perfect bosom.

He'd forgotten exactly what had brought him into the house, and had stomped from the kitchen after a few moments to return to his fields and animals.

She was a worrisome woman, he thought as he stood atop the hay wagon in the midday sun. He wondered what she was up to now, what foolishness brought about the peals of laughter sounding from within his house. Holding the reins in his hand, he listened again to the voice of his son and the chortling noises his daughter was prone to make. And above them both was the laughter of the woman he had brought here.

The horses responded to the slap of reins on their backs, and he turned the wagon to the lane, heading for the hay field where the rows of dried alfalfa lay waiting for his arrival. Already two of his hands had gone ahead, raking the hay into piles, readying it for the wagon. He cast a look at the sky, where clouds were forming on the western horizon. There was time to get it all under cover before nightfall, as long as the rain held off.

They worked for long hours, ignoring the dinner bell at noon, finally sending Lars Nielsen, Bonnie's younger brother, back to get a jar of water and some bread to hold them over. Lars was a tall, sturdy lad of eighteen, saving his money for a farm of his own someday.

He'd returned after half an hour, driving the team of horses, Leah at his side on the padded leather seat of the red wagon. She handed down a wicker basket to Gar and he eyed her with misgiving.

Was she angry that they had ignored her call to eat? It seemed not. Her smile was like a benediction, and the water she handed him was cool against his parched throat.

"I wondered if you would have time to eat. It looks like rain, doesn't it?" She glanced worriedly at the clouds that were scudding across the sky in the west.

"We'll take ten minutes," Gar said, sliding to sit against the wagon wheel. "What did you bring?"

"There is hot soup I put in mason jars I found in the pantry. I thought you could just tilt it up and drink it that way. I made sandwiches, too," Leah said, unwrapping thick slabs of beef on sliced bread. She passed them around, leaving Karen to sit in the back of the wagon, where she scooted from one side to the other.

"She is beginning to crawl," Gar said, watching as the baby gripped the side wall and peeked down at her father. With a thump, her bottom hit the wooden floor of the wagon, and she uttered a howl of protest.

"It will be awhile, but she's learning," Leah agreed.

Benny Warshem and young Lars ate with gusto and thanked Leah profusely for the meal, handing up the basket to her, along with the assortment of jars and towels they'd used.

"Thank you, Mrs. Lundstrom," Benny said, for the third time. His grin showed wide, white teeth, brilliant against tanned skin.

"Yes, thank you, ma'am," Lars added, blushing as he grinned at his boss's wife.

"We should be done in five hours or so, Leah," Gar said. "Another four loads should do it." He eyed the big field. Over half of the alfalfa it had held was now under cover in his barn. "Send Banjo out to help us when you get back to the house."

The third man had been busy in the hayloft, readying it for another load. Leah's directions had sent him to the house where a sandwich waited on the kitchen table, along with a bowl of soup.

By now he was probably hard at work in the barn once more. "Yes, I'll send him out," she told Gar, lifting the reins to turn the wagon around in the field.

His gaze followed her, noting the graceful movement of her hands on the leather straps, the watchful glance she cast into the back, warning Kristofer to tend to the baby.

"Mrs. Lundstrom!" Gar called, holding his hand to his mouth to funnel the sound in her direction.

She stood, pulling the team to a halt, and looked back over her shoulder. "Yes, what is it?" Her hand lifted, shading her eyes against the bright sunlight.

"You haven't painted those flowers on the wagon yet, I noticed," he called, hands on his hips, hat tilted back, teeth gleaming.

She frowned, then grinned suddenly as she caught his meaning, waving at him with good humor. He watched the wagon roll across the field. Watched as his men went back to work, his eyes on the woman who was setting his life topsy-turvy, even as she brought sunshine inside the walls of his house.

Chapter Six

"Did you have a busy day?" Gar spooned potatoes onto his plate, then passed them to Leah.

She wrinkled her brow. "No, not really. I cleaned the parlor and did the ironing. Oh, and put yeast bread to rise." She mashed green beans into a spoonful of potatoes and offered a bite to the baby.

"Nothing else?"

Leah looked up quickly. "What are you after, Gar? Yes, I helped Kristofer with his alphabet during Karen's nap and I sorted out your worn socks for mending." She bit down on the chicken leg she held as if her teeth were set on devouring it whole.

"Who was here this afternoon?" Gar asked, lifting his head to speak, fork uplifted. His eyes watchful, he waited until Leah stopped chewing and sipped her coffee. "I saw a surrey in the yard earlier."

Her brow rose and irritation drew color into her cheeks. "It was Mrs. Thorwald, my old neighbor. Orville Hunsicker brought her out to see me." She placed her fork with care on the table. "Why? Am I not allowed to have callers?"

"Am I not allowed to ask after visitors to my house?"

Leah's eyes glinted, like sparks on steel when he used his grindstone vigorously. "Of course," she conceded. "It is, after all, your house. But when you asked me what I had done, I thought you wanted a detailed list of my household chores."

"I do not keep track of your work, Leah. This is your home, after all."

"Ha! I am allowed to live here as your wife. But now I can't have visitors without permission, is that it?" Her tone glistened with sarcasm and her tilted chin punctuated each sentence with a jab.

"That is not what I meant, and you know it." The woman could turn a phrase, he admitted to himself. She had a gift with the English language, and not for the first time had left him feeling the ogre.

"Then what did you mean? Shall I give you chapter and verse of what we spoke of? Would you like to know how many cups of tea she drank in your kitchen?"

"It is not my kitchen. I turned it over to you on the day I brought you here." His voice boomed across the table, and Kristofer slid from his seat, heading for the screen door at a run.

"Now see what you've done," Leah whispered, glaring at the man who was gritting his teeth and glaring in her direction.

She rose quickly, hurrying from the house, and caught the boy halfway across the yard. Her hand clamped on his shoulder, bringing him to a halt.

"I don't want you to fight with my pa," Kris cried, turning to face her. "I don't like it when people yell at each other. My mama didn't like it, either."

"And did your papa yell at her?" Leah asked quietly, her fingers soothing the nape of the boy's neck.

Kristofer hesitated. "Only sometimes, when she did things she wasn't supposed to do. Like when she got up and cooked and then fell on the floor and he had to carry her up to the bed."

"She fainted?" Leah asked, imagining the woman who must have pressed her strength to the limit in caring for her family.

Kristofer lifted sad eyes to the woman who watched him. "She was tired a lot of times, Miss Leah. Pa didn't act mean with her. He just got all loud and bossy when she wasn't happy."

"A typical man's reaction," Leah said, almost to herself. "When men don't know how to handle a situation, they tend to shout and carry on," she told Kristofer. In her limited exposure to the male creatures in her life, she had found that to be the rule rather than the exception, and Gar Lundstrom appeared to be of that breed.

"He was mad at you." Kristofer's mouth pouted, and he glanced back at the house.

"Come in, both of you, and eat your dinner." Gar was on the porch, hands low on his hips, glowering across the distance between them. A note of frustration shaded his words and Leah nodded, willing, this once, to be acquiescent.

Her arm slipped across the boy's shoulders, and she nudged him in the direction of the porch. "Come, Kris. We'll let him bluster while we eat." Her words were spoken against his head as she bent to whisper them as a secret between boy and woman.

"All right." Sliding from her grasp, he ran to the house, past his father and into the kitchen.

"And you, too, Miss Leah?" Gar asked, his eyes blue

as a robin's egg, a pale, color-washed hue that silvered in his anger. "Will you share your dinner with me if I promise to mind my tongue?"

It was an apology, unexpected and welcome, and Leah grasped it eagerly. "Yes, of course. I only wanted Kris to be aware that you were not angry with him."

"He is soft sometimes." Gar held the door open for her and followed her to the table they had abandoned so hastily. He offered his plate. "May I have some hot gravy to warm these potatoes, Miss Leah?"

She took it from his grasp, her fingers touching his. He had the ability to anger her and then soothe that fire with such touches of humility, as if he begged her pardon in an oblique manner.

She placed the plate back before him, hot gravy steaming, and he nodded his thanks. Her own food was edible—not hot, but warm enough to slide down easily—and she ate quickly, aware of the ironing awaiting her in the basket. Karen would sleep for another hour or so, and if she hurried, Leah could have the bulk of Gar's shirts pressed and folded and in his drawer by then. Kristofer's things only required folding, and she had but three dresses for herself to iron.

"Are you still sulking, then?" Gar's words penetrated her thoughts and she looked up quickly.

"No, of course not," she denied. "I was only planning my afternoon work. We will have stew for supper, and biscuits on top."

He nodded, casting a glance at Kristofer's bent head, his fork busy at the task of filling his mouth. "We will talk later, all right?" His eyes scanned her, and she wondered what he saw. Whether he rued the day he had brought her here. If he thought his bargain a distasteful one, with a contentious wife instead of the calm, sedate woman he must have thought her to be.

"We'll talk," she agreed, rising to take her plate to the sink. He was gone when she turned back to the table, and Kristofer was wiping his mouth on his sleeve, sliding from his chair.

"I'm going out to check on the new puppies," he said. "Then Pa said I should pull weeds in the garden."

"Kristofer." She bent low, bringing her face to his level. "Your father loves you very much."

The boy nodded his agreement. "I think he likes you too, Miss Leah, even if he hollers sometimes."

"Yes, I suspect he does," she answered, standing erect once more. And perhaps more than he had expected he would, she thought. For unless she was blind, Gar Lundstrom had made note, more than once, of her physical attributes. And he seemed, in some odd way, to enjoy their verbal jousts.

They would talk later, he had said. She walked to the window, watching as Kristofer jumped from the porch, heading for the barn where the puppies awaited his inspection. Just inside the big doors a tall figure moved, disturbing the shadows, and Leah felt a clenching where her heart did its business, beating in a routine manner.

It gave her pause that the sight of Garlan Lundstrom should disturb the natural course of events within her body. And not for the first time, she admitted to herself, had her heart done double time in his presence. The man held a strange sway over her emotions, with his pale eyes intent on her movements, his words of instruction to her tempered by the frustration she read in his gaze.

Gar was a man without a woman to ease his hurts, a man who lived in need of that which he had scorned upon entering this marriage. Whether he sought penance for the death of his wife, or perhaps what had come before that time, Leah could not know. But that his need was great was a fact she would be willing to stake her future upon.

If that need were slaked upon the altar of her body, she would have some tall explaining to do. Her shroud of widowhood would be torn forever, and Gar would be the one holding it in his big hands.

But unless she walked with Gar Lundstrom down that path, she would remain forever a spinster bride.

The sun was almost below the horizon, only the pink and azure colors staining the sky to tender it farewell. In a porch swing made for at least two to share, Gar's proximity made Leah almost wish for a larger perch.

Her feet clear of the floor, she allowed him to set the tempo for their dalliance, for such did she consider it. To sit at the end of the day with nothing to do but catch a stray breeze and enjoy the scent of honeysuckle from the trellis near the milk house was indeed a treat. Gar touched the floor of the porch with his boot, and the swing moved at an angle.

"I need to sit closer to the middle to do this right," he said with a trace of humor.

"That's all right," Leah answered quickly. "I don't mind sitting still."

"I want to ask you something, Leah," he said after a moment. "About where you came from. How you happened to be a healer, I guess."

"From Illinois," she said, her gaze on the hens scrabbling on the ramp to the chicken coop. "And I learned what I know from my mother."

"I think what I wondered was why you came here?

Of all the places you could have gone, why Kirby Falls?''

She pleated her skirt with finger and thumb, her mind abuzz. "Why not?" she asked with a forced bit of laughter. "It seemed a likely place."

His even glance speared her with its disappointment in her words. A look that might have been frustration turned his amiable visage to solemnity, and he deigned to reply, repeating after her. "Yes, why not...indeed, a likely place." He sighed. "I ask you because I want to know you better, Leah. Don't begrudge me that much."

It would be the first step on the road to his discovery of her past, and she took it unwillingly. "I was born here, in Kirby Falls, thirty years ago, Gar. Were you here then?"

He shook his head, his eyes sharp with interest as he turned his full attention in her direction. "No, I came from the East with my family when I was still wet behind the ears, twenty years ago. My father thought he would like New York, but then he heard of the communities here that were more like home, in the old country."

"Well, I was gone from here before you ever arrived, then," she said softly. "My mother took me with her, and we lived together in the city. She was a healer and a midwife, and I learned what I know from her."

"And is she well, back there in the city?" he asked, his words slow and hesitant, as if he knew the answer already.

Leah raised her head, her eyes leaving the fabric of her skirt that she had folded into neat pleats. "She died four years ago. I carried on her work, and then decided after...well, later on...I decided to move from the city." Her hand lifted and the fabric fell from its folded pattern, her fingers smoothing at the faint wrinkles she had created.

"And your husband?" he asked, wary as he stepped on ground not yet disturbed.

"He died there, not long after my mother." The lie stuck in her throat and the words were broken, perhaps sounding as if she mourned him yet. One falsehood would require another to support it, her mother had often said. Leah hoped there would be no more tonight.

Gar cleared his throat and shifted on the swing beside her. "You have borne grief, Leah, more than you deserve, maybe. I hope you can forget it here, and find peace."

The night bird sang in a tree just beyond the porch and its mournful melody underlined the words he spoke. Leah only nodded, guilt at her duplicity tugging at her.

"Then you left the city to come here?" Gar prodded after another few moments.

Leah drew a breath, willing to tell this part. "I knew I'd been born in Kirby Falls, and I thought…well, no matter what I thought, I came here to live. You know the rest of it, how I took in laundry and sewed up cuts and dabbed salve on infections and lived in a little house alone."

"Were none of your mother's people left here?"

She shook her head. "My father is dead, and she had no one here. I doubt anyone even remembers Minna Polk." She considered for a moment. "There is no Polk family hereabouts that I've heard of, so perhaps she was right, that there was no one of my father's family here to miss her when she left."

His gaze rested on her hands, fascinated by their movements. Narrow, they were, her fingernails short and neatly trimmed. He was aware of the faint calluses she bore, brought on by wringing out clothes over a scrub board, and marring the smoothness of her palms. And he knew that those same hands were tender and loving when they dealt with his baby daughter.

Leah's hair was down tonight, her braid over one shoulder, the end loose with a handful of curls evident. She'd touched them, wrapping one then another around her index finger, and he wondered how that silken lock would feel, clinging to his own rough skin.

The sky was darkening and her hair was golden in the twilight, seeming more fair as the shadows deepened around them. His hand lifted from his knee and then settled there again, his palm aching to lay claim to the rounded slope of her shoulder, wishing he dared to draw her closer to his side.

And why not? he asked himself. She was his wife, all legal and binding. And yet, there was a bridge he was not ready to cross. He'd told her he would not expect her to occupy his bed, and now, less than a month into the marriage, he was eyeing her like a randy boy.

She fit in well here. She suited him, and Karen and Kristofer were enamored of her. If there were a chance of sending her on her way, he daren't risk it. He would not go back on the bargain he had made with her.

Leah leaned into the corner of the swing and lifted one foot, tucking it beneath her bottom. "I suppose this is the life I yearned for back in the city, Gar. I didn't like the dirty factory smoke in the air, and the streets so full of horse droppings that they had to clean them with a crew of men every few days."

He chuckled, and heard the sound with a sense of surprise. Was he so bereft of humor in his life that he must be amused by tales of horse droppings? And yet, it seemed tonight that he could put aside his austere manners and relax with Leah, here in the almost-dark. She too had relaxed her guard, and he watched her, the lamp from the kitchen spreading its glow to silhouette her face.

She was pretty, this woman he'd married. More than pretty, he decided, his eyes taking in the clean lines of her profile. Her nose was straight, her chin just a bit prominent—he smiled at that observation. She led with it often, he decided, that stubborn part of her giving away her tendency to dig in her heels.

"Do you miss living in town?" he asked, urging her to speak her mind with him.

"In Kirby Falls? No…only that I enjoyed talking to the ladies at the store and having tea with Mrs. Thorwald and Eva Landers sometimes." She turned her head and met his appraisal.

"I love your children, Gar. I appreciate the lovely home that you allow me to share. I even like you sometimes," she said, adding the qualifier with a small pursing of her lips.

"That's about as good as it will get…between us, isn't it?" His gaze was focused on her, and he watched for a reaction, his jaw clenching as he fought the strange sadness that gripped him.

Her eyes lowered as if she feared she had daunted his mood. "I do like you, Gar. I think this will work out for us both, this being married and sharing a home with your children."

Perhaps it was comfort he needed, more than just the pleasure she brought his eyes.

Gar's hand clenched, and he forced it open, feeling a tingling in each fingertip, swallowing the reluctance that nudged his conscience. His palm lowered to touch her, skimming the narrow line of her shoulder, his index finger tracing the ridge of her collarbone. She lifted her chin, her eyes wide and startled. Her tongue, that fascinating bit of flesh that never failed to intrigue him, slid across her upper lip, then retreated.

Promise, be damned! He leaned forward, touching his mouth to her temple, the soft curls at her forehead brushing his nose. He inhaled her scent, a fresh air and rainwater aroma. It was sweet, yet not like the honeysuckle or the early roses by the porch. Better—like a woman's flesh, fresh from washing at the end of day, when she rinsed away the dust and perspiration her skin had gathered.

He saw her in his mind, this woman of his, stripped to the waist, standing before her washstand, drying the dampness from her skin, her hair free and loose from her braid, long strands outlining the soft contours of her breasts.

Those breasts that were only inches from his hand.

His fingers stilled their roaming, one barely brushing the side of her throat. "Leah." He'd never heard that sound in his voice before, harsh yet pleading. With only inches to travel, his index finger touched beneath her chin and tilted it to his pleasure.

Her lips were soft beneath his, unmoving yet not unresponsive. She was hesitant, as if she waited for him to tell her what to do. Her breathing stilled, and then her lips twitched and were motionless once more, as if she experimented with the sensation of their flesh touching. A sigh escaped her mouth and he inhaled it, then pushed against her softness, sensing a reluctance as his lips would have eased between her own.

He moved his mouth, seeking another angle, his teeth touching her bottom lip. She shivered, a soft sound of surprise making him smile. His caress moved to her cheek, and he closed his eyes, brushing lips and nose against her soft skin, murmuring words he'd almost forgotten how to speak, in the language of his birth.

"Gar?" She was breathless, her movements awkward as she shifted away from him. "I didn't think we were going to do things like this."

"We are allowed to share friendly kisses, Leah," he said quietly. "I'm sure it was a part of our bargain."

She shook her head. "No, I don't think so."

Straightening, he looked at her, his attention taken by the startled look she wore. Almost as if she were fearful of him, she drew back—as if his kisses had frightened the young girl she had been half a score of years past.

If he hadn't known better, he'd have judged the Widow Gunderson to be no more knowledgeable about the ways of marriage than a virgin bride. Perhaps her husband had not warmed her for his taking. Maybe she had not spent hours dallying beneath the moon, and more long minutes beneath the sheets before her woman's flesh was made his.

At that thought, Gar's foot stilled the movement of the swing. Suddenly he could not bear to think of this woman beneath another man. He rose to his feet. "You are right, Leah. I took advantage of the darkness and the warm night. I beg your pardon." His head bowed in a semblance of apology, and he watched as she rose and made her way to the kitchen door.

"I'll see you in the morning," she said, her breathing just a bit ragged. His tongue touched his upper lip and he tasted the residue of her flavor there. He was right. She was sweet. Just a bit tart beneath the surface, but sweet, nonetheless.

Dr. Berg Swenson attended Sunday church with regularity, occupying his customary pew. Leah flashed a glance in his direction this morning. How could he face God within his sanctuary and not be stricken by heaven's power? This man, who worshiped and nodded and spoke so kindly to the townsfolk, was the vilest of all creatures, in Leah's private record book.

He picked and chose his patients, caring for those who paid well and presented small challenge to his talents as a physician. And that Hulda Lundstrom had not rated high on his scale of need would forever be held against him by the woman who had witnessed her death.

Now, in the aftermath of the morning service, during which Leah had sung favorite hymns and listened to a long sermon that had half the congregation shifting in their seats, she was approached by the man for whom she felt only scorn.

"Mrs. Lundstrom." He was pompous, never considering that she would not reply...although she was sorely tempted.

Her manners won out and she turned to face him. "Good morning, Dr. Swenson."

"I have a case I would like to discuss with you," he said in an undertone.

"Oh?" Her surprise was genuine.

"Will you step aside with me?" She nodded and he grasped her elbow, turning her to one side of the churchyard, away from the lingering crowd of parishioners.

"I have a patient whose illness has resisted my attempts at healing. I thought you might stop and see him with me."

Leah bit her tongue, monitoring her words, lest she gain an enemy by this meeting. "What makes you think

I can help someone you are unable to treat? Surely, you are more prepared than I to handle illness."

"He has a fever, and nothing I give him eases it. I fear that he is growing weaker by the day."

"How long has he been ill?" Leah asked, her mind darting over the remedies she knew to be of value.

The doctor frowned. "That's the problem. It's only been three days since he called me in, and the fever has drained him beyond what I would have expected."

"I don't know if I can be any help," Leah said quickly. "I have tended bruises and cuts and bound up broken bones. Fever can be a worrisome thing."

"He will pay you well."

Leah stiffened. If money was the final argument in this favor he asked of her, the doctor was in for a surprise. "If I see him, I won't ask a fee. I will do it as a service because I am able."

"Leah, what is the problem?" Gar stood at her back, holding Karen in his arms, the scent of leather and horses and store-bought soap making her aware of his presence even before he spoke.

She turned her head, including him quickly. "The doctor wants me to visit a patient of his and see if I can suggest anything to aid his recovery." She took a step back to include Gar in the circle. "Will you mind if we do it now?"

"Who is ill?" Gar asked the doctor, looking around the churchyard as if he would discern which among the townspeople were absent from the crowd.

"Eric Magnor."

Gar's brow lifted. "Eric? I had not heard. Surely he's not…" He frowned.

"No, nothing beyond a fever that lingers, I think. I thought your wife might have a suggestion to offer."

"Yes, we can stop by on our way home. Will he be expecting her?" Gar asked.

"I've told him I would suggest it," the doctor said.

"And he agreed?" Leah asked.

Doctor Swenson nodded. "He was more than agreeable. He'll be waiting for us."

Karen's head nodded, and her eyes closed as she used Gar's shoulder for her pillow. Kristofer waited in the surrey, watching them as they walked from the churchyard.

"I'll put her down on the seat by Kris," Gar said quietly. "She should sleep for an hour or so, I would think."

The big house sat on the edge of town, far removed from the sawmill that had made its construction possible. White, with tall pillars across the porch, it spoke of wealth and power, an image only enhanced by the presence of a butler who opened the door to the Sunday visitors.

"Mr. Magnor is expecting you, Mrs. Lundstrom." His regal tones welcomed Leah, even as his chilly demeanor excluded the two men who accompanied her. "Will you gentlemen wait in the parlor?" He motioned to the wide doors leading to the formal room just down the hallway.

"Leah?" Gar's low utterance of her name was a question she understood.

"I'm fine," she said quietly, for his ear only. "I won't be long." Picking up her skirts, she followed the stately figure of the butler up the curving staircase to the second floor, looking back for a moment to meet Gar's gaze. His nod was one of encouragement, and she allowed a half smile to touch her lips.

The room to which she was led was spacious, with windows open to the sun and fresh air. Eric Magnor was dressed in a fine robe. His trouser legs showed beneath its hem, as if he would hold his illness at bay by being clothed, instead of lying abed as he probably should have been.

He sat before the fireplace, but no fire lent warmth to the room. His head turned as Leah entered the doorway and he waved a hand at the butler, signifying his dismissal.

"Will you sit down, Mrs. Lundstrom?" His voice was far from strong, and he failed to rise, a lack Leah could only blame on his condition. For beneath the flags of color that rode his cheekbones, Eric Magnor was pale and wan, his eyes sunken in his head, his lips dry and cracked from fever.

He looked more than his age today, his graying hair lank against his head, the few wrinkles in his brow prominent.

She stepped closer to him, scorning the seat he offered. Her hand touched his forehead, and she felt the heat radiate from his flesh even before her palm made contact with the lined skin above his eyes.

"You have had no relief from the fever?" she asked.

He shrugged, a fatigued movement of his shoulders. "It comes and goes, and I'm tired to death of the pills and potions our esteemed town physician has to offer."

Leah stepped back and watched him, noting the lax position of his hands on the arms of the chair. As if the man had no strength to spare, he leaned his head against the high chair-back and lifted heavy eyelids to gaze upon her.

"Do you have any remedies to suggest, ma'am? I

understand you are a healer of sorts. Do you claim success in treating fever?''

Leah nodded. "I have a bag that contains various…'' She paused. ''If my husband will give me the use of his team and surrey, I'll go home and bring it back with me. For now, I would suggest you have your butler or some other servant help you to bed and then wash you with cool water. It may ease the fever. It certainly won't hurt.''

''My stable man can take you,'' Mr. Magnor said, lifting a hand toward the doorway, where the butler had apparently waited, unseen by Leah.

''Sir?'' the man asked.

''See Mrs. Lundstrom downstairs and do whatever she asks,'' Mr. Magnor said wearily.

Leah rose, darting one last look at the ailing man. ''I'll return as soon as I can,'' she promised. ''Please do as I suggested, sir.''

His hand waved again, as if speech were too tiring to attempt, and Leah left the room.

Gar stood at the doorway of the parlor, his expression wary as she descended the stairs. ''What is it, Leah? Can you help him?'' He walked to meet her and offered his arm.

She took it, pleased by the gesture, and nodded at the doctor, who came from the parlor to join them. From beyond the front door a child's voice called out. ''The children?'' she asked.

''Karen awoke and a maid went out to them. She is playing with them in the yard. I doubt they've missed us.''

''Would madam care to be escorted by the stable man, as Mr. Magnor suggested?'' the butler asked, his bearing more subservient, his glance in Leah's direction almost friendly.

"No, I'll take Mrs. Lundstrom home myself," Gar said brusquely.

Leah's fingers tightened against his sleeve, and she halted him with a look. "Gar…I must come back. I'm only leaving to get my bag from the house."

His jaw set and he looked about him with a harried glance. "I had not expected that, Leah. Perhaps the stable man had better follow us and bring you back. He'll have to make the trip twice, getting you home later on, but that can't be helped. I can't leave again, with the baby to tend to."

Gar's mouth tightened, and Leah felt a stir of aggravation at his gesture of impatience. They stood before the stoop under the scrutiny of the butler, and Gar's hand clenched into a fist, the muscles of his arm rigid beneath her touch.

"This is important, Gar," she said softly, seeking his understanding.

"So is your family, Leah," he blurted, but then had the grace to look abashed at his harsh rejoinder.

"Dinner is almost ready to put on the table. By the time you and the children finish eating, I should be back."

His nod was almost imperceptible as he turned his gaze upon her. "I'm sorry. I'd looked forward to this afternoon, when we could spend time without worrying about the barn or the crops. I'm being selfish, I know. And Eric Magnor is a friend. I shouldn't begrudge him any help you can give."

"He's pretty sick, Gar," she said, following him toward the surrey.

"Madam?" The butler hurried to catch up with them.

"Am I to send the stable man along to bring you back?"

"Yes." Gar spoke abruptly.

He offered Leah his hand and she climbed the iron step into the vehicle. Within minutes they were well on their way home, the doctor making a more leisurely path to his house near the sawmill.

Chapter Seven

It was hours past dark before the fever broke, and Eric Magnor slept. Leah sat beside his bed, watching her patient, her gaze drawn to the austere features of the man she had met only this noontime.

He'd been more than a gentleman with her, instructing his housekeeper and butler to do her bidding. And so they had worked together, she and these two servants who obviously held their employer in high esteem.

Eric had swallowed the tea obediently, a blend of dried elderberry blossoms and boneset that Leah's mother had set such store by in years past. He had endured the cooling towels as his fever rose, and had shivered without complaint as his butler fanned him in the warm summer evening. The debilitated state of the man was frightening, Leah decided, watching as her orders were carried out. And not until he broke out in a sweat that drenched him thoroughly did she relax her vigil.

"I think he is better," she said softly to Thomas. The tall man tended his employer with unstinting effort, having just changed the sick man's nightshirt and bed linens.

Thomas nodded. "Yes, ma'am, I believe he is. This is the first he's really slept in three days."

"Lord bless him," Sarah Perkins, the housekeeper whispered. "He's never ailed like this before, not in all the years I've worked for the man."

Leah rose and stretched, aware suddenly of the tight muscles that protested her taut posture over the past hours. "I must be on my way home. I hate to ask your stable man to go out at this hour, but my husband will be concerned by now."

Thomas cleared his throat and glanced at the doorway. "Mr. Lundstrom is waiting for you downstairs, ma'am."

"He is?" Leah's movements were stiff as she walked past the servant. "How long has he been here?"

"I let him in several hours ago, at twilight."

Had she been so wrapped up in the man she cared for that she'd missed Gar's arrival? So it seemed, and that thought hastened her steps as she moved down the staircase and across the wide foyer.

"Gar?" Her whisper was not enough to rouse him as she walked to where he sat near the window in the parlor. Her hand touched his shoulder, and he tensed beneath her fingers.

"Leah." As if he'd recognized her touch, he awakened and spoke her name in the same instant.

She tightened her fingers, holding him still as he would have risen. "Shh…rest a moment." Stepping before him, she sank onto a small footstool and leaned one arm against his knee. "Who is with the children?"

"Benny brought Ruth to the house. She said she would spend the night. I told her to sleep in your bed."

Leah nodded. "The sheets were clean yesterday,"

she said. It would not do for a visitor to sleep upon sheets wrinkled by a week's use.

"Is he better?" Gar asked, dropping one hand to touch his wife's hand. At her nod, he ran his index finger across the narrow span, then turned it over to touch her palm. "These are healing hands, aren't they?"

"Sometimes, when they do as they are bid," she answered, her breath taken by the movement of the single finger that smoothed a path across her palm and up the length of each finger.

"You have a calling, Leah. It was wrong of me to be selfish earlier, when I sulked at your choice to return here."

She smiled at him, and felt a kindling within as his eyes met hers. "He is a good man, isn't he? His servants treat him tenderly, Gar. That sort of care is merited by more than good wages."

Gar nodded. "Eric Magnor is a fine man. He has a sadness in his eyes, but we have never spoken of it." His voice lowered to a tone just above a whisper. "I've heard his wife was not happy here, that she left him and never returned."

Leah shook her head. "How tragic for the man. He has this big house and money aplenty, and no one to share it with."

"He shares it," Gar corrected her. "The townspeople vie for a chance to work at the sawmill. He pays them well. And the church fares nicely from his generosity. I suspect he looks after this town more than any of us know."

Leah smothered a yawn and felt her eyes dampen. She blinked then lifted her free hand to stop a second telltale yawn from escaping. "I am weary, Mr. Lundstrom,'' she said, yearning to lay her head against his muscled thigh. She dismissed that errant thought and struggled to her feet.

"Is it safe to leave him?" Gar asked, rising quickly at her movement and holding her arm to steady her balance.

"He is sleeping soundly. I think he is over the worst of it."

Gar led her to the wide parlor doors. "What was wrong with him?"

Leah shook her head. "I don't know. He had only a soreness in his back, and that may have been from muscles tensed with his fever and chills. Whether he had an infection of the throat or perhaps elsewhere...it's hard to say." She turned to watch as Sarah came down the stairway.

"Make sure he drinks water every hour, Sarah. His body needs to be flushed out, to be rid of the illness. And make up the tea for him if he even begins to become warm again."

"Yes, ma'am, I'll do that. Thomas will stay with him now. I'll take him up a decanter of water." Even in her weariness, the housekeeper was erect and proper, opening the big door to the pillared porch and nodding her farewell as Gar and Leah passed before her.

"I'll be by on Tuesday," Leah said. "Unless he is worse tomorrow. If so, send your stable man out and I'll come."

Sarah nodded. "Yes, ma'am. We'll take good care of him. And he'll be pleased to see you return, I'm sure. He'll want to thank you and settle up with you."

Leah stumbled as she stepped down to the driveway, where Gar's horses waited, still in harness before the surrey. His hand slid around her waist and he held her against his side.

"Are you all right?" His words were coated with concern, and without awaiting her reply, he lifted her to the seat.

Leah nodded, feeling a great weariness overtake her. Spending her strength was nothing new to her. It left her in overwhelming waves when she treated a patient for a number of hours. Tonight, she felt its loss, as if the very essence of her spirit somehow joined with that of the man she had guarded so closely. Her gaze swept upward to the window on the second floor of the house where, behind filmy curtains, two men shared that beautiful room, one watching, the other asleep.

"Lean on me," Gar said, his voice growling in his throat as he lifted his reins. She felt the surrey jolt into movement as her head touched Gar's shoulder. As her eyes closed, she heard his voice again.

"Leah…" Just the sounding of her name, but uttered in a tone so warm, so comforting, it touched a chord within her.

Leah…

The baby rode her hip comfortably as Leah walked into the general store. Karen's arm around her neck clutched the braid Leah had allowed to hang freely down her back, and her other hand waved at the women who greeted her. There was nothing like a baby to pave the way to friendships, she thought, answering smiles and nods as she made her way to the counter.

Bonnie Nielsen watched her closely, frowning a bit as she reached to tweak Karen's nose. "You look weary, Leah. Have you caught up on your sleep?"

"Of course," Leah answered, scoffing at the concern.

"I only took a short nap yesterday and I was fine. Poor Gar was the one who worked all day in the fields with the men."

"My brother says your Gar is a fine man," Bonnie whispered, leaning over the counter. "He works hard, Lars says, and pays well."

Leah nodded her agreement. "He seems to have no problem with finding hired hands. He even helped Benny Warshem build a house for himself and his wife, just beyond the hay field. Banjo goes home every night, but he and your brother are there right after breakfast every morning."

"Are you in town alone?" Bonnie asked, peering over Leah's shoulder toward the door.

"No, Gar sent Lars along to get lumber from the mill. He's building new stalls in the stable for his mares."

"And have you visited your patient yet?" Bonnie wanted to know.

A cessation of voices in their vicinity told Leah that more than one shopper had heard the question and awaited her reply. "No, I'll go there next and Lars will pick me up when he finishes at the sawmill."

"I heard Dr. Swenson asked you to visit Mr. Magnor," Mrs. Pringle said eagerly. "Is his house elegant?"

Leah brushed aside the woman's question, answering only as courtesy would allow. "Yes, I saw Mr. Magnor."

"He's a kind man," Eva Landers said, walking toward Leah from her desk in the corner of the store. She held an envelope in her hand, and Leah's heart picked up an extra beat. "This is for your husband," Eva said.

Leah breathed deeply, accepting the mail, her pulse settling to its normal rate. It had been weeks, almost two months, since the arrival of Anna Powell's letter.

Perhaps her worry was in vain. Perhaps there had been no more inquiries into her disappearance from Chicago.

She could only hope.

"Do you have a list for me?" Bonnie asked, her glance excluding the women who had gathered in the vicinity.

Leah pulled the wrinkled paper from her pocket. "I hope you can read it. Karen was bouncing on my lap as I wrote."

Bonnie scanned the items written in Leah's hand and nodded. "I'll have it ready when Lars comes by. You go on ahead, Leah."

Karen gurgled and waved at Bonnie, peeking over Leah's shoulder, and Eva accompanied them to the door, stepping out on the sidewalk with them.

"He's a good man, Mr. Magnor," Eva said quietly. "I'm glad you were able to help him."

"There's something about him." Leah spoke in a low tone, lest she be overheard. "He's sad. Not just from his illness, but as if some great sorrow has brought him much pain. Gar said it's because his wife left him."

Eva nodded. "I've heard that. It must have been a lot of years ago, though, before Joseph and I came to live here."

"I'd better go," Leah said, sensing she would hear no more on the matter. "I don't know why…there's just something about the man, something that makes me yearn to see him smile."

"You're as kind as he, Leah," Eva told her, hugging her shoulders as she dropped a quick kiss on her cheek. "You make a good pair." Her grin was roguish. "But not as good a pair as you and that handsome husband of yours."

Leah's cheeks warmed as she heard the teasing

words. "You're a caution, Eva Landers, talking that way. You know Gar Lundstrom only married me because he needed someone to cook his meals and care for his children."

"Did he, now?" Eva asked archly. "I think I see him look at you as if he enjoyed more than your ability as cook and nursemaid."

Leah swatted at her friend amiably. "Go on with you. You'll make me blush."

Eva stood still and watched as Leah left her side. "Mind what I say," she said cheerfully. "Pay attention, Leah."

The big house was a good half mile from the general store and Leah's legs were weary, what with toting Karen on her hip and being called aside several times to pass the time of day as she walked through town. The folk were friendly, more than one of them curious to ask after Eric Magnor.

The pillars were gleaming in the morning sun as Leah stepped to the front door, barely lifting her hand to rap on its white surface before it swung open before her. Sarah stood in the doorway, a smile lighting her plain features.

"Mrs. Lundstrom! He's been asking after you since he ate breakfast. I'll tell him you've arrived." She ushered Leah into the foyer and hastened toward another set of doors across from the parlor.

"Mr. Magnor, sir. Mrs. Lundstrom has arrived."

The growl of a male voice followed the announcement, and Leah watched as Eric Magnor stepped into view. "Mrs. Lundstrom." He took her hand and bowed low over it. "Please come into my study." His gaze touched Karen, and he glanced at Sarah.

"Let me take the babe," Sarah offered quickly.

"She'll be fine. I'll take her to the kitchen and coax her with a pudding."

Leah turned over the child willingly, her arm aching from the weight of her, and followed Magnor into his domain. Shelves full of books covered two walls, the third a blend of windows and French doors, with draperies pulled back to allow the air to enter. A large desk sat to one side, its surface covered with papers and ledger books. Before the cold fireplace, two chairs sat at an angle, and it was there that he led her.

"Won't you sit down, my dear." His voice was rough, perhaps from the illness, she thought.

"Thank you, sir." She chose the chair nearest the door and sank into its comfort. "The baby weighs more now than she did half an hour ago," she said with a chuckle. "My arms grew weary before I got here. Next time I'll use the wagon to your front drive."

"Where is your conveyance?" Eric Magnor asked, his forehead creasing into a frown. "Why did you walk, carrying a heavy child in your arms? I could have sent a carriage for you."

Leah shook her head. "Oh, no! It was nothing. My husband's wagon is at the mill. He sent Lars along to pick out boards for new stalls, and I came on ahead. Lars will pick me up here shortly."

"I didn't want you inconvenienced in any way, Mrs. Lundstrom. I owe you a great debt." Mr. Magnor leaned forward in his chair and spoke quickly. "I have called upon Berg Swenson before when illness has visited this house, but never have I been so upset with his incompetence as now. He had no notion of what to do for me. He wanted to spread salve upon my forehead and feet to allow the fever to escape." His look of aggravation spoke volumes to Leah.

Eric Magnor stood and paced to the fireplace, his hands thrusting into his trouser pockets as he watched his visitor. "I owe you, Mrs. Lundstrom," he repeated. "But, besides that, I feel we should become friends. I want you to know that my resources are at your disposal."

Leah felt a warmth well within her. "I ask nothing for what I did here, Mr. Magnor. Your offer of friendship is payment enough. I have no need of anything but your recovery to give me satisfaction for what I accomplished. But it is comforting to know that I can call on you again, as a friend."

"You are a gifted woman." He paused and his jaw worked, as if his emotions were torn by this visit. "May I call you Leah? I don't mean to be presumptuous, but I feel we have a sound basis for an acquaintance."

"Leah will be fine," she answered. "I came back today to be sure you are fully recovered, Mr. Magnor, and because I said I would return. You have no more fever? Or pain?"

He shook his head. "None at all. I awoke yesterday morning, or rather, well into the afternoon, feeling much refreshed. Perhaps that was due to the gallons of water my help poured down me. At your orders, I understand."

Leah smiled at his humor. "My mother always said that an inward cleansing with copious amounts of water was the best cure for many things. I'm pleased that it aided in your recovery. Did you require any more of the tea?"

"No, that vile stuff seemed to do the trick, though. It tasted strongly of something bitter, I thought. But, whatever its source, I am thankful for the potency of the treatment. Be assured, dear lady, that I will never send for Dr. Swenson should we be in need of a healing hand in the future.''

Leah flushed at his words. ''I'm sure the good doctor has many talents. Not everyone uses the medicines my mother taught me about, Mr. Magnor.''

''Your mother. She was a healer also?'' His voice contained a semblance of caution as he stepped closer to where Leah sat. ''Where did you live, you and your mother?''

Leah forced a smile to her lips. ''In the city. We went there many years ago, and Mother…'' She lifted her hand from her lap and moved it in a dismissive manner. ''You don't want to hear all of that, I'm sure. Suffice it to say that I came back here several years ago. The city was not to my liking.''

''You feel at home here?'' he asked quietly, his eyes kind as he watched for her reply.

''Yes.'' Leah met his gaze, noting the veil of sadness he wore. ''You must save your strength, sir. Won't you sit down?''

He nodded, accepting the other chair, crossing his legs as he leaned back. ''I'm still a little weak, but my appetite is good, Leah. As I said, I think your medicine was responsible for my well-being today.'' He touched his fingers together and formed a peak, touching the tip of his index fingers to his lips. ''I would be pleased if you come to visit me again. I enjoy your company.''

She bowed her head, perhaps to hide the smile his words brought to her lips. She'd never been so readily accepted by anyone before, except for young Kristofer and Karen, of course. Even Gar…

And there her thoughts began to churn. Gar would be waiting for his lumber and his dinner. That Ruth was available to put the food on the table was immaterial.

It was Leah's job to tend her family, and sitting here, in this magnificent home, whiling away the time while her husband waited at home, was not to be tolerated.

"I must leave." She rose and motioned her host to remain in his seat. "Please, Mr. Magnor, don't get up. I can find my way out. I'll just need to locate the baby first." Her smile was quick. "I'm sure your household is not prepared for Karen. She tends to upset schedules and keep everyone on their toes."

Eric Magnor leaned forward. "Are you happy, Leah?" His words were urgent, spoken in an undertone, as if he feared to be overheard, and his look spoke of deep interest. "I know it is none of my concern, but I truly care about your well-being."

Leah turned to look fully upon the man who had asked her friendship, and found no guile in his demeanor. He was sober but benevolent in his manner, almost as a favorite uncle might appear.

"I have a good life," she assured him hastily. "Mr. Lundstrom treats me well."

Eric nodded. "I thought as much. He is a man of honor, so far as I know."

Leah turned to the door, only to find Sarah there, her arms full as she cuddled Karen to her breast. "She went sound asleep," Sarah whispered, obviously reluctant to return her charge.

The transfer was made, nevertheless, and Leah was let out the front door. The big farm wagon was halfway up the driveway as she stepped from the porch, and in moments she was settled on the wide seat with Lars beside her, Karen still asleep in her arms.

She glanced back as the wagon turned in a wide circle before the house and caught a glimpse of a dark figure standing in the shadows, just inside the window of Eric Magnor's study. She lifted a hand in farewell and smiled as the man returned her salute.

He was well, almost returned to good health, and she felt a surge of satisfaction at that thought. Gar would be happy to hear the news.

"He wants to be your friend? You have lady friends, Leah. Eric Magnor can be my friend. It isn't proper for a woman to visit with a man alone."

She never should have told him about her conversation with Eric, Leah decided. Her supper was late, due to the day being half over before she'd arrived back at the farm. She'd put chicken on to cook, stewing an old hen who was intent on hiding her eggs under a bush in the yard.

This was no time of year for a cluck to be nesting, and by next year the creature would be too tough to grace the dinner table. So, with hatchet in hand, Leah had dispatched the hen quickly. Today's supper would be chicken, with fluffy dumplings on top of the kettle.

Now she wondered why she had gone to all the trouble of fussing over a meal for the sourpuss who sat at the head of the table. Gar Lundstrom was in a snit. There was no other word for it. Leah's mouth was set as she plopped his plate down before him.

"I didn't mean to imply that I would be spending hours on end visiting with the man, Mr. Lundstrom. He simply thanked me for my help and asked if I would consider him a friend. I thought I could not have too many of them on hand, so I accepted his offer. Now, if you don't like it, you'll just have to lump it!" She turned away from him, and his growl was the only warning she received.

Fool woman! She thought she could prance around

and twitch her skirts and act the flirt with him and then throw Eric Magnor in his face—and he should like it. Gar Lundstrom was filled to the brim and overflowing with an enormous amount of anger, most of it directed at himself.

She'd been gone all morning, and even though his common sense told him that the trip had not taken much longer than necessary, he'd kept a close watch on the road, lest he miss the approach of his farm wagon. He told himself it was the lumber he waited for so impatiently. But in his heart of hearts, he knew he was yearning for the sight of Leah, the woman who held herself from him.

The kiss he'd stolen on the porch had not been enough. And yet it had been too much. And how she could be such a puzzle was beyond his comprehension. She had him in a tizzy, that was for sure. And now she had the nerve to tell him he could *lump it*...whatever that fine phrase was supposed to mean.

He stood, ignoring the chair that fell to the floor at his rising. In two steps he was upon her. In another second, he had lifted her to settle her plump little bottom on the kitchen dresser, where it vied for space with the second largest pickle crock and the coffee mill.

"Gar Lundstrom! What are you doing?" she shrieked, her tone tempered by the palm of her hand that covered her mouth.

"I'm setting things to rights in my kitchen," he returned sharply.

"My kitchen," she corrected him. "Just put me back down on the floor this minute."

"When I get good and ready," he told her, leaning to look fully into her eyes. "You have a sassy mouth for such a bright lady. Did no one ever tell you it would get you into trouble someday?''

''Pa? Are you mad at Miss Leah again?'' Kristofer asked from his seat at the table.

''Now see what you've done,'' Leah spouted.

''I'm not the least mad at Miss Leah, Kris,'' his father answered mildly. ''Just tend to your supper there.''

Leah leaned forward until her nose almost touched his, and Gar inhaled her scent, that of starched cotton, and cinnamon from the apple tarts she'd put in the oven only minutes ago. Mixed with the fresh smell of her skin, it served as an aphrodisiac to his vulnerable body, and he met her mouth with his own. One day he would subdue the fire that burned between them.

For now, he would add to its flame.

Her lips were warm and soft, and unless he missed his guess, they were willing to be tasted and subdued with the touch of his. He sucked softly at her bottom lip, then transferred his attention to the upper, finally seeking entry between the two for the tip of his tongue.

Her whimper was that of a woman made aware of a new and urgent need, and he gloried in the evidence of her feminine nestling as she leaned into his chest. Her breasts were full and firm against him, and he subdued the groan that begged to be let free from his throat.

His mouth widened over hers and he covered her lips with his own, searching out the even, smooth surface of her teeth, the crevices of her lips and tongue. And then he retreated, swiftly and without due care, as he heard the knock at the kitchen door.

''Yes?'' His mouth was wet with her flavor, and his trousers strained at the fly front.

''Gar? There is a young heifer caught in the mire.''

The voice of Banjo Kemmel was abrupt, its message that of a man who awaits an immediate answer.

"I'll be right there," Gar answered, his narrowed eyes upon the woman who even now was in his arms. His nostrils flared as he inhaled sharply, his head swimming with the passion her mouth and the curves of her body had set into motion.

Her gaze was wary, as one hand lifted to touch her mouth. Her other hand levered against his chest, and she whispered soft, broken words that spoke of her confusion. "Gar? What are...I don't know...Gar?"

He lifted her to the floor, steadying her with strong hands at her waist. "I must go out and see to the heifer, Leah." Even to his own ears his words were harsh, as if he were uncaring of her, and she reacted accordingly.

As though each movement pumped new strength into her spine, she straightened, her chin lifting, her hands pushing at him. "Turn me loose," she said quietly. Her eyes slid to rest on the table where Kristofer watched, his features blurred with bewilderment.

"Kristofer and I will feed Karen while you take care of your animal," she said. Glancing at Kristofer, her tone of voice softened. "Eat now, Kris."

"Yes, Miss Leah," the boy said obligingly. He bent to with a will and filled his fork with a chunk of chicken, gravy dripping between the tines. "It sure looks good."

"Yes, it does," Gar offered, regret coloring his words. "Keep some warm, if you don't mind, Leah. I'll probably bring Banjo back for a bite, too. He's late going home. Those brothers and sisters of his will have cleaned the pots by the time he gets there."

"Yes." Leah's head was bent as she lifted a bit of

dumpling on her fork, eyeing it as if it were somehow defective.

Apparently, that was going to be the extent of her reply. As answers went it wasn't much, Gar decided, but it was probably about as good as he could expect after the mess he'd made of this encounter.

Across the barnyard, Banjo was trotting at a quick pace, heading for the hapless cow, and Gar set off in his wake. A detour to the horse corral netted him a strong gelding, and he swung up on the horse's back, guiding him by a rope he'd snatched from the fence and tied onto the animal's halter.

He overtook Banjo just about the time the hired hand made it to the swampy area, a low spot in one corner of the pasture. Beyond him, the young cow was knee-deep in muck and mire, bawling her head off.

There was no way around it. If he couldn't toss a lasso that far, he'd have to wade through the mud until he was close enough to throw the rope over her head. Gar looked down at his boots and sighed. Might as well take them off now, and the stockings, too. No sense losing them in the mess he was about to get into.

Chapter Eight

The mud caked on his feet and legs as he walked, and each step took more effort than the last, the boots he carried weighing more than he remembered. Gar was bone weary, his mind set on the chicken still sitting in the pot at the back of the stove. The dumplings would have lost their fluffy texture by now, but as hungry as he was, that mattered little.

Banjo was just steps behind him, cheery and garrulous in his praise. "Yessir, you just snaked that rope right over that li'l darlin's head, just slick as a whistle, Mr. Lundstrom."

That he had had to slog through mud almost to his knees to accomplish the task lessened Gar's joy in the matter, and his reply was muttered into his chest.

"S'pose Miss Leah saved us somethin' to eat, Mr. Lundstrom?" Banjo headed for the pump, levering the handle with enthusiasm. He bent his head to slosh water over his nape, wetting down his hair and splashing his face liberally. His fingers ran through his hair, and he scrubbed at his hands with gusto beneath the cold water.

The thought of washing up in that chilly waterfall turned Gar's feet toward the porch. "Leah!" She'd been scurrying around in the kitchen just moments past. Maybe there was warm water left in the reservoir, enough to wash up with anyway.

"Leah!" he called again, only to see her pressing her fanny against the screen door as she backed from the kitchen to the porch. She must have read his mind, he decided in a moment of thanksgiving. In her hands she held her largest basin, filled with water that looked to be steaming.

"I'm here, Gar! You didn't give me a chance to answer. I had to sort out things to find a basin large enough for your feet."

"My feet?" He stood in the grass just below the bottom step and watched as she lowered the wide container to the porch. A towel was slung over her shoulder, a washrag with it. She dug in her apron pocket, pulled out a bar of store-bought soap and offered it to him.

"I'll push the pan closer and you can wash your hands and face first, then come up on the porch and we'll do your feet."

"We'll do my feet," he repeated, his weariness preventing his mind from comprehending her plan. The cloth was sudsed in no time, and the hot water was a welcome relief. His skin itched like a son of a gun wherever the mud had touched it, and the hot water dissolved the residue as he scrubbed at his face and head alike.

"You're looking more like a human being already," Leah said, her voice teasing.

Relief shot through him. She wasn't mad. She wasn't upset at him kissing her then leaving her as if she'd come down with a case of the measles.

Her voice softened and touched him with concern. "You look about worn-out, Mr. Lundstrom."

"Yah, I am. But the heifer is back on solid land, and I am almost clean once more, thanks to you." Bending over the basin, he poured double handfuls of water over his forearms and wrists. "I was dreading the cold pump water."

"I need me a good wife, Mr. Lundstrom," Banjo said from behind Gar. "Seems to me you get treated mighty fine."

Gar cast him a glance, his mood enhanced more than a little by Leah's thoughtfulness. "You'll have to look around for a woman of your own, boy. Mine's taken."

"Step up on the porch, Gar," Leah told him, moving the basin from the edge. "Get hold of the post there and stick one foot in the basin for me."

He looked at her, puzzlement alive in his mind at what she was brewing. One foot in the basin, he held the post and watched incredulously as she knelt at his feet, competently rolled his pant leg another turn, then soaped the cloth. Her hands worked rapidly, soaping the calf of his leg, her face hidden from his view as she murmured instructions to lift his foot.

He did as she asked and she quickly scrubbed at his ankle, then his toes and the long length of foot between.

"Here," she said, placing the towel on the porch and motioning him to place his clean foot there.

Within a minute, she had finished the other leg and foot and rose to toss the dirty water from the end of the porch. The washrag she hung on a short rope she kept stretched between two posts for that purpose. Then, hands on her hips, she cocked her head at him.

"I only wash. I don't dry," she said pertly. "Supper's ready." She picked up his boots and thumped them on the side of the porch, watching as dirt cascaded over the ground below. Then, placing them next to the wood siding, she sailed through the door, allowing it to slam shut behind her.

"I suspect you better dry your feet, Mr. Lundstrom. Miss Leah's dishin' up," Banjo said, following in her wake.

"Yah, I better do that." Stunned to the core of his being, Gar watched through the screen as his wife placed Banjo's food before him, then turned back to the stove. With several well-aimed swipes, he dried his feet, slung the damp towel over the line and entered the kitchen.

Leah placed a plate before him. The dumplings still looked more than edible, and he set to with a will. The chicken was well-done, and he ate generously of the carrots and onions she'd added to the stew.

Banjo finished quickly, cleaning his dish with a slice of bread, every bit of gravy and every smidgen of food wiped up and delivered to his mouth. He rose and handed Leah the empty plate, then turned to the door.

"I'll be here in the morning, sir," he announced cheerfully. "Thanks again for the supper, Miss Leah."

He was gone, and Gar ate more slowly, his stomach pangs easing. He watched as Leah brought Karen in from the parlor, where her quilt was left spread open on the carpet. She played there sometimes in the evenings with her assortment of toys. The baby reached for her father, and Gar took the miniature hand in his and shook it playfully.

"She missed you at supper," Leah said, sitting in the rocking chair with the child. A nightgown and fresh diaper were at hand, and with deft movements, Leah readied the baby for bed.

"I've never had anyone wash my feet before," Gar

said, the words slipping past his lips before he thought to hold them back.

"I'll bet your mother did, more than once," Leah said, kissing the palm of Karen's hand, peeling the fingers back to find the sensitive center, then causing the little girl to laugh as she bit at the plump flesh.

"You know how to do all the right things with her," Gar said, spearing the last bite of his chicken and lifting it to his mouth. "I have to stop and remember the way Hulda played with Kristofer. I don't think she made up the kind of games you do."

"You probably just didn't notice," Leah answered, watching him over the baby's head. "I'm sure she was a wonderful mother."

"Yah, she was good with the boy. But she was always so quiet, so…almost sad, it seems like." He rose from his chair and took his plate to the sink. "I shouldn't talk about her with you, I guess."

Leah shook her head. "You can talk about your first wife all you please, Gar. She was a part of your life, and mother to your children."

"This one," he said, his finger pointing at Karen. "This one will never know her. She'll think—"

"We'll tell her when she's old enough," Leah cut in. "She needs to know that her mother gave up her life so that she could live."

"Is that the way you look at it?" he asked. Somehow that explanation had never occurred to him. That one life was given so another might exist in this world. And yet, it made sense. Hulda had known what a risk she took, and she did it gladly.

"Of course. Hulda wanted to give you a child, and she did. I think she died happy, Gar. She knew the baby was alive. She heard her cry, and then she kissed her brow. Her lips were on Karen's forehead when Hulda died.''

He hadn't known that. He hadn't known that Hulda had seen the child. All he remembered of that night was the blood that covered the bed, the ashen look of Hulda's face and the terrible mess that Leah had cleaned up all by herself.

''You wouldn't even let me help,'' he said, his mind skimming the surface of those terrible hours.

''It was no place for a man to be,'' Leah said, rocking with Karen, easing the child into sleep. ''My mother said men were useless in the face of childbirth.''

''It was my fault, though,'' Gar said, the words spoken aloud for the first time. He ground his teeth against the doubt that had ridden him lately. ''I blamed you, Leah. I wanted it to be your fault that she died, so I told you it was so. Now I look back, and I don't know what I believe. One thing I do know, though. She got in the family way because of me.''

Leah slanted a glance at him. ''She got pregnant because she wanted another child, Gar. She told me so.''

''I think I'll carry the guilt for the rest of my life.'' He walked to the door, looking out on the darkening night.

''She didn't want you to, you know. She'd want you to be happy, Gar. I don't think the woman had a selfish bone in her body.''

He acknowledged the truth of that with a nod. ''I didn't treat her as I should have, though. She was a good woman, and I didn't have a great love for her.'' He turned to Leah. ''I liked her, though. And isn't that a thing to say about your wife, that you liked her! Her father and mine made a pact that Hulda should marry me, and neither of us had a choice in the matter.''

"You could have said no, couldn't you?" Leah asked.

"I was taught to do as my father said," Gar answered. "He left me the farm when he died. And for that inheritance, I did as he asked. It was the way things were then." His words were solemn now, as if he made a pledge in her hearing. "I'll never raise my boy that way. He'll have a choice."

"Yes." Leah nodded her head. "You're a good father, Gar. Your children love you."

"I never had anybody wash my feet before," he repeated, the thought circling his mind and surfacing as a thing to be spoken of.

"I just didn't want you to track mud in all over the kitchen. I seem to spend a good share of my time sweeping up behind you." Her tone of voice belied the scold she delivered, and he caught a smile lurking at the corner of her mouth.

"I'll try to be neater from now on," he promised.

"Don't get all carried away with yourself," she warned him. "I may hold you to it."

"Do you want me to carry Karen up to her bed?" he asked, watching as Leah rose from the rocking chair. The baby was turned neatly to sleep on Leah's shoulder, and a small quilt covered her from the evening breeze that came in from the west.

"No, I can take her up. You might want to help Kristofer with his numbers. He's sitting at the library table in the parlor. I gave him a slate full of figures to add."

Gar watched her leave the kitchen, listened to her soft footsteps on the staircase. His gaze followed the sway of her hips until she reached the top of the flight of stairs. She moved past his bedroom to where Karen's door stood open, and turned to look down at him. For a long moment she was unmoving, framed in the door way, only the pale form of her dress and the golden glow of her hair visible in the dusky light.

She was his woman, his wife, and he felt a thrill of ownership at the thought. Not that her body was his property, but that her very life was committed to him. It was a commitment he had no doubt she would keep. And he would be the better for it.

She was a contentious woman sometimes, quarrelsome and stubborn. She scolded him for the least little thing, caused him to lose his temper more than he'd ever done before, with her standing toe-to-toe with him the way she did.

And now she'd gone and done something that took his very breath from his body.

She had washed his feet.

"You have a letter, Leah," Eva Landers called from her desk where the morning mail was in the process of being organized. Boxes behind her bore the names of all the townsfolk, and as she spoke, Eva sorted letters, circulars and postcards into the various cubicles.

"All right," Leah answered, her fingers fumbling at the coins in her small purse. Suddenly numb, her fingertips refused to function as they ought, and she bit at her lip as she shook the money into the palm of her hand.

"I must have the correct change here, Bonnie," she said, her mind going blank as she attempted to recall the amount the storekeeper had asked for in payment for her groceries.

Bonnie leaned over the counter and picked at the assortment. "Got it!" she announced, dropping the coins into her cash drawer.

"Thanks," Leah said, tucking her purse away. "I'll just step over and get my letter."

"You're really getting popular, Leah," Eva teased. "Two letters in one year." The envelope was simply addressed to Leah Gunderson, in care of General Delivery, with no return address. She folded it once and stuffed it deeply into her pocket, thanking Eva politely.

"Someone from the city?" Eva asked.

"Probably." Leah searched for a smile, settling for a twitch of her lips. "I think Gar is about done at the mill, Eva. I'd better get my things together. Thanks, again."

Dropping her bundles on the edge of the sidewalk, Leah peered down the street toward the sawmill. Saturday morning in town was always busy. Today seemed even more so, with buggies and wagons coming in from four different directions.

"Morning, Miss Leah." Brian Havelock tipped his hat and paused a respectful distance from his former laundry lady. "I heard tell you paid a visit to Mr. Magnor last week. Got him back on his feet right soon, I understand."

Leah nodded. "I was glad to be of service, Mr. Havelock." Surely Gar was on his way by now. The red wagon was not hard to spy, and she stepped into the street to look from a different angle.

"I'll bet he paid you a pretty penny for making a house call on Sunday, didn't he?" Brian asked, pushing his hat back and chewing on a toothpick.

"I beg your pardon?" Leah was shocked at the crude remark, and disappointed in the man she'd thought was a friend.

"You know what I mean. Everybody knows he's loaded to the gills with money. I'll bet it was worth a bundle to him for you to get him back on his feet so quick-like."

"You overstep, Mr. Havelock," Leah said coldly. "I fear we have nothing to speak about."

He moved a few inches closer, and his hand snaked out to clasp her wrist. "I've been wondering what the big farmer man has that persuaded you to marry him, Leah. He's pretty well set, out there on that spread of his, ain't he? Bet you're gonna be fixed for life."

Leah tugged for freedom, but Brian tightened his grip. "Is it worth it to sleep with the big lummox?" His chuckle was low and mocking. "I offered you a good time and a nice place in town, not to mention a healthy specimen of manhood to keep you happy. You never even came to the dance that time, when you promised me you would." His laugh was low and filled with bitterness as he mocked her. "You missed your best chance, ma'am."

"I find nothing attractive about you or the proposal you offered me, Mr. Havelock," Leah said tightly, fearing that their conduct was becoming a spectacle for the passersby's entertainment. "As for the dance you speak of, I had other things on my mind the night of that dance, as you well know. Furthermore, I think my husband would be more than angry if he were to hear of your remarks."

"Well, I doubt you're gonna tell him, are you? Just remember, when you get tired of the old farm boy, come see me. We'll have a good time, honey."

Leah broke the grip of strong fingers and backed away from the man. She felt a trembling overtake her that had nothing to do with fear but much to do with a furor she could barely contain.

"Don't ever put your hands on me again," she said

in a low, controlled voice. "I have access to several firearms, and I'm sure I can figure out how to shoot them without too much trouble."

Brian teetered back on his heels. "Are you threatening me, honey?"

Just beyond the man's shoulder, a red wagon came into view and Leah turned her back on her erstwhile suitor, hailing Gar with an uplifted hand. When she glanced at her bundles and then back at the street, Brian had moved from sight, and she heaved a sigh of relief.

Gar Lundstrom would more than wipe up the dust of the street with the young man if he had heard just one remark that had fallen from Brian's mouth. Becoming a public spectacle was far from Leah's aim in life, and she whispered a prayer of thanks for Gar's appearance.

"You about ready, Leah?" Gar asked, jumping down from the wagon.

"Yes, my things are there," she said, pointing to the bundles. "It took me two trips."

"You about bought the store out, didn't you?" His muscles flexed as he lifted two packages at a time, holding them by the string that was wound firmly and tied on top of each bundle.

Leah watched as he loaded them all then looked expectantly at her. "We ready?" he asked.

"Yes, just about. Do you still have to stop at the blacksmith's?"

"I'll only be ten minutes or so," he said, holding her arm as she climbed inside the wagon box.

"I'll wait outside, if you'll park in the shade," she offered. "It'll be time enough for me to check over my lists again."

The horse chestnut tree stood just beyond the big double doors of the blacksmith's shop. Glowing coals marked the forge Sten Pringle worked, and his muscular arms glistened in the sun, his shirtsleeves torn off at the shoulder. The various instruments of his trade hung on an iron rack, and Sten handled them with ease. His body was honed by the hours he spent swinging a heavy hammer, forming the horseshoes and metal fittings. He was an awesome sight to behold.

Leah sat atop the red wagon, idly waving a folding fan she'd found in her reticule. A souvenir of George Thorwald's funeral three years ago, it was but one of many to be seen on this hot afternoon. It was a lazy day, dust motes floating in the air, and even the blacksmith's dog was too warm to investigate the visitors to his domain.

Leah's gaze admired Gar, her thoughts taken with the man she'd married, watching him as he spoke, his hair gleaming in the sun.

Although a tall, strong man in his own right, he was almost swallowed up in the figure of Sten Pringle as he conducted horse business Leah hoped would not take too long. She swatted at a fly buzzing near her ear. They gathered in this area, probably due to the number of horses here and at the livery stable next door.

It was to that establishment Eric Magnor rode his black horse, a stallion if Leah knew anything about it. Her eyes flitted to the animal's obvious male structure and away, a feeling of awe overcoming her reluctance to view such a physical trait.

Eric looked to be fit and capable, especially for a man his age, Leah thought. Her gaze touched upon him as he dismounted from his horse and led it to a hitching post available there.

"Mr. Magnor!" Sten called out, waving the heavy

hammer he held. "I'll be with you in a few minutes, soon as I finish up with Mr. Lundstrom here."

"No hurry," Eric said, waving in return, tugging at his reins to reinforce the knot he'd formed. He glanced around and saw Leah. He lifted two fingers in a salute and walked in her direction.

"Mrs. Lundstrom!" His greeting was jovial and his eyes scanned her rapidly as she sat primly on the wagon seat. "Would you like to descend and wait for your husband on that bench over there?"

Leah shook her head. "No, thank you, sir. He won't be long." His eyes were clear, the circles beneath them almost too faint to notice, and his skin color was healthy. "You look as though your illness has left you with no permanent effect," she said, relieved to see that he appeared to have completed a full recovery.

"I'm fine, Leah," he answered, using her given name as he stepped closer to the wagon. "I can't thank you enough for the care you gave me. My housekeeper and Thomas are still singing your praises. I fear they've spread the word. I only hope you're not inundated by folks seeking your help. I doubt Mr. Lundstrom would appreciate your absence from home on a regular basis."

Leah smiled, pleased by his words of praise, sensing a strength and vitality in the man that drew her interest. Almost as if he spoke to a part of her that hungered for words of friendship and admiration, she felt herself liking him more and more.

"How is the little girl?" he asked. "My housemaid was quite taken with her, and the boy, too. I expect they keep you busy, don't they?"

She nodded. "They're at home today with the wife of one of Mr. Lundstrom's farmhands. And, yes, they do keep me hopping. It's almost as if they were really my own, Mr. Magnor. I've had the care of Karen almost since the day she was born, and Kristofer has spent a lot of time with me.''

''Lundstrom is a lucky man to have found you, and an even smarter man to have married you, Leah. I hope you are happy with him.''

The statement sounded almost like a question and Leah met his gaze for a moment before answering. A look of expectancy lit his eyes and he watched her soberly. ''Leah? Am I being too bold, asking such a thing?''

She shook her head. ''Oh, no! Not at all. Gar Lundstrom is a fine man—you're right. A good husband, and a wonderful father.''

His brow drew down and he tapped his fingers against the rim of the wagon bed. ''If there is ever anything I can do for you, I want you to know that my door is open to you. Anytime, Leah. Anytime at all. I owe you a great debt,'' he added quietly.

Leah felt a flush cover her cheeks and she whispered her thanks. ''You don't owe me anything, Mr. Magnor, but I appreciate your kind words.''

''Leah?'' Gar's voice was stern, and Leah lifted her gaze to meet his, noting his downturned mouth and narrowed eyes.

''Are you ready to leave now, Gar?'' she asked, folding her fan and making a great show of replacing it in her reticule.

''I was just telling your wife how much I appreciated her help last Sunday,'' Eric told Gar, turning to him with an outstretched hand.

Gar clasped it, shook it once and murmured his thanks. ''She was pleased to help you, I'm sure,'' he said with barely a trace of civility in his tone.

"I'll tend to my business now." Eric turned to the blacksmith. "Good day to you both." He tipped his hat in Leah's direction, and she was again struck by the depth of his scrutiny, the firm line of his mouth and chin.

Gar climbed aboard the wagon and turned it about beneath the tree, cutting a sharp curve back onto the road toward home. "What was all that about?" he asked Leah after a few minutes.

"All what?" she asked, knowing what he wanted but unwilling to repeat the words she'd shared with the mill owner.

Gar's eyes struck sparks as he looked at her. His hands were clenched tightly upon the reins, his anger in evidence. "What did Eric have to say to you, Leah? His business with you was finished last Tuesday. He had no reason to approach you today."

She turned her head away, looking out across the fields that held wheat in abundance. A rabbit ran across the ditch and headed for the wagon's path, halting just as it reached the side of the road. Eyes bulging and whiskers twitching, the small creature looked like prey for any hungry hawk, not to mention the half-wild barn cats that roamed the hedges.

Leah looked back over her shoulder, feeling a strange kinship with the gray bunny, watching as it hopped across the road to safety. So might she seek the security of her room once she got back to the farm, she decided. Gar seemed determined to have a fuss over Eric Magnor. And she was equally set against the idea.

"Leah," Gar said, his tone softening a bit. "I don't think it's proper for you to spend time with a man like Magnor."

"How about spending time with Brian Havelock,

then? He had quite a bit to say to me today, and you didn't raise a fuss over that, Mr. Lundstrom.''

"Well then, what did he say to you?" Gar asked, as if he must humor her.

"I don't believe I'll tell you," she answered after a moment's silence.

"Are we going to have an argument, Leah?"

"I think you'd do well to leave it alone for now, Mr. Lundstrom. I'm willing to ride with you in silence. I am not willing to hear you fuss at me all the way home.''

He snapped the reins in the air over the backs of his horses and the team set out at a rapid clip, the wagon rolling easily behind. Wood bounced in the back, wide boards and square posts and bags of what Leah supposed were nails and fittings.

"The blacksmith will be out tomorrow to shoe several of the horses," Gar said. "I have invited him to have the noon meal with us. Will that be all right with you?" He looked straight ahead, and Leah was forced to answer aloud, knowing he would ignore a nod of her head.

"Yes, certainly. It is your house, after all—all but the kitchen, since I am the one who works there. You have the right to invite anyone you choose to share the table with you.''

The growl issuing from his throat was interspersed with words Leah could not decipher—nor did she want to. In fact, if she was not mistaken, her irate husband was swearing up a storm, and she could only look aside, unwilling to allow him access to the smile that threatened to turn to laughter.

Anger brewed slowly in Gar Lundstrom, and she suspected she was in for a period of silence that would only be shattered by heated words and more of Gar's rigid notions of the proper behavior for his wife.

She had been Leah Gunderson for too many years to bow to a man's whims at this stage of her life. Gar was in for a battle royal, and she hoped fervently that she was sturdy enough to hold her own.

Chapter Nine

"Mama!" As clear as a bell, the word burst forth from Karen's lips as Leah entered the kitchen door. From behind her, she heard the indrawn breath of the man who followed her.

"Mama," the baby chortled, her plump arms waving as she sat in the middle of the kitchen floor.

"I told her that Mama would be home soon, and she picked up one word from my whole long lingo," Ruth said cheerfully from where she stood, stirring a kettle on the stove. "She's been calling for you ever since."

Leah's heart beat rapidly as she bent to pick up the child, wrapping her in her arms and dropping numerous kisses against the pale curls. "Did you miss me, sweetkins?" she crooned.

"Will you help carry in the rest of your packages, Leah?" Gar asked from the doorway, where he had just eased his two parcels to the floor.

She swung her head to look at him. Gar was glaring at the child she held, as if she were foreign to him, and Karen, totally oblivious to the tension that strung tightly between Gar and Leah, waved in his direction.

"Papapa…" Her lips smacked on each syllable, and she squirmed in Leah's arms, reaching for her father.

"Whoa, now!" Leah admonished, shifting her grip lest the wriggling child cause her to lose her hold.

Gar stepped closer, lifting Karen into his arms. "Did you behave for Ruth, little girl?" He turned his back on Leah, speaking next to the woman who had spent half the day with his children.

"Thank you for watching her, Ruth. We did not mean to be so long."

"Saturday in town is always busy," Ruth answered. "It always takes extra time with so many folks around and about." She gave the contents of the kettle a final stir and placed the spoon on the edge of the stove. "I thought you'd be hungry, Leah, being gone from home so long. I made you some soup with that ham bone you had in the cooler."

"Thank you, Ruth." For a moment, Leah felt almost a stranger in her own house. Anyone could cook a pot of soup. Gar was proficient at handling his daughter, and it seemed the only thing left for her to do was carry in the last two bundles of supplies she had purchased at the store.

She walked past Gar and across the porch. Her feet felt heavy as she trod the stairs to the yard and shuffled through the grass to where the wagon stood. The parcels were heavy and she lifted them from the wagon, only to lower them to the ground in order to get a better grip.

"I should not have spoken harshly. I'll take them." His voice was gruff. "Take the baby from me, Leah."

She shook her head. "You asked me to bring in the rest. I can do it, thank you." With barely a glance in his direction, she slipped her fingers under the string and hoisted the bundles, walking back toward the house.

From the barn, Kristofer's clear voice rang out a greeting, and she turned her head. "Miss Leah, wait up! I'll help you!" He was a blur of blue shirt and dark trousers as he ran toward her, his smile eager and welcoming.

"Pa! We got all the frame built and the stalls are ready for the boards," he said to his father. "I been workin' hard all day with Benny."

His warm, agile fingers slid in to lift the weight of Leah's burden from her left hand and he laughed as they carried the package between them. "Wow, you musta had a long list today, Miss Leah. Did we get any candy?" His blue eyes were hopeful as he reached for the screen door, his fingers closing around the spool that served as a handle.

"You don't like peppermint sticks, do you?" she teased.

"I sure do, ma'am."

"As soon as we eat some soup and maybe some bread and butter, you may have one, Kris."

Gar came through the doorway behind them, silent and frowning. "Get the baby's chair up to the table, Kristofer. And then wash up for dinner."

The boy cast a quick look at his father, then glanced at Leah. "Yes, sir, I will," he said, then hurried to obey.

Dinner was quiet, only Karen disturbing the silence as she chewed on a bread crust in between bites offered from Leah's spoon of mashed beans and slivers of ham that floated on the broth. It was a relief once the meal was finished and the silence was broken by the slam of the screen door, signaling Gar's departure from the house.

"Is Pa mad at us?" Kristofer asked from the doorway, where he had hesitated in his father's wake, toeing the throw rug into place.

"No, of course not," Leah answered, wishing the words were true. And they were, to some extent. Gar's anger was directed at her, not at the children.

"He's probably just got a lot on his mind," Kristofer said, his eyes suddenly wise for his years.

"Yes, you're right," Leah agreed, forcing a smile to her lips. "The blacksmith will come tomorrow. Maybe he's thinking about that."

The boy's face cleared, his worry dissipating as he accepted her theory. His wave was quick as he pushed the screen door open and jumped from the porch.

"And now there's just you and me, Karen," Leah said, running her fingers through the golden hair of the child who sat perched in the high chair.

She was rewarded with a grin and upraised arms, and for her own comfort, Leah lifted the baby and settled into the rocking chair with her. "Your papa may be angry with me, but you are always my sweetheart, aren't you?" she whispered against the sweet-smelling cheek.

A ruffled sigh greeted her words, and Karen's head fell heavily against the fullness of Leah's breast. A bubble escaped her infant lips and blue eyes shuttered as the baby relaxed against the warmth and softness of womanly curves.

Leah's voice lifted in a muted melody as she soothed the babe into slumber. The chair creaked as it rocked, and the sunlight poured through the window to crown the golden heads with twin halos.

To the man watching from the porch, it was a scene he could barely resist. And yet, within his breast churned a deep resentment that this woman should hold

the hearts of his children so easily. That this daughter
of his should reach out for Leah, calling her the name
that should have belonged to Hulda. That she who had
not been able to save the mother should now bask in
the adoration of the child.

Perhaps the greatest resentment of all was that he was
so mightily drawn to the woman himself. That his loyalty to Hulda had gone by the wayside sometime over
the past months, since Leah had come to this house and
lent it her beauty.

It had drawn him to her from the first, that honey-
colored hair, the pure line of her profile and the lush
curves of her body. And not only him, he decided. She
drew the eyes of men wherever she went, it seemed.
From the boy, Brian Havelock, who so obviously had
been taken with her, to Eric Magnor, whose wealth and
position would make him an attraction for any woman.

Even the blacksmith, Sten Pringle, had cast an eye in
her direction as she sat in the wagon beneath the chestnut tree this morning. She was golden and fair, this
woman he'd married. And for all that she lived in his
house, she did not belong to him.

And that was a situation he tired of more with each
passing day.

For now though, he owed her words that would be
hard for him to speak. It would not do to be jealous of
his own child, not even for Hulda's sake. And that had
been at the front of his mind for the past hour.

"Leah." He spoke her name without thinking, watching as she lifted her head to gaze at him through the
screen.

"It was not enough that Karen called me Papa. I was
upset that she called you Mama," he said quietly,
knowing that he must have this small thing out in the

open. "It made me hurt to know that Hulda never heard her say that word. But, I need to tell you, it's all right. I shouldn't have let it bother me, and I'm sorry."

Leah's eyes widened at his words of apology and her mouth opened to speak.

"Don't say anything," he told her quickly. "I don't apologize for anything else, just this one thing. The rest of our quarrel is still sticking in my craw. We will talk about it later. For now, I just came to the house to get my extra gloves from the wash room."

Leah watched him as he came in the door and walked to the small lean-to where the washtubs and scrub board were kept. He bent to sort through a box full of gloves and mufflers and caps Hulda had kept there for extra use, finding the ones that would fit closer to Kristofer's size.

With barely a look in her direction, he left the house and settled his mind on the stalls that would take shape before nightfall.

Hulda...who had deserved to live. Who had tried and failed, over and over, until her gamble had resulted in death. Leah brushed her lips against Karen's soft cheek, whispering words of love to the child, aware of hot tears cascading down her own cheeks that mourned the loss of a mother.

She shifted in the chair, reaching for the handkerchief she kept in her pocket. A rustle of paper met her fingers and greeted her ears at the same time.

The letter. She'd been so at odds with Gar since this morning that she'd totally forgotten the letter. Her handkerchief wiped the tears and she blinked away the moisture that remained in her eyes. One long finger slipped beneath the flap and she opened the envelope.

A familiar scrawl met her eyes and the signature of

Anna Powell was scribbled across the middle of the page.

The message was simple. She'd been careless, leaving her small book of friendship, which Leah had signed, on her desk—only to come into the house and find it missing. Someone had broken in, and the book was the only thing taken, so far as she could determine.

Did Leah think there might be someone desperate enough to find her that they would stoop so low?

Too well, Leah recalled the words she had written, words of friendship and caring, signing with her name and the address where she could be reached.

"Yes, there is someone," Leah whispered, crumpling the single sheet of paper in her fist.

The sun had set in a fiery ball, and darkness was fast overtaking the outbuildings as Leah settled Karen in her bed for the night. Rocking her to sleep was probably pretty close to spoiling the child, but the joy she found in the warmth of those small arms around her neck was excuse enough, she'd decided.

Spoiling was easily undone, farther on down the line, when, like Kristofer, Karen grew too old to want the comfort of loving arms and a lullaby at bedtime.

Leah stepped close to Kristofer's door, rapping lightly on the wooden panel. "Kris? Are you in bed already?"

"Come in, Miss Leah," he answered. She opened the door and met his sleepy smile with an answering nod.

"I see you're just about ready for the sandman," she teased.

"I never heard about the sandman before you came here, Miss Leah," he told her, rising up on one elbow. "Can you tell me about him again?" His eyes were hopeful and Leah sat on the edge of his mattress, reaching to brush a wayward lock of hair from his forehead. Perhaps he was also needy of some spoiling tonight, she thought.

"Of course, I can," she said as she bent to kiss the spot she had bared. "Just put your head on the pillow and close your eyes, and he'll visit you in no time."

The boy did as she bade him, settling against the pillow. "It smells good in my room at night," he murmured against his pillow. "Like flowers, I think."

Leah smiled, weaving the tale with soft words and a simple melody, singing and speaking the story her mother had taught her years past. In minutes, Kris had relaxed against his pillow, his mouth opening just a bit as he inhaled the scent of honeysuckle that climbed up a trellis beneath his window.

"It makes for sweet dreams, little boy, that honeysuckle your papa planted." She straightened the sheet over his chest and touched his hand lightly, tracing the length of his index finger with her own. Then she rose from the bed to face the man who watched from the doorway.

He lifted a finger and beckoned her, this big, husky man who was but a larger version of the boy she loved so well. If it took cajoling him into a good mood, she could do that, she decided, so things would be well between them.

She followed him from the room, closing the door almost shut behind herself, then made her way down the stairs, intent on his broad shoulders as he led the way. He went through the kitchen and out on the back porch, and she was close on his heels as he turned to face her.

"I am not a jealous man, Leah," he began, looking down at her from his great height.

"You could have fooled me," she blurted out, and then bit at her tongue, which had betrayed her so quickly. Where was the meek and mild woman she had thought to be for this occasion?

"See? This is what I mean! You are ever ready with these smart remarks that rile my temper. Why can't you listen and be obedient, maybe just once in a while?"

"I'm not Hulda, Gar." That much she had to say. To that extent she had to defend herself. "You didn't marry an obliging, easygoing woman this time. I didn't promise to bow to your temper every time you got in an uproar over something."

"Well, this time you will listen to me," he said, his voice rising with each word.

She shook her head at him admonishingly. "Don't shout at me, Gar. You'll wake the children, and they don't need to hear you having a tantrum."

His big hands snaked out and settled on her shoulders, and for a moment she thought he would shake her. She braced herself and lifted her chin, the better to meet his gaze. His grip was strong and bruises might appear by morning, but since he wouldn't see them, it didn't matter much, she decided.

"I am not having a tantrum. I am only telling you that it is not seemly for you to speak to men on the sidewalk in town and lure them to the wagon while I do business."

"Lure? I lured Eric Magnor to the wagon? You must be dreaming, Garlan Lundstrom. I spoke to the man for a moment, and that's all. I told him you were a good husband and a wonderful father to your children. Is that so bad?"

His fingers eased their grip and she relaxed beneath the weight of his hands. "He likes you, Leah. He looks at you in a certain way."

"Well, I'm glad someone likes me, Mr. Lundstrom. You certainly don't seem to share his feelings."

He shook his head. "You don't know how I feel about you. How can you know, when I don't even…" He transferred his hands to his hips and his jaw jutted as if he were ready to face an opponent.

"You get me all in an uproar, Leah, with your ideas. I always thought women should be happy to tend to the house and not want more. And then you come along with your independence and people looking to you for help, and I'm left to wait while you prance off and take care of someone else."

She was stunned by his vehemence. "It isn't just Eric, is it, Gar? You don't want me to treat folks who need me, do you?"

"I thought they would find it too far to come, once you moved here from town. Like Hobart coming here, all flustered, looking for a cure for his wife's womanly ills last week, and Lars taking home salve for Bonnie's cut finger. I certainly didn't think they would go so far as to drag you from the churchyard on Sunday morning to do your healing."

He caught a deep breath and his eyes accused her. "You belong to everyone else and not to me, Leah. Even the children…" He halted, his words coming slower, his eyes shadowed with pain.

"I belong to you, Gar. I'm your wife," she answered, sensing more than a jealousy in him. "I like Mr. Magnor. He is my friend, no more than that. I must help those I can, when they need what I can give. And most

of all, I love your children, and they love me in return.
I can't help that they turn to me."

He shook his head, as if her words were not what he
wanted to hear. "You have smiles for everyone but me,
it seems, Leah. For me you have sassy words. And you
turn away and swish your skirts until I want to take
hold of you and..."

She backed from him. Surely the man did not intend
to lay hands on her. Bad enough that his fingers had
perhaps left their mark already. He was not a harsh man,
not cruel certainly, but in his temper, he might do something he would regret.

Gar Lundstrom lived with enough regret already. She
would not be the cause of more.

"I'm going to take a walk," she said, sidling past
him to the porch steps. "Maybe you'll feel better if you
sit on the swing and think about things for a while."

"No, I don't want you out in the night by yourself."
He moved to grasp her arm, and she slid from his touch.
"I mean it, Leah. Come and sit with me and we'll talk."

She shook her head. "No, this time I'm right, Gar. I
want to walk by myself, just out to the orchard and
back." She slipped down the stairs and started across
the yard, only to hear the clatter of his boots on the
wooden steps as he followed her.

"I'll come with you," he said in a harsh undertone,
his hand touching her shoulder.

She shrugged away from beneath his touch and ran,
her feet slipping on the damp grass, her breath catching
in her throat. Deep within her a flame of excitement
came into being, and she felt its flush against her breasts
and throat, climbing to her cheeks.

Then the stable was before her, the big door open
only a crack, and she headed there, pushing her way

inside, knowing as she did that he would follow. The sound of animals settling for the night surrounded her and she blinked in the darkness, wary of stumbling over something and falling.

Behind her, the door was shoved open farther, and a beam of moonlight slanted past. Then the door was closed with a clatter and Gar was there. "Stand still, Leah. There are boards in the aisle and tools on the sawhorse."

He spoke the truth. The glimpse she'd had of the floor ahead of her had revealed a veritable maze of obstacles, and she hesitated. Her heart pounded, not from the exertion of her race to this place, but from the presence of the man who stood behind her, whose scent surrounded her.

He was a man of the earth, his clothing bearing the smell of leather and animals and sunshine. But tonight, he wore another aroma, one not yielded by the weave of his shirt and trousers, but coming from the flesh beneath them. A heady, masculine scent she was not familiar with, but one that flared her nostrils with its potent allure.

"You will not walk away from me now," Gar said, his whisper husky in her ear, the words a promise.

How had he stepped so close without her knowing it? How had his hands become so urgent yet careful against her arms, as if his anger had eased into another, stronger emotion?

"You have chosen the place for this," he said gruffly, as if his voice were changed by whatever feeling had replaced his anger. "It is not what I would have preferred, but you have led me here."

"What are you talking about?" Surely that thin, wispy little voice could not be hers, she thought, stepping away from his touch. But he would not allow it, his hands sliding to her waist and turning her in his arms.

"I cannot let you go, Leah. My body aches for you, and I have watched you for too long, wanting to touch you and hold you like this."

She stumbled as he pulled her closer, until their bodies were meshed, with only the layers of clothing between them. His hands were strong as he held her upright, those long fingers tracing the outline of her spine, down past her waist to cup the fullness of her hips, then back up to the curve of her ribs.

"Put your arms around my neck…please," he said, his voice an urgent whisper.

Some last trace of stubborn will nudged her to rebel. "No! I will not be taken in the barn like a mare in one of your stalls." Yet, even as she spoke, her arms obeyed his request, sliding upward to meet at the nape of his neck.

"I am glad you are being obedient tonight." His words were soft and teasing, but his body was firm, his manhood pressing urgently against her belly, hard and prominent, and she was put in mind of the stallion Eric Magnor had ridden this same day.

She trembled, the image blending with the very real presence of Gar's masculine arousal, her head tilting back as the hot, forbidden scent of his body reached her.

"Will you be able to live with this tomorrow, Gar? Are you sure this is what you want? You told me you…"

He inhaled sharply, his arms loosening from around her, and she was almost free of his touch. "Leah…ah,

Leah, I told a great lie.'' His voice was a shuddering sound, as though his whole body spoke her name.

"I thought I could live with you and not take you to my bed, and I was wrong. You have tempted me every day since I brought you here." His hand touched her cheek and she leaned into the tenderness of his caress.

"You have not come to me, not once," she cried.

"No, I haven't, and all that stiff-necked behavior has gotten me nowhere. Now I am reduced to stumbling around in the dark, when I want instead to be in your bed. I have had to watch as the men in town admire you. And I cannot find it in me to do without you any longer, Leah."

"Do without me? Sometimes I think you don't even like me!" she wailed, her frustration at his hardhead-edness surfacing in a cry that roused the horses in their stalls.

"Ah, there you are wrong, Mrs. Lundstrom," he whispered, his words even more potent for their soft-ness. "I more than like you. I have a need for you that overcomes my honor, it seems. I have come close to claiming you tonight without your permission, and for that I find myself not liking Garlan Lundstrom.

"I watch you every day, wishing I could go back on my word and take you to my bed."

"I need you, too," she whispered.

"Don't tempt me if you don't mean it, Leah. Don't tell me you are willing if you are not." His voice was softer, hopeful, not unlike that of the small boy she had tucked into bed earlier. As if he stood waiting for the single word that would make his world come to rights.

"I am more than willing," she said quietly. "But I must tell you something."

"Later, you may speak all you like. For now, you

have told me what I wanted to hear,'' he said, lifting her, cradling her within his firm hold and making his way carefully down the aisle.

''Where—'' The single word was halted by his command.

''Hush. I will not put you in a stall, Leah. There is fresh hay against the wall, waiting for the morning. I would not lay you on the floor without softness beneath you.''

She was lowered, and felt herself sink into a measure of hay that allowed her comfort. But before she could catch her balance within the soft nest, his hands were on her clothing, his big fingers clumsy at the buttons of her dress.

It was dealt with readily, the sleeves shoved down so her arms could escape, her underwear his next target. He undid the buttons of her chemise more easily. His callused fingers opened it fully, the edge of his nails brushing against the rise of her breasts.

She caught her breath, her flesh responding as his hand splayed wide on her chest, then slid beneath the fine lawn fabric of her chemise to enclose the generous curves beneath.

''You have beautiful breasts, Leah,'' he whispered, and in the deep shadows his head was a darker form, bending to her as a supplicant might, his mouth damp against the virgin flesh of her bosom.

''How can you tell, here in the dark?'' Was that her voice? That sound that whispered from between her lips?

His laughter was low, breathed out against her damp skin. ''I have looked at them every day, and now I feel them against my lips and tongue and hold them in my hands. They are more beautiful than I dreamed.

"My Leah…this is a part of marriage I thought I could live without." His voice turned bitter as he continued. "I made do without a woman's touch for a long time, until the night Hulda came to me, well over a year ago. Since then I have been without hope, with no way to be a man as I should be. Until you came into my life."

He lifted his weight from her, his mouth making a trail against her throat and pressing hot kisses against her flesh.

"Let me take your dress off," he whispered. "Lift up, Leah."

And she did, following his instructions, sitting silently as he spread the wide skirt beneath her bare back, and shivering as his warm hands lowered her once more to the bed of hay.

His fingers were agile, loosening the ties of her drawers, and his hands slipped them down her legs with deft movements. Words escaped his lips, a blend of English and his native tongue, and she heard his voice break as his hand brushed the curls where her thighs met, pressed tightly together.

"Too soon, too soon," he murmured, as if he chastised himself. "Ah, Leah! You are so much woman, so soft, almost ready for me." He covered her with his body, lifting to touch and tease her breasts for long moments. Then his mouth found her, his lips and teeth forming the pouting crest as he suckled.

Leah's hands threaded through his hair, and her eyes closed. Torn between the sudden shaft of pure pleasure that darted through her body and the knowledge that the deepest secret of her life was about to be revealed, she cast aside the apprehension that had gripped her. She could not bear it if admitting to the deceit in her life now were to call a halt to this pleasure he offered. If there were consequences to be borne, she would handle them later.

Leaving the bounty of her bosom, he moved upward, his mouth skimming her throat, her shoulder and then her lips in a kiss that was tender yet eager. She met the thrusting of his tongue with her own, and her fears dissolved beneath the heated exploration of her mouth. He left her lips after long moments—reluctantly it seemed—and yet, as if he had other worlds to conquer, he moved on.

His lips suckled beneath her ear, then his tongue probed within, and she laughed softly at the sensation he offered.

His open lips pressed hot caresses the length of her neck, then his teeth opened against her shoulder and she shivered at the firm edge that raked her flesh. "I would not hurt you," he whispered. She clutched him closer, eager for whatever he might do, her body yearning for whatever he gave.

His hands measured her, widening against her stomach, then sweeping over her belly to linger where her womanhood wept for his touch. She held her breath as his fingers explored, heard the high, keening note of surrender that escaped her lips as he penetrated that hidden place, and then shivered at the pleasure he brought to her.

His breath was warm, his mouth urgent, as if he would savor the taste of her flesh. Then he caught the tight crest of her breast within his lips and her hips rose in a reflex she could not control, whispering his name as he suckled.

"Ah, Leah!" His breath was hot, his words muffled against her breast. "So soft, so warm." He slid upward, his hand leaving her woman's flesh as he rose to his knees, spreading her thighs to allow him room. His hands were between their bodies and she heard the rustle of his clothing. Then he bent low, spilling kisses across her stomach, his hands lifting her legs.

She was churning within, her arms and legs unable to do her bidding, only capable of obeying his dictates as he moved her beneath his body. "Put your arms around me, Leah," he whispered, and she did as he asked.

"Lift your leg, just a little more." His big hands were gentle against her tender skin, and she obliged him willingly.

The fire he had kindled within her belly raged unquenched, his caressing hands and seeking lips only adding to the flame that threatened to burn her beyond redemption.

And then he pressed against her, there where no man had entered.

His groan was muffled against her throat as he bent over her, his words of praise like music to her ears as he whispered of her beauty. She pressed upward against him, seeking his manhood with every ounce of her strength, accepting the piercing of her flesh.

The pain was small and easily ignored, for she had known it would come, but the rapture of his possession radiated throughout her body. Hot tears of joy slipped from her eyes as she celebrated this moment with the man she had married.

He was within her, pulsing and full, and she wrapped her legs around his, holding him fast against her as his big body jerked above her and his seed found its home. And then he retreated, slowly and with reluctance, it seemed.

"Gar?" she asked, bewilderment lacing the single word. Surely there was more, more than this ache that remained within her.

"You were a virgin, Leah. How is that possible?" His hands were still buried in her hair, clenching now as he rose over her.

"You are not what you have pretended to be. I think I deserve to know what manner of woman I have married."

Her words trembled, tears melding with anger that he could turn such beauty into ugliness. "You married a virgin, Garlan Lundstrom."

"But why?" He rolled from her, leaving her bereft, the hay swallowing her form, and for a moment she was tempted to pull great handfuls of it to cover her nakedness, lest he see her in the dark.

"It was a lie, my marriage," she admitted quietly. "I could not be a midwife and be unmarried. It simply is not done, Gar. There is no husband buried in the city."

"Why didn't you tell me that? Do I mean so little to you that such a secret should remain between us?"

"You told me when we married that you would sleep alone and I would do the same," Leah reminded him.

"But tonight, when you knew what I intended…" His growl of frustration was loud in her ear as he rolled back to her side. "I was not careful with you, Leah. I could have hurt you badly. Surely you know that!"

"Weren't you?" She lifted her hand to twine her fingers through his hair. "You took my maidenhead with care, Gar. I thought you showed me great tenderness. I wanted to tell you, but then I could think of nothing but what you did to me. My mind was not on the lie I told, but the truth I was about to discover."

"Truth? What truth, Leah?"

"That the blending of man and woman is a joyous thing, Gar. That a man is made to be taken inside a woman's body, to bring pain and pleasure combined."

"I fear there was no pleasure for you." He touched her face with his fingertips, his words soft with an unspoken apology. "I fear I hurt you, no matter what you say."

"Only a little." She tugged at the lock of hair she held.

"Come with me now," he said gruffly, rising to his feet. He adjusted his clothing, then reached for her. His hands were gentle as he helped her into her dress, shaking it out and dropping it over her head.

"My chemise…" She caught sight of a pale shadow against the floor as Gar bent to pick it up.

"I have the rest of your things," he told her, turning her toward the door. His arm was firm against her waist, his hand inches from the curve of her breast, and she leaned into his strength.

They walked in the moonlight. He watched her, meeting her gaze but not answering her smile. As if he spoke words that pronounced their future, he paused at the porch, gaining her full attention.

"You have slept alone for the last time, Leah. Tonight we'll sleep together in the room I built for my wife. For the first time," he said, lifting his hands to cup her face, "I will open my eyes in that room in the morning and find my wife next to me in that bed."

Chapter Ten

Gar watched as creamy gravy was ladled over biscuits, wondering if Leah was aware that her hand trembled. She brought the plate to him, standing beside him as it thumped from her grasp to the tabletop.

"It slipped," she said faintly, turning aside. But not quickly enough to escape the hand that enclosed her wrist with a firm grip.

"Leah? Will you look at me?" he asked. It hurt that even now she could not meet his gaze. That she had looked upon him with wide, startled eyes upon awakening and then buried her head beneath the sheet to escape his touch.

Or so it had seemed at the time. Now that he thought about it, she had behaved exactly as a blushing bride would on the morning after her wedding. And he had been too big a dunderhead to see it. And so he had left her there, instead of searching her out beneath the covers and claiming her lips as he'd been tempted to do.

He'd carried her to the house last night and up the stairs, feeling like a man on his wedding night, whispering those words as they crossed the threshold. He had explored her body with curious hands, his memories of those hurried minutes in the barn too incomplete to suit him.

She had allowed it, had drawn in her breath several times and moved beneath his palm. But she was too new to this game of loving, and he would not give her pain while the hurt was fresh inside her body.

At dawn he'd left her in the big bedroom he'd built for his bride, left her with the sheet covering her sun-streaked hair and forming itself to her curves. And then he'd thought of nothing else but that luscious form as he milked his cows and let them out into the pasture for the day.

She sat down across the table, her words directed at Kristofer and the baby, and Gar reached to touch her hand.

"Leah." Her name was soft, he decided, listening to the sound he breathed.

Her gaze touched their hands, his atop hers, his fingers darkly tanned, thick and long, hers slender and golden beneath. And then she looked up at him. Like those of a startled fawn, her eyes found his, then darted away.

"Are you well?" he asked, and watched as a blush climbed to ride the ridge of her cheekbones.

"Yes, of course." She leaned to Karen. "Open wide, sweetkins. The oatmeal is good this morning."

"Oatmeal?" Even to his own ears, his voice sounded hopeful.

"I made it for the baby, with a little for Kristofer. She can't eat sausage and gravy yet. It is too spicy for her and Kristofer isn't overly fond of it."

"If there's any oatmeal left over, I could eat a little," Gar said, digging into his plateful of food.

"You can have mine, Pa," Kristofer offered.

"I thought you liked oatmeal, Kris," Leah said, frowning as the boy shoved his bowl across the table.

"I do," he said, sliding from his chair. "But Lars said his sister is coming with him this morning to pick out a puppy, and I want to be in the barn when she gets here."

"Don't let her choose the last female," Gar cautioned, "and be sure to tell her she can't have the pup until he is weaned."

"She knows that, Pa. She just wants a pick before we sell them all."

The screen door slammed behind the boy, and Gar turned back to Leah. "You didn't answer me." He reached for Kristofer's rejected bowl and dug his spoon into its depths.

"I'm fine."

"You move slowly today, Leah. I fear I hurt you last night."

"Do we have to talk it about, Gar?"

"You don't look at me when you speak, Leah. Have I made you angry with me? You hid beneath the sheet this morning."

The spoon Leah held hit the table with a clatter, bits of oatmeal splattering the oilcloth. Karen laughed aloud, obviously pleased by this turn of events, reaching for the spoon. Only Leah's quick action kept the baby from attaining her goal as she rose, gathered Karen to her bosom and turned from the table.

"Go out and tend to your animals or cut hay or something! Your blacksmith friend is coming, remember?" Leah's words were muffled against Karen's head as she hurried from the kitchen. Gar watched her walk away, noting the faint hitch in her step.

He went after her, catching her against himself in the hallway, his long arms encircling both woman and child. His head bent to allow him access to her cheek, his hands cuddling the baby she held tightly to her breast.

"Please, Leah. Let me know what your thoughts are. I fear you are angry with me, and I don't want it to be so. I care about you. You are my wife, Leah."

She slumped in his embrace, turning her cheek so his lips touched the slope of her jaw. "I didn't consider this happening when we married, Gar. I know it is a natural thing for husband and wife to…" Words seemed to fail her as she shivered within his arms.

Karen's chubby hands reached for her father over Leah's shoulders, fingers tangling in his hair, her wide smile evidence of her joy in this encounter with her parents. Gar laughed aloud as he allowed the child liberty.

"Karen is pleased I am hugging you, Leah," he said, breathing the words into her ear. "I am pleased my arms are around you. That leaves only your opinion to be aired."

"Maybe I'll be more used to this in a day or so," she managed to say after a moment. Gar's arms loosened their hold on her and she used the additional space between them to turn around, facing him.

Her blue eyes met his squarely. "Karen and I both like your arms around us." A smile trembled on her lips. "I will do better at this, Mr. Lundstrom. Give me time, please."

Time? He was already counting the hours until dark should come again and he could find his place beneath the sheet on her bed. His body responded to his thoughts, reflecting her nearness, and he backed away from close contact. He would not offend her in any way, this woman who had become his wife with such sweet surrender.

"My arms have been empty for too long, Leah. They have ached for your warmth. Don't turn from me."

She nodded. "I won't refuse you, Gar."

"That's not what I mean." He searched for the words that would reveal his need of her. "I find myself wanting to touch you, Leah. Not just for what passed between us last night in the barn, but so I can be warmed by your affection. So you will put your arms around me and kiss me, perhaps, and whisper that you like me a little?"

"I don't need to whisper those words. I do like you. I respect you, and I enjoy spending time with you. I thought you knew all that already."

He smiled, admiring her rosy cheeks, her eyes that reminded him of cornflowers and blue skies, and most of all, the honesty in her words. "I did know that. Maybe you can find other things to whisper to me," he said, cocking his head to one side.

Her blush deepened, and her eyes crinkled with the force of her smile. "Why, Garlan Lundstrom, I do believe you are flirting with me!" Gone was the hesitancy in her speech, and in its place he heard a welcome assurance. Perhaps she needed his words to make her know he thought her worthy of his desire.

And that thought brought all sorts of possibilities to mind. The long nights of his celibacy had left him with yearnings aplenty, and the thought of spending his passion on her willing body was almost more than he could stand still for.

"I will share your bed tonight, Leah," he whispered.

"We will be truly husband and wife from now on. And I will be sure you enjoy our coming together this time."

Bafflement vied with curiosity as she considered him. What was the man talking about? "I enjoyed…" She could not finish the words, her experience not fitting her for such talk between a man and woman.

There was no need apparently. Gar's laughter rose to shatter her thoughts. "You know so little, my wife." His eyes lit with a teasing light, and she tilted her head back to consider him.

"I know I am truly your wife, Gar."

He shook his head. "Perhaps, Mrs. Lundstrom. I will ask you tomorrow if you have learned anything new."

She backed from him and he let her go, his arms reluctantly falling to his sides. "I must tend to my animals, and what else was it you told me to do? Yah, and 'cut hay or something.' And I have not forgotten that Sten Pringle is coming."

A dimple appeared in his left cheek that she had not noticed before. Perhaps his smile had not been wide enough to bring it into being until now. The temptation to put her finger into the small dent was sudden, and Leah smothered it.

"I must change Karen's diaper, Gar, and then get busy with my bread making. I don't have all day to waste just standing around talking."

"I will be in for dinner when you ring the bell. I have told the men to take their noon meal with us from now on. The days will be long for the rest of the summer, and they need more than a piece of bread from home to tide them over until supper time."

She nodded. That would mean more for dinner than she had planned, but if Gar asked it, she would do it.

* * *

The men filled the kitchen, dragging in extra chairs from the big dining room to settle upon. Their praise was profuse, and Leah wallowed in the attention her food garnered. Gar touched her shoulder with his big hand as he stood behind her at the stove, and then slid his arm around her waist when she poured his coffee at the table. It warmed her heart, and that was an altogether satisfactory condition, she decided.

The talk was of the three-year-old fillies that Sten had shod that morning and the training they would undergo now that Gar considered them old enough to ride. Leah listened avidly, wishing for long moments that she were able to climb upon the back of one of those beautiful creatures and ride like the wind across the pasture and down the road.

She tended to the dishes, watching and listening as the men finished their meal, her gaze drawn by the handsome man who kept a watchful eye on her. He rose finally and stepped to the door, waiting as the three hired hands trailed outside to the porch, Sten bringing up the rear.

"I'm going to follow Sten into town, Leah. I need new hinges for the big door. The ones I used when the barn was built are not sturdy enough. And I must arrange for a new harness to be made for the black mare."

"May I go with you?" she asked. "I just need to punch down my bread and set it to rise again. And I'd better wash Karen a bit."

"I can wait for you. I'll tell Sten to go on ahead." He paused at the door. "I'd better tell Kris. He'll likely want to go, too."

But Kris refused the offer, and Leah was strangely pleased by his reply. He was busy with Benny and Lars, and Banjo had promised him a ride later on to inspect the far pasture where young bullocks had been penned. They would be grass-fed with extra hay brought to them, to fatten them up for market.

Perched high on the padded wagon seat, Leah waited for Gar. She bounced Karen on her lap, keeping time with the song she sang to the baby.

"That's a new one on me," Gar said, swinging up beside her. "Where did you hear the songs you come up with?"

Leah laughed, her mood more than joyous. "My mother sang to me once in a while. And our neighbors always sang while they worked in their houses and yards. It seems that I spent about as much time with the ladies who lived near us as I did at home when I was small."

"Your mother was not with you?"

Leah hurried to correct his notion. "Only when she had to go out on a case and I was still too small to tag along."

"You did not have an easy life, did you?" He nudged his team into a quick trot, and the wagon jostled along the road. His arm slid to enclose Leah and the baby in its grasp, and he pulled them closer to him on the seat.

"It was hard for her, especially at first. I got a taste of that when I came back to Kirby Falls. People were so used to Dr. Swenson they were afraid to trust someone new. It took awhile before they realized I could help them."

"And in the meantime?"

Her laugh was rueful as she cast him a sidelong glance. "In the meantime, I got along as best I could. I took in laundry and lived very frugally. I almost changed my mind a few months after I arrived in town, and decided to go back to the city. I had even begun to pack my things, when Hobart Dunbar called on me to help an ailing hotel guest. Dr. Swenson was gone on a long house call and a man staying at the hotel had fallen down the stairs and cut his head open.''

''So you stayed.'' Gar's arm tightened its grip on Leah's waist. ''I wonder when that was...if it was before I knew you existed.''

''Perhaps.'' She felt her heart race at the idea of having left before Gar came into her life. ''It must have been meant to be, Gar, that I stay on here. Things picked up for me. Some of the bachelors from the mill came to me with their baskets of dirty clothes. Then Dr. Swenson sent me cases he didn't want to bother with—cuts and a few broken bones.''

Gar snorted at her words. ''I think some days he bothers too much with his whiskey bottle, Leah. He is getting old, and sometimes he isn't fit to go out on house calls.''

''Doesn't he have a family?''

''Yah, but they are all grown and gone. His wife is dead...maybe six or eight years now.''

They rode in silence for several minutes before Gar cleared his throat and shifted in his seat. ''I'm glad the doctor would not come when Hulda needed him.''

''You said he wasn't available,'' Leah reminded him quietly.

''He had been drinking, Leah, and he told me he had vowed not to deliver another dead child from Hulda's body and refused to come with me. He said he had warned her not to get in the family way again, and it was her fault if she was having a hard delivery.''

''How did you ever walk away from him and leave him standing?''

''I wanted to kill him. Right then I wished for a gun

and the courage to pull the trigger. But I didn't have the time to go to all the trouble. I just came to you instead.''

''What made you think I would do it?''

He looked at her squarely, his eyes dark and discerning, as if he were searching for something within her gaze. ''You have a kind heart, Leah. People said you were good with the art of healing. Then, too, you never looked back when the men made eyes at you, and I liked that about you. You have always been a lady, spoken well of in town.''

His praise brought a thrill of delight to her heart. Her own words were diffident, her eyes slanting a wondering look in his direction. ''I thought you never noticed me before that day.''

''I noticed you,'' he muttered, further answering her with a look that encompassed her face and hair, then focused on her lips. ''But I did not carry it further. You were not my woman, Leah, and I had no right to pay you any attention. I had to watch the young bucks eye you up and down, and mind my mouth. I had to listen to that scallywag Brian Havelock make his big boasts, even though I knew he was not the man for you.''

''I thought you hated me, Gar, the night Hulda died, and for a long time after that.''

''I hated myself. I blamed you so I would not have to accept all the guilt myself.'' His frown was dark and he spoke slowly, as if the words were torn from him. ''I still hold a lot of anger, deep inside. It comes on me sometimes, and I don't know what to do with it. Perhaps now I feel guilty for another reason.''

She concentrated on the gleaming horses that pulled the wagon. Their tails swished, almost in tandem, and their feet picked up quickly, holding a fast clip. Beside

her, she could sense Gar's attention upon her and she
knew he waited for her to speak.

"I will sleep with Karen before I cause you guilt,
Gar Lundstrom," she said quietly. "And I will deny
forever after that you have cause to suffer one minute
of blame."

"Hush! There will be no talk of sleeping with the
baby. Maybe my problem is that my need for you is far
greater than any I ever knew before."

Karen interrupted his words with a babbling
monologue, reaching for the reins he held. Her shriek
of anger was long and loud when Gar rescued the
leather straps from her grasp. It was an interruption
Leah welcomed. He'd revealed more than she wanted
to hear. Poor Hulda had suffered from more than the
pain of childbirth, for surely she knew her marriage
lacked much.

The wagon rolled past the hotel and Hobart Dunbar
waved a greeting. Gar nodded and tipped his hat. Leah
wisely concentrated on holding Karen immobile, the
baby squealing at the activity around her and wiggling
to get down. She had best ignore the friendly gestures
of the men in this town, Leah thought, if there was to
be peace in her household.

The store was crowded, and, as usual, Karen received
attention in abundance—even the men around the stove
tweaking her toes and poking at her round cheeks.

Leah made her way through the store, finally reaching
the counter where Bonnie took her list. "Let me see
your hand," Leah said, reaching for the ailing member.
Bonnie removed the small bandage, allowing Leah first
to inspect the cut, and smiling as she pronounced it well
healed.

The womenfolk surrounded Leah, the friendly circle noisy with women's talk. Lula Dunbar was one of the curious, casting her bait with agility. "So, how does marriage agree with the Widow Gunderson? Do you find a farmer preferable to the big-city man you had the first time around?"

As insulted as Leah tended to feel at the bold inquiry, she was obliged to answer sweetly. "I'm an old married lady, for months now. Do I look like I'm suffering from Gar Lundstrom's cruelty?"

She flirted her eyelashes as she spoke, bouncing Karen in her arms. Her cheeks pinkened; the attention showered on her bringing confusion and embarrassment to the fore.

"I'd trade all of your old customers for one day with Gar Lundstrom," Mrs. Pringle said in a loud whisper, bringing gales of laughter from the women who bent close to hear her words.

"You can have Hobart," Lula Dunbar offered. "I'll spend some time over the washboard if you want to take him off my hands tonight."

Bonnie Nielsen lifted an eyebrow at Lula's words. "Don't be so quick to give him away, Lula. You might find a taker. A good man is hard to find these days."

"Leah didn't even have to go looking," Eva Landers said, stepping up to the group of ladies.

"She had men falling all over her before Gar Lundstrom came along," Bonnie said cheerfully. "Leah's always had her pick."

"Stop all this nonsense," Leah protested. "You'd think I was a new bride, the way you all talk. And as to having a beau, I never made it my business to dally with anyone before I married Mr. Lundstrom."

"Not for lack of men trying, though," Mrs. Pringle

said. "They don't linger nearly as long around my porch as they did yours."

"You ought to be ashamed of yourself," Mrs. Thorwald said, hearing only the final words as she neared the counter. "Leah Gunderson is a good woman. She never played backdoor games with anybody. I should know, living right next door for all that time."

She turned to Leah and squeezed her arm. "How are you, Leah? I've missed your homemade soup, you know. And I didn't know what to do for the carbuncle I had last month."

Leah bent to hug the woman. "You should have called on me, or sent word to the farm that you needed my help, Mrs. Thorwald. I'd have come to you."

"Well, I soaked it good and put on a bread-and-milk poultice. Seemed like you had told me about that some time ago."

Leah nodded. "It usually works well. But next time, get hold of me if you need me."

"Heard tell Eric Magnor had reason to appreciate your healing skills, Leah," Lula Dunbar said, her face losing its smile. "We'd be in a bad sort of way in Kirby Falls if anything happened to him, what with the sawmill keeping so many of our men working."

"He's a good man," Leah said, unwilling to elaborate further.

She turned to Bonnie Nielsen, remembering an idea she'd been considering during this trip to town. "I thought I'd bring in some butter for you to sell over the counter, Bonnie. I'm churning more these days. I hate to give the pigs the milk when they do just as well with the buttermilk after I churn."

"I can always use fresh butter for sale," Bonnie answered. "Bring in all you like. Are your chickens laying good? I always need more eggs, too. These town ladies don't like to feed chickens. They'd rather buy them from a crock on the counter.''

Lula shuddered delicately. ''I cannot abide the odor of a henhouse. I vowed the day I married Hobart I'd never again shovel chicken poop.''

. Everyone laughed aloud. ''I never thought I'd hear you say such a thing,'' Eva said after a moment. ''You always look so dignified, Lula.''

The hotel owner's wife leaned closer to the circle of ladies. ''I came up the hard way. Marrying Hobart was the smartest thing I ever did, but don't anybody dare tell him I said so. I've got him thinking he's lucky to have me.''

Behind them, the door opened again, admitting a tall figure, and Bonnie held up a silencing hand. ''Leah, your husband is here, probably looking for you.''

Leah turned around and met Gar's gaze. His face was sober, his finger beckoning her with a familiar gesture. ''I must go, ladies. Bonnie, do you have all my things together?''

Bonnie nodded. ''Let me have a minute to figure this up, and I'll bundle it for you.''

Leah walked to where Gar waited and offered him the weight of the baby she carried on her hip. ''She's heavy, Gar. Will you take her for a few minutes?''

He nodded, lifting the plump child into his arms. ''The sheriff wants to talk to you, Leah. He's outside. Do you want me to come with you?''

Leah felt the color leave her cheeks, as if a wave of cold water had splashed all the warmth from her flesh. She shook her head, slipping through the door to the sidewalk, looking in either direction to locate the lawman.

Morgan Anderson was a quiet man, his presence seldom made known to the townspeople, since crime was not an issue in Kirby Falls. The occasional drunkard might spend the night in his jail, and once in a while the sawmill workers got into a set-to at the saloon on payday, but that was the extent of it.

He was a stranger to Leah, and only the fact that he wore a badge pinned to his gray shirt identified him as the town sheriff. She walked to where he stood, leaning against a post near the barbershop next door.

"My husband said you wanted to see me." She waited as he straightened and slid his hands into the back pockets of his trousers. His look was appraising but respectful as he scanned her quickly, his dark eyes meeting hers with questions alive in their depths.

"I had a visitor yesterday, Mrs. Lundstrom. He asked about you. I wasn't sure what I should tell him, but when he threatened to scout around town, offering a reward for information about you, I thought I'd better pay him some attention."

"Who was he?" What if it was Sylvester Taylor, finally locating her after three years? His vindictive words still haunted her dreams. Taunting her with threats of prison, he had followed her from his house that fateful night. "Murderer" and "liar" were only two of the names he'd hurled after her as she fled his presence.

And who would believe a woman accused by a rich man, an influential man who could hire lawyers, and probably judges, if it came to that?

"Who?" she asked again, her lips dry, throat closing around the word she uttered.

"A detective from Chicago," Sheriff Anderson said quietly. "Let's take a walk, ma'am." He turned and waited for her reply, and Leah nodded, stepping to his side and keeping pace as he strolled down the sidewalk.

"I'd rather hear what you have to say, Mrs. Lundstrom, but the fact is, the man seems pretty sure of his client. Said you had delivered a child to a Mrs. Mabelle Taylor and were careless, killing the boy at birth."

"I won't bother to defend myself to you, Sheriff," Leah answered. "I'll only say that it's not true. What did the detective say? Am I to be taken back to the city in shackles?"

A grin twisted the corners of Morgan Anderson's lips. "No, I don't think we'll have to go that far, ma'am. I told him I knew where you were, and once we hear from the courts, we'll go on from there."

"So I live in limbo for now?"

"Unless you want to set about proving your innocence before we hear from Chicago, that's about it."

Leah shook her head. "I have no way to prove what happened. It will be my word against Mr. Taylor's. I can only tell you that his wife is a demented woman. Any creature who can kill her own child is not worthy of being called a woman. And Mabelle Taylor did just that."

"That's a nasty accusation to make, ma'am."

"That's the truth, nevertheless, Sheriff."

He halted before the hotel. "Shall we walk back? I see your husband out in front of the mercantile looking for you."

"Yes, certainly." Her heart was beating rapidly, and panic was quickly overtaking her. She had to get to Gar. He'd know what to do.

And yet…would he believe her? Given the circumstances under which they'd met, given the death of his first wife to consider, would he be willing to accept her story without hesitation?

Or would Garlan Lundstrom look at her askance? Would their fragile relationship shatter before it had even begun to flourish?

Chapter Eleven

"Will you tell me what Morgan Anderson wanted, Leah? Or am I not to know?" Gar's silence had lasted for the full half hour it took to travel home from town. Not until he helped Leah from the wagon seat did he ask his question.

She met his gaze and nodded. "Yes, of course I'll tell you. I'm just confused right now, and my thoughts are all in a jumble, Gar." She stepped back from him and his hands dropped from their grip on her waist. Karen clung to her neck, whining at the sudden awakening, and Leah shushed her, jiggling her in her arms.

"I'll be in later on," Gar said, grasping the harness of his lead gelding and walking toward the barn. The back of the wagon still held the results of their shopping.

"Bring in my things when you come," Leah called after him, and he nodded.

She trudged to the porch and up the steps, the sounds of Kristofer's excited voice from the barn barely penetrating her fog. What to do? How could she talk to Gar about the detective? She settled Karen in her lap and rocked the baby back to sleep, her lips silent. There was no song in her heart, no melody in her soul. Only the heavy weight of fear.

By now, the detective was back in Chicago, had probably already spoken to Sylvester Taylor. How long would it take for the man to arrive in Kirby Falls with his accusations? She cuddled the child against her breast and rose from the chair. A quilt on the parlor floor supplied a resting place, and Leah placed pillows from the sofa on either side of Karen to give comfort, lest she feel abandoned and alone should she waken.

Supper was going to be a quick affair, with corn bread and side pork cooked with fried potatoes. She sliced the slab of white meat, streaked with rosy stripes throughout, and put it in the iron skillet to cook. The boiled potatoes were left from the day before and she sliced them into the grease as the pork fried.

Deep in the back of the pantry Leah found a hoard of applesauce, the quart jars filled with the pink bounty from the orchard. Gar had not worked hard today and would not be overly hungry. They would make do.

Kristofer burst through the door just as she drew the pan of corn bread from the oven, his eyes sparkling, his eager words pouring forth. "I had a long ride with Banjo and we looked at all the fences and counted the cows and I helped him a lot. He said he couldn't hardly get along without me."

Leah's smile came easy and she hugged the boy against her breast. His hair was sweaty and smelled of horses and saddles and hot sunshine. He carried the same scents as his father, she thought, closing her eyes to better retain this single moment in her memory. He would grow so fast, this small replica of Garlan Lundstrom.

In years to come, she would bring to mind this day

this year in her life, when good and bad were wound so tightly together it seemed impossible to separate one from the other.

She released him from her embrace, and his grin was as pure as sunshine. "I sure am glad you came to live with us, Miss Leah."

Her hand ruffled his hair, then smoothed it into place. "I am, too, Kristofer. I am, too."

"I didn't know if you would come to my room tonight, Gar."

He stood in the doorway, one hand gripping the edge of the jamb, the other holding the glass doorknob. "Why did you doubt my word? I said it would be so."

She stood before the dresser, watching him in the mirror, her hair a veil over her shoulders, curling and waving to her waist. Her hairbrush was still uplifted, frozen in place, as it had been since his knock and immediate entrance to her room.

"I thought…" She lowered the brush to the dresser top and pulled her hair over her shoulder to form the braid she wore nightly.

"You thought—?" He prompted her, closing the door quietly behind himself. She watched as he slid his suspenders from his shoulders and undid the front of his trousers.

"I don't think it matters, now," she told him, suddenly aware of her own lack of clothing. The gown she wore to bed was of fine batiste, an extravagance on her part, but one she gloried in. That a man should see her in it had not been part of the plan when she bought it from Bonnie Nielsen. Now it felt like cobwebs against her skin, its fullness floating like a gauzy cloud around her body.

He sat on a chair near the door, and all she could see of him was his head and chest as he lifted one foot to pull his sock off. He repeated the action with his other foot, then stretched his legs before him, his arms crossed against the width of his chest. Her hair became too much of a problem to cope with suddenly, and she allowed it to fall from her hands.

"I want to know what you are thinking, Leah. Is it that you need to confide in your husband? Or that you have secrets better left hidden? Secrets that only the sheriff in town should know?"

She swung to face him, noting the way his eyes narrowed and swept the length of her body, lingering on her bare toes for just a moment. "I thought you would not want to come to me tonight. That you were angry with me because I didn't talk to you on the way home from town."

A flush rode his cheekbones and his eyes made a trail from her feet upward, seeming to delve beneath the gown to find her hidden secrets. The air was still, the night birds silent outside the window, and his movements were slow and deliberate as he rose from the chair.

He unbuttoned his shirt rapidly and shrugged it from his shoulders. Beneath it he wore only pale skin, with a tightly furred triangle covering his chest, a narrow strip of darker hair disappearing beneath his gaping trousers.

"My anger cannot compete with what I feel right now, wife."

Her mouth would not form the words her mind whispered inside her head. If anger was not foremost in his thoughts, what did that leave? His eyes burned darkly, his flesh drawn tightly over his jaw, that firm line bespeaking a tension she could not fathom. And his hands had formed fists—large, formidable weapons that could easily render a man unconscious if he so desired. What havoc could they wreak on a woman?

And yet, he'd said he was not so much angry as…what?

"Are you going to thump me until I tell you what you want to know, Gar?" Even as she spoke the words, she knew the thought was ridiculous.

"I will never strike you, Leah. I only curl my fingers into my palms in order to keep them from touching you until we speak."

"Must we speak tonight?" In that moment, she could think of nothing more enticing than to have Garlan Lundstrom's hands touch her. Beneath the fine fabric of her nightgown, her breasts peaked in readiness for those long fingers to enclose their weight. The memory of his muscular thighs pressing to find space between hers brought to life a heated thrumming in the very depths of her belly.

She shifted, moving her legs, unsure if the bones they contained were strong enough to carry her weight. Her breathing was affected, her lungs suddenly incapable of supplying the air she required. And surely that was not her heart, skipping and quivering within her breast.

"I think you are right, Leah. I think we can speak tomorrow. Tonight is not made for talking, but for allowing our bodies to know each other." He nodded at the bed, his unspoken message clear and deliberate.

Leah levered herself away from the dresser, her hair flowing freely. She began to braid it once more, her fingers quickly twining thick sections together.

"Leave it loose."

Her fingers set free the waving strands and she sat

on the edge of the bed, watching as he walked to stand before her.

"Move over, Leah. I will sleep on this side." His hands pushed trousers and underwear from his body in one motion, and he stood before her, this arrogant, bossy man who had married her.

Within her rose a surge of rebellion that he should tell her to do this, to move here or there, that he should think himself the master of her body and order her to accede to his demands.

Yet, what else would she have happen this night? Would she banish him from her room, this room he had made ready for a bride, then left empty for so many years? No, she could not. Arrogant or not, proud or humble, Garlan Lundstrom was her husband and she would do as he asked, for there was within her some small voice that cried for his touch, that yearned for his body to possess hers.

If she would ever come to love him fully, she must fully be his wife, and Gar had said she had much to learn. But this much she knew: the desire he set to churning within her body could only be quenched by the force of his passion, and the need to be joined to him was but one part of the puzzle.

Tonight she would allow him to teach her the solving of it.

He waited until she moved to the middle of the bed and then slid in beside her, gathering her into his arms as if he would take her very essence into his body. Between them her gown was a thin wall that offered little resistance, the tiny buttons yielding readily to Gar's fingers. He was adept at this, she decided as he spread wide the bodice, revealing the slope of her breasts.

His hand slipped beneath the material and he weighed the curve of her fullness in his hand, a growl of appreciation signifying his pleasure. His head nudged her cheek and she looked up at him, fascinated by the pale heat of his eyes as his gaze encompassed her face. He bent to her, his mouth hot against her own, his lips soft yet assured.

She opened to him, the sensation of another's tongue touching where only her own had dwelt holding her in thrall. He explored, nudging her into a reaction she delighted in.

He retreated slowly, the candlelight glistening on his damp lips. "Ah, you learn fast, my wife." His teasing words pleased her, and she smiled. "I don't frighten you?" She shook her head, a minute movement. "Will you learn more?" Her hand lifted to slide behind his neck and she tugged him closer, fitting her mouth to his once more.

He traced the edge of her lips with his own, as if he would commit them to memory. His hand tightened its hold on her breast, one finger moving in a circular fashion around the pink, sensitive bit of flesh.

She inhaled sharply when his tongue touched the crest that had been prepared for it. His mouth enclosed the firm, pebbled surface and tugged at its length, and Leah was cast into a sea of sensation beyond her wildest fancy.

A thin wire seemed to stretch the length of her body, from her breast to the hidden secrets where soft folds of her flesh craved his touch. She shifted against Gar, felt his leg ease between her thighs and submitted to the pressure he exerted there. There, where she knew only a tingling, burning need that begged for relief from his teasing torment.

His hand smoothed its way down her back, then lifted her thigh to accommodate his touch. His leg held her so, and she knew a moment of panic as his hand parted the veil of curls that protected her woman's parts.

A long finger slipped easily against her tender flesh, and he murmured a word against her breast as he plied that clever fingertip. She was still, as if frozen in his hands, but the heat of her body yearned for a cooling breeze and she tugged the sheet from her. His hand was motionless, seeming to await her pleasure, and she shifted her hips restlessly, seeking the elusive sensation he brought her.

"Leah, roll to your back," he whispered, his fingers cupping her, as if he could not bear to release the treasure he had discovered.

She obeyed, caught up in the fabric twisted around her body, and with a muffled phrase she could not understand, Gar released her, his powerful hands lifting her and stripping the gown over her head. He flung it to the floor, and with unerring precision, his hand found its place once more.

His mouth returned to hers, warm and seeking, suckling at her lips, then smoothing its way over her cheek to her temple, charting a path with teeth and tongue that delighted her. He had not treated her so last night, for there in the barn he had taken her more rapidly, as though he must stake a claim upon her body.

She had gloried in his touch then; now, she reveled in it, her body seeking whatever he offered. He urged her submission and she granted his wish, opening to his possession. His hands delivered warmth and tender touches, then sought her compliance, even as he demanded her response.

Clever fingers invaded the tender depths of her body,

pressing with gentle friction until she gasped for breath. Her hips surged upward, and she cried out, knowing such pleasure could not be possible, not in this lifetime or in the heaven to come.

But he proved her wrong.

He was the giver of joy, and she received it. He lavished her with his gentleness, and she welcomed it. He sought and found the secrets she could not conceal from his greater knowledge, opening to his touch as he coaxed her to his will. He supplied the wings that empowered her release, and her body took flight, soaring within his embrace.

She trembled beneath him, aware of his weight as he moved over her, finding his place. He lifted her, hands firm upon her hips, and with a groan that seemed wrenched from his depths, he filled her with the very essence of his manhood.

His thrusts were accompanied by murmurs that escaped his lips, words meshing with sounds of pure pleasure. He was within her, her captor, his weight pressing her into the bed as he came down over her body, his forehead touching hers, his hands surrounding her face.

She held him within her arms, strong hands clutching him, fingers pressing to bring him ever closer to her yearning, straining body.

They were equally the victors in this, he with his taking, she with the giving of herself. And in those final moments, as she knew herself to be the recipient of his seed, she was truly his bride. What had come to pass between them tonight far overshadowed their coming together in the darkness of the barn.

Here, in the light of candles, with his harsh face above her, she had seen the man exposed, as he gave himself into her keeping. And knew a moment of delight as she took his vulnerability to herself, aware in one brief second of clarity that the possession was not one-sided. She had possessed him as well.

For there was a hidden, vulnerable part of this man, and it would forever be hers.

Leah slept in his arms, and when she awoke, he watched her, leaning over her on one elbow, holding tightly to the sheet as if he forbade her to cover herself from him. Leah smiled as she felt the flush rise to paint her cheeks.

"You blush again, Leah. Does your memory hold pleasure this morning?"

She nodded, unable to speak of the night past.

"Hold it fast, wife. No matter the storms that come, this part of our life will be sacred, a place we will visit for pleasure and comfort, where we can forget all else but this desire that draws us together."

She'd never heard such beauty spoken aloud. That this gruff, arrogant man could speak such words in her hearing was almost not to be believed. Leah touched the back of his head and drew him down for her caress. Her lips brushed against his in a soft kiss of thanksgiving, no desire tainting its purity, only a whispering graze of fragile flesh, still swollen from the night past, when their kisses had been passion filled and seeking.

He smiled, his blue eyes seeming to see within her soul. "I think you may be the woman of my heart. Know that I have never spoken those words to another, Leah."

The fancy black buggy arrived midmorning, when Gar and his men were hard at work with the second cutting of alfalfa in the farthest hay field. Leah wiped her hands dry on the flowered apron she wore, peering through the kitchen window at the driver.

He sat with reins in hand, hat pulled over his forehead and one foot propped against the front of his vehicle. His bay mare twitched her tail and bent her head to sniff at the clover growing by her shod hooves. With agile strength, Eric Magnor leaped from the buggy and tied his horse to the rail.

Leah watched with mixed emotions, one part of her welcoming the visitor, the other dreading telling Gar of his visit. Her gaze swept over Eric, noting the well-tailored clothing he wore, his clear-eyed appraisal of his surroundings and his confident air.

The screen door was a fragile barrier between them as he stepped onto the porch, and Leah opened it without hesitation.

"Come in, Mr. Magnor. What brings you here?"

He walked past her, his eyes meeting hers for less than a second, then he scanned the kitchen. He pulled a chair from the table and paused beside it. "May I sit down, Leah?"

"Yes, certainly." There was a disturbing note in his voice, and she hesitated where she stood, framed in the doorway.

He removed his hat and gloves. "Sit down, Leah. We must talk."

"What's wrong?"

"Sit. Please." He watched her as she stepped to the table and sat down across from him. His eyes traveled the distance from her hands, clenched before her, to where her teeth bit at her lower lip.

"I have heard rumors in town, Leah. I fear you are in need of help. What can I do?"

"Rumors?" Surely the sheriff had not spread the news of Sylvester Taylor's detective.

"A detective has offered a reward for your whereabouts, and one of the men is bragging about the money he will come into once his telegram is received in Chicago."

"What do you mean? Who would do such a thing?"

"You scorned a surly young fellow before you married Gar Lundstrom, didn't you? The man works for me. Brian Havelock. Perhaps I should say, he used to work for me."

"Brian? Brian would do this to me? Surely not, Mr. Magnor. There must be some mistake. How would he even know the detective from Chicago was there, looking for me?"

Eric shook his head. "Such a thing to happen in our town, Leah. There was a poster put up at either end of town, with your description and your name, offering a reward. They tell me Brian saw it and sent a wire within minutes to the detective agency."

"Sheriff Anderson didn't tell me about the posters."

"He didn't know. They were put up without his knowledge. He tore them down in no time, but it was too late, my dear. The damage had been done."

"What will I do?"

"What does Gar want you to do?" He looked out the screen door. "Where is he, Leah? I should be telling him about this, too. He needs to be prepared for what will happen next."

"He doesn't know." As if those words condemned her, she lifted her hands to cover her face, overwhelmed by guilt. "I meant to tell him, but we..." She shook her head, thinking of the hustle and bustle of early-morning preparations for the haying. They had been late rising, and Gar had been impatient, barely waiting for breakfast before he left to join his farmhands on the hay wagon.

"This is something you cannot keep from him, Leah. These are serious charges, according to the sheriff."

She lifted her head, aghast at his words. "You know about it? The sheriff told you?"

He nodded. "Yes. I went to see him when I heard about it this morning at the sawmill. The town is abuzz with gossip, and I knew I must hear the truth from your lips."

"Oh, God!" It was a fervent petition, her head bowed, hot tears washing her eyes.

"Leah, the sheriff says you are being accused in the death of a newborn child."

She lifted her head, dreading the accusation that must surely be aimed in her direction. Blue eyes, filled with sadness and seeming to peer within her very soul, met her gaze. "As God is my witness, I delivered a live child, only to find it with a broken neck, less than half an hour later.

"The mother accused me of the death, and I feared for my life. Mr. Taylor is a rich man, an influential man, and he desperately wanted a son."

"Then why did he call you to take the case? Surely, his wife had gone to a physician in Chicago during her pregnancy." Eric's brow was furrowed.

Leah's hands spread flat against the tabletop as she rose. "I don't know. He came to me late in the evening, and I went home with him. I'd never delivered a babe in that section of town before. Most of my clients were poor as church mice, and he took me by surprise, offering me five dollars for helping him on such short notice."

"That's quite a sum for a lying-in, isn't it?"

She nodded. "More than I'd ever made before. It was too much for me to turn down, even though I wondered why he didn't call on one of the doctors who work with folks in that part of the city."

"What happened? Did she have a difficult time with her delivery?"

Leah shook her head. "No, not really. She'd had a baby before, and for some reason, it died." She closed her eyes, remembering the hateful look of Mabelle Taylor's face. "I think she must have killed that child, too, Mr. Magnor. She's an evil woman. When I put the baby beside her, she drew away, as if she didn't want to touch him. When we heard her screaming just minutes later, and went back upstairs, he was dead."

Tears overflowed to cascade down her cheeks as she recalled the tragedy of that night. Her voice broke as she finished the story she had never told to another living soul. "His head was twisted to one side, and she pointed at me and said I'd delivered him dead and tried to make her think he was just sleeping."

"What does Gar say to all this?"

"I told you. He doesn't know."

"You've told me something that you've kept from your husband? Why, Leah? Surely he deserved to know."

Her mouth worked as she sought words to explain. "When I came here to help Hulda, she was almost beyond my control. Karen was a breech birth, and Hulda was hemorrhaging terribly by the time I was able to deliver her."

"And Gar blamed you?"

She turned from him, walking to the door, shoulders slumped in despair. "Yes, of course. I would have taken the blame, but I knew better. No one could have helped her. And Dr. Swenson didn't even try. He refused to come that night.''

Eric rose and walked to where she stood, his hand rising to rest on her shoulder. ''You thought Gar would believe the worst of you, didn't you? You were afraid he might not have enough faith in you to hear the truth from your lips, about the baby in Chicago.''

''I've never told anyone, Mr. Magnor.'' The warmth of that hand was a comfort, and she stood immobile, lest he rescind the gesture and take from her this small emblem of his faith in her.

His fingers squeezed gently. ''It's time for you to tell Gar, Leah. Past time, I'd say.''

''I should have told him yesterday, after I talked to Sheriff Anderson, but things happened, and I put it from my mind.''

''None of us can hide from our past forever, my dear. We all have secrets. Yours are sadder than most, but one day you will know that mine are equally hard to live with.''

His hand left her and he walked from her, his footsteps quiet against the kitchen floor. She turned, her curiosity taken by his words. ''You have secrets, Mr. Magnor?''

He stood beside the table, hat in hand. ''You may know the answer to that sometime, Leah. For now, though, I want you to talk to your husband. Tell him what you have told me. Honor him with your trust.''

''I cannot go to town again,'' she cried, suddenly aware of the ostracizing she would face.

''Your friends will stand by you, my dear. The rest of the folk will only need to be told the truth.''

''Will I be taken to Chicago, do you think?'' The

thought was appalling, but the chance of it happening was very real.

"Not if I can help it," he said grimly. "I told you I was your friend, Leah. My resources will be at your disposal should there be further trouble." He looked over her shoulder as she faced him at the back door, and his words brought horror to her soul.

"Come in, Gar. There is much for you to know here. Your wife needs you."

"What trouble is afoot?" Gar asked grimly, his voice causing Leah to shiver. He opened the door behind her. "Move from my way, Leah. Must I have your permission to enter my own house?"

She stumbled, her feet refusing to obey, and only his hard fingers gripping her elbow kept her from falling to the floor.

"I will leave you," Eric Magnor said formally. "Leah is waiting to talk to you, Gar. She is in need of your understanding, I fear."

"And do you understand her, Eric Magnor? Has she already given you her confidence? Did she tell you what the sheriff wanted with her in town yesterday? Or am I to be the first to know?"

"Gar!" Leah turned to him, her fingers gripping the fabric of his shirt. "Don't be rude to Mr. Magnor. He came here to help."

"Do you need his help, Leah? Mine will not do?" He covered her hands with his own and plucked them from his clothing.

"I will leave you," Eric said again, his gaze tormented as he looked into Leah's eyes. "I cannot help you with this, Leah. You must face your husband and make things right with him."

The older man walked from the kitchen, brushing

past Gar and donning his hat as he stepped from the porch. His gloves were drawn into place before he untied his mare and climbed into his buggy.

Leah watched the black buggy disappear from sight, her eyes focusing on the dust that followed in its wake. Beside her, Gar was silent for long moments, until the vehicle was gone from view.

And then he spoke. "Now will you tell me what Sheriff Anderson wanted with you yesterday—now that Eric Magnor has given you permission to confide in your husband?"

Chapter Twelve

Her world was collapsing around her, and from the sounds of him, Gar would not be any consolation. Leah dragged a chair from the table and eased herself onto the seat. She watched as Gar walked to the other side of the room and leaned against the kitchen dresser.

His arms were folded across his chest and his eyes were like ice. He provided a formidable image, one she knew held no sympathy or succor for her state of mind. His gaze touched her impersonally, as if he saw a stranger in his home.

"I need to tell you a story, Gar." She folded her hands neatly on the table and sat very straight in the chair, wanting to present a credible picture to his doubting countenance.

"I prefer the truth to a tall tale, Leah. No excuses, no dallying with the facts, just honesty, plain and simple, if you please."

"This is the truth, Gar. I want you to listen to the whole story before you say anything."

His nod was cool, his posture indolent, as if he expected little to come of this encounter.

Leah's voice broke before she had finished the first

sentence. By the time she had told of that night in Chicago, and the discovery of the baby boy's death, tears were flowing freely.

Gar's attention never wavered from her face. His expression remained stoic, as if he weighed her words and found them wanting.

She struggled on, reiterating the night of Hulda's death. "I had no reason to confide in you then, Gar. No one in town knew about the incident in Chicago. It wouldn't have helped anything for me to make it public, and I feared what would happen if Sylvester Taylor found me."

"And no wonder," he said dryly. "He lost a child. At least he still had a wife."

"You continue to blame me?" she asked, searching his face to find the answer.

His eyes were bleak. "I have no reason to doubt your word, Leah. I would have thought you could tell me this before now, but perhaps you had your reasons."

"Yesterday," she continued, "when the sheriff called me outside the store, he told me a detective had come to Kirby Falls to find me."

"Ah…and that, too, you could not bring yourself to speak of? What good am I to you? What is a husband for, Leah?"

"I didn't know what to do, what to say. On the way home from town, I was so frightened, Gar. And then, last night…"

"Yes, *last night.*" His hand sliced the air in abrupt dismissal of her words. "And what of this morning?"

She grew impatient. "You know you were in a hurry this morning. You barely took time for breakfast."

"So what great news brought Eric Magnor here to visit with you?"

"The detective put up posters in town. Brian Havelock saw one and sent a wire to Chicago. I'll no doubt be hauled away by Sheriff Anderson once Sylvester Taylor gets word of where I am."

"You will be hauled nowhere, Leah Lundstrom. We will find a lawyer for you and settle this thing." His tone gave little clue to his state of mind, nor did his expression, from what she could see through the veil of tears that flowed unceasingly.

"You will get me a lawyer?"

He nodded. "You are my wife." As though that settled the matter once and for all, he stood and approached her, his hand touching her shoulder. "We will have a river running through the kitchen soon, Leah, if you do not come to the end of your crying."

He tilted his head as she looked up at him, and his voice softened. "But there is good reason for your tears to flow, for they have a healing power. Perhaps they will wash away the fear from your heart."

"I've lived with fear for a long time, Gar. It would have been better if I'd shared it with you before this. If I'd thought you would understand, I might have."

One eyebrow rose. "Eric Magnor—he understood?"

She was silent before him, her head bowing at his query. His hand on her shoulder squeezed lightly, then released its hold. "You are the woman I have chosen, Leah. We will find our way through this thing."

As assurances went, it left something to be desired, but she could not fault him. He would stand by her; his name would protect her. She was his wife.

Dinner was quiet. Only Kristofer provided conversation, his talk of puppies and the tree house he was planning filling the void. Leah stood throughout most

of the meal, serving the men, refilling bowls of vegetables, pouring coffee and dishing up the berry cobbler
she had baked right after breakfast.

"That cream is pret'near as yellow as egg yolks, Miss
Leah," Banjo announced as he viewed his brimming
bowl. His spoon plunged into the cobbler and he lifted
it to his mouth, licking the juicy residue with appreciation.

"Mr. Lundstrom bought that new Jersey for the
house," Leah told him. "She doesn't give as much milk
as the Holsteins, but it is richer."

Banjo eyed the pan of cobbler on the stove. "You
sure are a good cook, ma'am. Maybe there'll be 'nuf
left for dinner tomorrow."

"There's enough for seconds today," Leah said
kindly, tempted to smile as the young man grinned at
her.

Benny pushed his chair back, obviously ready to
leave the house for the more cheerful outdoors. "Gar
will be charging you to work here if you don't stop
eating so much, Banjo."

The youth flushed at the reprimand and shot a look
of apology at Leah. "Didn't mean to be eatin' more
than my share, ma'am."

"Good food makes for good workers," she said
quickly. "I'm sure you'll earn every bite by the time
the afternoon's over, Banjo."

Mollified, the youth rose, still savoring the last bit
from his bowl. "I believe Lars ate more than me, Miss
Leah. I just talk more and he keeps right on puttin' it
away."

Lars winked at Leah as he carried his plate and bowl
to the sink. "I learned a long time ago to keep my
mouth shut and pay attention to business."

The men clattered across the porch and Leah swept up the debris they'd managed to track in on their boots. She poured hot water into the dishpan and within minutes had her kitchen back to order. The warm dishwater was dumped on the floor, and she mopped with vigor as she rid the wide planks of dirt.

Karen watched from her high chair, chewing on a piece of bread and pushing bits of vegetables around on her tray. "Mamama," she called, waving her crust in the air.

"Yes, sweetkins, Mama will be right there," Leah responded from the pantry, where she hung the mop from its nail on the wall.

"Leah? Are you in there?" A woman's voice calling from the back porch brought Leah quickly into the kitchen, wiping her hands on the front of her apron.

"I'm here." She crossed to the screen door, her fingers brushing at the tendrils of hair that had escaped her braid. "Eva! Come in, won't you."

The postmistress stood on the porch, her husband's big wagon sitting beyond the pump, two horses waiting within their harness. "Do you have time for me?"

"Of course! I'm so sorry I didn't see you coming. Be careful you don't slip on the wet floor. The men track in so much, I have to mop every day."

Eva Landers walked gingerly toward the table, pausing to ruffle Karen's golden curls with the tips of her fingers. "Such a beautiful child." She pressed a kiss on the baby's temple, and Karen responded with a verbal barrage that brought laughter from the two women.

"Can you understand what she says?" Eva asked, settling in a chair next to the baby.

Leah shook her head. "Not much of it. Only 'kiss-kiss' and 'papa.' She calls me 'mama.'" The last was said softly, and Leah felt a surge of love as Karen repeated the word, chortling at her own cleverness.

"You may not have given birth to her, but you certainly gave her life," Eva said stoutly. "You're a good mother, Leah."

"You didn't come here to tell me that," Leah said quietly, bringing two cups of coffee to the table.

Eva shook her head. "No, I didn't. But I suspect you may already know about the happenings in town. I saw Eric Magnor's buggy head this way early this morning."

"He was here. And yes, he told me about the posters and about Brian spreading the word all over town and wiring Chicago with the news of my whereabouts."

"It's even worse than that, Leah. Lula Dunbar suggested Hulda's death should have been investigated, instead of just taking your word for her condition."

"Who would have known what to investigate?"

"Dr. Swenson was not about to come out here, that was for sure," Eva said. "Mrs. Thorwald spoke up for you in the store, told Lula that probably the baby would have died, too, if you hadn't been here for the birthing."

"Bless her heart." Leah's eyes filled with tears as she thought of the elderly neighbor she'd looked after. "She's a loyal soul, isn't she?"

"There're a lot of other loyal folks in town, but you know people like something to talk about, Leah. Now Brian's suggesting Eric Magnor has taken a fancy to you, and once the word got back to Mr. Magnor, Brian got himself fired. He's having a hissy fit now, because he says it's your fault he was let go."

"Well, I'm not about to take the blame for him being so hateful about things and lying about Mr. Magnor. I treated Brian as well as I could," Leah said soberly. "I just couldn't marry the man, and he was determined to get a foot in my door every time he stepped up on my porch.''

"He may grow up one day," Eva predicted. "But in the meantime, he's carrying gossip. And if he isn't careful, he may have your husband's fist in his mouth for his trouble.''

"Gar will hear about this, won't he?''

"I guess that's why I felt I needed to come out here and tell you what's going on, Leah. He'd do better to hear it from you than some busybody in town.''

"Eva, I want you to know Mr. Magnor doesn't have that sort of regard for me. We're friends, and that's all.''

Eva's hand shunned the words, silently warding off Leah's protest. "You don't need to even say so. He's a good man, and if he wanted to look for a woman he'd have done it a long time ago. Not that he shouldn't have, mind you. But I think the man is still married, to tell the truth. No one's ever heard tell that his wife died.''

"How long ago did she leave?''

"Oh, I guess twenty-five years or so. Maybe longer. Took her little girl and got herself a ride south on a wagon that was passing through. Eric Magnor never got over it, I guess.''

As if she felt his pain for that long-past act of cruelty, Leah's heart went out to the man and she wiped another tear as it tracked down her cheek. "I could never leave Gar. He'd have to kick me out the door for me to walk down that lane.''

"I doubt there's much chance of that," Eva said with a smile. "He'll fight for you—and maybe with you, but I don't see the man ever putting you out of his life.''

* * *

"Eva was here today, Gar."

"I saw Joseph's undertaker's wagon outside. Thought maybe you had plans for me." His head was bent as he pulled his stockings from his feet, then stood to remove his trousers.

Leah looked into the mirror, her hand stilled in mid-air, brush clutched tightly. "Such a thing to say."

"As mad as you are with me, I thought it was appropriate, maybe."

"I'm not angry with you. I just think you make foolish accusations, Gar." She resumed her ritual, closing her eyes and relishing the pull of the brush against her hair.

"So, what did Eva have to say? Is young Havelock still stirring up trouble?"

"Eric Magnor fired him from the sawmill."

Gar stepped out of his trousers and kicked them aside impatiently. His fingers were busy with the buttons on his shirt, but his face was intent as he approached Leah.

"Why was he fired? Was it because of you, Leah?"

She nodded, meeting his gaze in the mirror. "He told it around town that Mr. Magnor was interested in me. And now, Brian is blaming his misfortune on Leah Lundstrom."

"When he becomes a man, he will accept the blame for his own actions. Right now, he is asking for a trouncing, like the child that he is."

"I don't want you to fight with him, Gar." She bent her head as his hands circled her neck, long fingers touching her throat.

"Come to bed, Leah. We will talk of it tomorrow."

She felt the warmth of tears against her cheeks. She'd shed more of them today than in the past four years combined. Gar's fingers left her throat to wipe her face, the callused surface of his fingertips careful against her flesh.

''I told you last night that our bed was a place of pleasure and comfort. Tonight it will be comfort we seek there, Leah.'' His wide palms gripped her shoulders and he urged her from the chair. ''Come with me, wife.''

She rose and turned to him, lifting her face, unmindful of the signs of her sorrow. ''How can you comfort me when you have so much anger in you?''

''The problems are put aside when we enter this room. If it cannot be thus, then this place is no longer sacred to our marriage. I told you how it would be, Leah. Didn't you believe me?''

She nodded, unable to speak, her eyes seeking out the message she yearned to find in his gaze. No tenderness met her search, but a quiet peace that, perhaps, pleased her more.

She watched as Gar blew out the candles, two on her dresser, one on the table beside the bed. The curtains fluttered and tangled in the breeze, and Leah shivered as she settled against her pillow. Against cool sheets, she lost the warmth of her body rapidly—a warmth quickly replaced by the arms of her husband.

He drew her against himself, tucking her bottom against his belly, and smoothing her gown around her legs. She was encircled by muscular arms, her waist held captive by one wide hand.

She felt Gar's voice rumble through her back as he spoke, the sound itself as much a comfort as the words he uttered. ''Now rest. You have shed enough tears for the whole year, wife. What has happened is in the past. We will get beyond it somehow. Tomorrow, or the next day, when we go to town, we will face whatever is there for us to hear."

Her frustration was alive in the words she spoke. "How can you put it behind you, Gar? How can you just ignore what Brian has done?"

"I have not ignored it. I will ponder it, Leah. Perhaps it is not all a big lie. There may be a kernel of truth in what he says. Eric is interested in you. Any fool can see that."

Leah drew in a shuddering sigh. "Your arms hold me as if you—"

"My arms will not let you go, wife. Even when we are apart, when I cannot reach you with my hands, my power over you will be stronger than Eric Magnor or Brian Havelock or any detective from Chicago. You are my woman, and I have vowed to protect you with my life."

"I have brought you trouble, Garlan Lundstrom." Her whisper was sad in the darkness, and she settled into his embrace, moving against his big body.

"I will give you more than trouble, Mrs. Lundstrom, if you do not hold yourself still. Rest now." His arms tightened, his hand sliding up to enclose the curve of her breast.

She closed her eyes, feeling the pressure of each finger as he palmed the weight of her with tenderness, the tenderness she had thought was missing in his gaze. How much more welcome it was now, evidenced in the touch of his hand.

Work took precedence over curiosity. Two days passed rapidly, the men working at breakneck speed to separate one large pasture into two, running fence and sorting out the occupants. Leah left the house, her steps quick as she anticipated the flavor of the early, young ears of corn that flourished in the field. The corn was high, the tassels turning rusty as the ears ripened.

She smiled as she pulled the largest from the stalks before the sun burned off the early-morning mist. Then, stopping at the end of the row, she stripped the ears. She blew distractedly at the silk that stuck determinedly to her fingers and flew to tickle her nose, sneezing in the bright sunlight.

"What are you up to?" Gar pulled his team up short, only a few feet from where she worked, and she shaded her eyes to peer up at him.

"Just picking corn for dinner. I like it best when it's young and tender. Later, when it's big and bright yellow, you can have it for your stock."

He smiled, the first cheerful look she'd seen on his face since their quarrel, and the dimple she'd learned to watch for almost appeared. "Many thanks, Mrs. Lundstrom. My animals will approve your generosity. Climb up," he offered. "I'll give you a ride up to the house."

She lifted her apron, heavy with the corn she'd gathered, holding it by the bib and the two bottom corners. "I should have brought out a sack to carry it in," she said, hoisting it to the wagon.

"Do you have enough there?" He took it from her hands and waited for her to join him, then placed it on her lap.

"Plenty. Two dozen and better." She wrapped her arms around the bundle and settled back to enjoy the ride. "It was going to be a long walk, carrying the corn. I'm glad you came by."

He slanted her a sidelong look. "I've been sticking close, in case we had visitors. The men are at the far end of the new pasture, finishing up the fence."

She peered back, barely able to see beyond the big cornfield. "The corn's too high to see the house from here, but I told Kristofer to ring the bell if anyone came. He's watching the baby while she sleeps.

"How did you know to find me out here?"

"I always know where you are." At her cynical snort of disbelief, he amended his statement. "Well, most of the time, anyway. At least lately. I've been watching the house, Leah."

For almost an hour she had put from her mind the worry she'd spent days mulling over. Now, in a few words, Gar had brought it to the forefront again.

"Maybe tomorrow we should go to town," he told her after a moment. "It is time to find out what the sheriff has to say."

"Yes, and I have eggs and butter ready to go."

"You needn't work so hard at churning, Leah. The pigs will use up the extra milk. It makes for good meat in the fall."

"I don't mind the work, and I don't keep the money, Gar. I've been spending it on things for the children."

He drew up the team near the barn and turned to her. "I didn't ask you to account for the money. If you churn the cream, you own the butter. You have little enough to show for the work you do here. I haven't seen you in a new dress since the day we got married, and only the one nightgown."

"Are you complaining about my wardrobe?"

His mouth pursed as he considered her words. "No, only that you deserve more than you take from me. You sew things for Karen and put new shirts on Kris, and still wear the same dresses day after day yourself."

She gathered up the apron, tying a loose knot to carry

it with and holding it in his direction. "Here, take this while I climb down."

"Wait, I'll help you." With an easy motion, he swung from the seat, sliding to the ground and striding around the head of his team. His arms lifted to her and she stood before him. "Now, give me the corn." She obeyed, watching as he placed it on the ground.

Then his big hands circled her waist, and with little effort, he lifted her to stand before him. His palms were warm and strong as he drew her against the length of his body.

"Do you still fear what will happen next?" he asked.

"I only know Sylvester Taylor is a rich man, an influential man in Chicago. And if he wants to punish me for what he thinks I did, he may very well swear out a warrant for me."

"He has no proof, Leah."

"Neither have I, Gar. It's his word against mine, and unless I miss my guess, he will hire a lawyer."

"We can do that, too." He loosened his hold on her waist and turned her toward the house, bending to pick up the corn.

"I won't have you spending your money on lawyers," she protested.

"You don't have a choice, wife. If we need a lawyer, we will hire one."

From beyond the house a horse neighed loudly, causing Gar's team to toss their heads and respond in a like manner. "I was right to stay close this morning. Someone is coming." Leah hurried to catch up to his longer stride as a horseman turned the corner by the back porch.

"Sheriff." Gar's word of welcome was answered in kind as the lawman stepped down from his gelding.

"Mr. Lundstrom…ma'am…I'm glad to see you both here."

Leah's steps faltered at his words. "Is there trouble?"

He held his reins loosely in one fist, the other hand tipping his hat at an angle. "Might say that, ma'am. Got a wire this morning from Chicago. Seems like that fella there who's been looking for you has decided to take you to court. You're going to have to appear there in two weeks."

"What can he do to me?" Her legs felt weak beneath her, and Leah slumped to sit on the porch steps.

Morgan Anderson looked apologetic, glancing first at Gar, then to where Leah sat. "He's accusing you of neglect, ma'am. And manslaughter. I've been authorized to take you to Chicago."

"Is my wife under arrest?" The words were soft-spoken, but Leah's quick glance at Gar's face revealed a cold, calculating visage. Even at his angriest, he had never looked so fierce.

"I didn't say that." Sheriff Anderson swept his hat from his head and slapped it against his leg. "I do think you might want to get yourself a lawyer, though. Maybe down in Minneapolis."

"What's wrong with right here?" Gar asked gruffly.

"About the only one in town worth his salt is Evan Dunwoody, the fella who works for Eric Magnor, over at the mill. Don't know if he takes on other clients or not."

"Does anyone else know of this?" Leah asked.

Morgan Anderson looked shamefaced, his mouth twisting as if he tasted something sour. "Pony Lathers, over at the rail station brought me the wire. I'd lay odds he's already spread the word."

"Perhaps we need to consider going to Minneapolis,

Leah." Gar's suggestion brought her attention. "We can ask Ruth to watch the children for two days."

"Can we do that? Or can I not leave here?" Leah posed the question quietly, aware suddenly of absolute silence in the kitchen behind where she sat.

"I don't see any problem with that," the sheriff said. "I doubt you'd leave these children alone any longer than it takes to settle your business, either of you."

"Yah, you are right."

"I can be ready tomorrow, Gar," Leah said. "I'll ask Ruth after dinner if she can stay."

"Sorry to bring bad news, folks. Seems like you've had enough to take care of, without adding to your load." The sheriff slapped his hat on and climbed into his saddle, turning his horse around. "Just let me know when you go, Mr. Lundstrom. I'll be interested to hear what you find out in the city."

Leah watched as the sturdy gelding broke into a quick canter, the horse and rider disappearing around the corner of the house.

"Your team is walking around to the back of the barn, Pa." Kristofer came out the door to stand in the shade of the porch, his hands hanging limply by his sides.

"Ach…" Gar spun to watch as the team he'd left untended disappeared with languid ease from sight, his words exasperated as he called to them. He set off at a trot, and Leah bent to pick up her corn, her enthusiasm for the early treat gone by the wayside.

"Are you going away, Miss Leah?" Kristofer's eyes were wary as he watched her, and he backed up to stand by the screen door.

"Were you listening from the kitchen, Kris?"

He nodded. "I didn't mean to, but I heard you talking

and I thought I shouldn't come out while that man was here.''

"We'll only be gone for two days," she said, "and Ruth will stay with you and Karen. Will that worry you, to have your father gone?"

"I never been alone here before," he said slowly, following her through the door into the house.

"You'll be all right," she assured him. "Ruth loves you and the baby, and we won't be gone long."

"Are you coming back, Miss Leah?"

Leah closed her eyes at the bleak query, aghast that such a young child should fear losing a mother's presence for a second time in his life. She was the only mother he was likely to have, and already she loved him with a fierce, protective yearning.

"Yes, of course I'll be back, Kris," she assured him. "I live here now, with you and your sister. Of course I'll be back."

And then she lifted her heart in a fervent prayer that those words would prove to be true.

Chapter Thirteen

"Who will take us into town?" Leah stepped from the porch, her small leather valise in hand. She'd worn the same dress the day she'd arrived in Kirby Falls, four years ago. A neat navy-blue jacket covered the white shirtwaist beneath, and she tugged it against her waist.

It fit as well now as it had then, and she repressed a small twinge of pride at that fact. She hadn't widened over the years, as women tended to do, and that fact was a source of consolation this morning, for some reason.

"No one. I will leave the horse and buggy with Sten Pringle." Gar gave her his hand, taking the luggage from her as he spoke. His own bag had come out earlier, when he'd gone to the barn to ready the black mare for the trip.

"Benny would not let me help with the harnessing," he told Leah. "He said I should not go to Minneapolis with the smell of a barn on my hands."

"Benny is a wise man." Her gaze measured Gar thoroughly. "You, on the other hand, are not only wise," she added, "but handsome as well."

His hair was like spun gold in the sunlight, his suit

pressed, with barely an iron mark showing. He was more than handsome, he was magnificent.

And to that he responded as she'd known he would. His face took on a ruddy hue, and he smiled, shaking his head in self-conscious denial of her words. "I am a farmer, Leah, plain and simple. Men who live in the city and spend their money on fancy clothing, those men are handsome."

He was becoming predictable, or perhaps she was getting to know him better. "Then maybe you are only a handsome farmer, Gar Lundstrom."

"You should have bought a new dress for this trip." His hands were firm as he helped her into the buggy and placed the valise near her feet.

"I am what I am, a farmer's wife. I have packed another dress that is sufficiently new."

Ruth held Karen in her arms, just inside the screen door, and Leah lifted her hand to wave at the pair. "I will miss her."

"Yah, but not so much as she will miss you," Gar said. "You are the sun in her sky, Leah."

Her eyes blinked, then teared without warning. She wiped a salty drop from her cheek. "I've never heard you say anything quite so…"

He lifted the reins and cracked them in the air, sending his black mare into movement. "So foolish?" he provided.

"No!" She shook her head. "That wasn't what I was going to say. Your words touched my heart, Gar. I don't think I'm easily moved to tears, but…" She swiped a second time at her face.

"You could have fooled me the other day."

"And that was a rarity," she said sharply. "I don't usually spring a leak that way."

His head nodded. "True. I'd never seen you cry before. But it was good for you, wasn't it?"

"I don't know. I'd just as soon it didn't happen again."

Whether his small talk was designed to take her mind from the trip they were about to undertake, or simply Gar at his most garrulous, Leah took advantage. She enjoyed the news of his work with the three-year-old fillies and discussing the prospective profits from the young steers they were fattening for market in the fall.

The sight of Sten Pringle signaled the end of their ride, and as Leah stepped down from her perch, she mentally marked it in her mind. Next would be the walk to the rail station and the purchase of two tickets to Minneapolis.

She felt a twinge of self-consciousness as she slid her hand between Gar's coat sleeve and chest. He was nicely muscled, his forearm long and sturdy beneath her fingers. She glanced up at him as they passed before the emporium. If pride was truly a sin, then she was knee-deep in its mire this morning.

"Good morning." Even Eva Landers could barely keep her eyes from the masculine presence before her, and Leah smiled at the other woman's admiring glance.

"Are you all dressed up for a reason?" Eva stood near the doorway, several pieces of mail in her hand.

"We're going to Minneapolis on the morning train," Leah offered.

"Let me walk with you as far as the hotel," Eva said. "I have letters for Hobart Dunbar."

The men sitting on benches watched as they passed, their hushed whispers following the trio as they approached the hotel door. "Don't mind the gossip," Eva said quietly. "It will pass, Leah."

"I've always felt welcome here before, but now there are eyes watching us, and I don't feel any warmth in them." Leah's good mood was gone.

"Only a few folks have paid attention to Brian's foolishness. And whatever that horrid man in Chicago has planned, I'm sure you'll be exonerated of any blame."

Her staunch support brought a faint smile to Leah's lips and she turned to hug her friend as they parted. Eva stepped inside the hotel lobby. From behind the desk, Lula Dunbar spoke loudly, for all to hear, as her gaze swept Leah's traveling suit, framed as she was in the doorway.

"Perhaps Gar Lundstrom will be sorry he married so quickly, once he finds out the truth in Chicago."

Leah's breath caught in her throat and she stumbled, only Gar's strong arm holding her erect.

"Don't listen to it," he muttered. "She is trying to upset you. Come. We don't want to miss the train."

Across the street, Brian Havelock sat on the steps of the barbershop, whittling at a piece of wood. "Enjoy your trip, Miss Leah," he called out, his disdain apparent even from a distance.

"You will not speak to my wife," Gar said loudly, as if this insult were the final straw.

"I was just being friendly. She likes friendly menfolk, I hear." Brian's chuckle was loud in the silence that contained the three of them.

"Come on. You said we needed to hurry." Leah tugged at Gar's arm.

Gar stood stock-still, his jaw a hard line, his forehead drawn into a frown as he considered the younger man's indolent posture. "I cannot let him speak this way about you, Leah." He took her hand from his arm and held it between his wide palms. "Stay here, please. I must settle this rascal's hash, once and for all."

His hands were already on the knot in his tie as he stepped into the dusty street. Midway across, he had unbuttoned his suit coat and was slipping it from his broad shoulders. By the time he reached Brian, Gar's shirtsleeves were unfastened and he was slowly and fastidiously rolling them up to a point just below his elbows.

"Do you think to fight with me, old man?" Brian said with a visible sneer as he rose from his seat.

"I think I will clean your clock," Gar said softly, handing his suit coat to the white-aproned barber who had stepped to the door of his shop.

Brian looked around the gathering group of men, several of whom had been awaiting the services of the barber. Seeming to take added strength from the murmurs of his audience, he struck a pose with fists cocked and ready.

"You and what army?" he jeered.

"I think I will only need these two soldiers," Gar told him, holding up his hands, then slowly flexing them and forming massive fists.

"Come and get it, old man," Brian said, repeating his disrespectful taunt.

"Yah, I believe I will." Gar took one step, his left hand countering Brian's right as the younger man threw a quick punch. Gar's right fist connected solidly, and Brian let out a loud yelp as he hit the sidewalk.

Gar bent, picked him up and slapped his face—hard, flat-palmed blows, once on either side. Brian's arms churned, his face crimson as he shouted defiance.

And then he hit the sidewalk again, the victim of a small flurry of blows that thudded against his face and body with unerring precision. His own fists made contact with little effect, as Gar meted out punishment.

The crowd shifted, gathering closer to the two men, and Leah found the combatants lost to her view. She backed against the hotel window, and one hand lifted to cover her mouth. How could such a thing happen?

"Gar had no choice." From beside her, Eva's voice spoke her own thoughts, and Leah turned to her friend.

"I don't want him fighting for my sake. He should have just ignored Brian."

"What did the foolish boy say?" A man's deep voice joined them, and Leah turned quickly to face Eric Magnor as he dismounted from his big black stallion. He tied the reins to the hitching post, and in two steps stood before the women.

His gaze swept over Leah, and she was comforted by his presence. Perhaps he could bring a halt to this folly before Gar went too far in his anger. "Can you make them stop fighting?"

Eric shook his head. "Young Havelock has been asking for trouble for several days now. I knew it would come to this before it was done." He stood beside Leah, as if his presence would lend support. "What did the fine young fellow say this time?"

"He said Leah liked friendly menfolk," Eva volunteered. "It was his tone of voice that offered an insult, Mr. Magnor."

From across the street, a roar went up from the watchers, and Leah saw Brian's husky body held high in the air. Garlan Lundstrom's strength was apparent to all who had gathered as he clutched the younger man's thigh and shoulder, lifting the considerable weight almost over his own head.

Loud yelps from the hapless man brought gales of

laughter from the onlookers, and only when Gar thrust the flailing form from him did the noisy crowd subside. Brian's body crashed against the side of the barber shop, and there was silence for a moment.

"Do you want to say anything more to me? Have you any more insults to offer my wife?" Gar thundered, and the watching men fell back from his wrath. Brian staggered to his feet, shaking his head, his clothing disheveled by rough handling.

"Are you ready to offer an apology to my wife?" Gar gripped Brian's shoulder and whirled him to face Leah.

She shrank back against the hotel. "No...don't do this, Gar." Her whisper was thin, uttered against the fabric of her glove.

From her side, Eric strode into the street. "I think Mr. Havelock owes an apology to more than Mrs. Lundstrom," he said loudly. His tall, dapper frame was set off by the splendid suit he wore, his hat at a jaunty angle.

The townsfolk waited, stunned by this gesture. Eric Magnor lived in regal solitude in his mansion at the end of town. Seldom did he insert himself into the everyday lives of its inhabitants.

Brian watched his former employer with one eye, the other already swollen shut from a well-placed punch. Gar stood behind the youth, and before them was the man Brian had spoken of in a disparaging manner. His shoulders slumping, Brian's stance was that of a condemned man.

Perhaps it was the hopelessness of his situation that made him brave the odds, for his chin lifted suddenly and his voice rang out in mocking tones. "Even the richest man in town is not immune to a woman's charm, is he, Mr. High-and-Mighty Magnor?''

Eric's stance was firm, his eyes clear as he scorned the man who accused him. ''I will not be accused of looking with adulterous eyes at any woman, Mr. Havelock. Least of all as it refers to Leah Lundstrom. For, in this case, the accusation would be that of an unspeakable crime.''

The men who watched and listened grew more intent with each word, and the women who gathered on the sidewalk murmured among themselves.

Eric stepped even closer to Brian. ''I will not be accused of such sin. Especially…'' he said in a chill voice Leah had never thought to hear from him. ''Especially, Mr. Havelock, when the woman involved is my own daughter.''

Brian hooted, almost hysterically. ''Your daughter? That's a tall tale, if I ever heard one. What makes you think you can convince anyone of that story?''

Leah's heart pounded within her chest, her head buzzed as though a million insects were battling to escape her skull, and her legs refused to hold her erect. Only when the air around her grew scarce and the sky turned black did she realize that she was falling to the sidewalk.

And then it was too late.

''Leah!'' It was a shout of dismay, too late for her to heed as Gar sprinted across the street. He fell to his knees beside her, one hand beneath her neck, lifting her head from the dusty walk, the other straightening her dress, pulling her legs from beneath her.

Eva was at his side, her slender fingers loosening the buttons that secured Leah's navy-blue jacket in place. Beneath it a shirtwaist bore an equal number of buttons, made of white pearl, and she opened the fabric to expose Leah's throat.

"Someone get some water," Eva requested, even as a full tumbler was pressed into her hand by Lula Dunbar.

"Leah?" Gar's hands were gentle, carefully supporting her head as he felt beneath her ear for a pulse. The crowd had transferred its attention to this side of the street now. As Gar looked up, his gaze met that of the barber, who still held Gar's suit coat over his arm.

Next to the barber, Eric Magnor watched, his mouth drawn into a thin line, his eyes narrowed as he waited for Gar's ministrations to have some effect. "Is she all right?" he asked after a moment.

Gar shrugged, shaking his head as he raised his wife to a sitting position on the sidewalk. He held the glass of water to her lips and called her name again, allowing a few drops of liquid to spill against her mouth.

Leah stirred, her eyelids fluttering as she inhaled a deep breath. "Gar?" It was a whisper, a thread of sound, but enough to insure Gar his wife was awake and aware, and that he need not worry for her well-being.

She licked at her lips and he tilted the glass a bit more, encouraging her to drink. She accommodated him briefly, sipping a few swallows, then turned her face away.

"Enough." She gazed down at her lap, then at the rough wooden boards upon which she sat. She looked up at Eva, and her lips trembled in a travesty of a smile.

"Let me help you up, Leah." Gar gave the water glass to a willing hand and, with his own hand at her waist, lifted his wife to her feet. He held her thus, feeling the trembling she could not subdue. His heartbeat slowed to a normal speed; she was all right.

"I'll send for my carriage." It was Eric, and Gar shot him a glance that brought a sudden halt to the other man's offer.

"I will take my wife home in our buggy. We will not be taking the morning train after all." Indeed, as he spoke, the sound of a whistle split the air, and just beyond the farthest building, a locomotive approached the train platform, belching smoke and trailing cars behind it like a string of dominoes.

"I need to speak with her," Eric said urgently, stepping a few inches closer to where Leah stood.

She shook her head. "Not now...not now, please." She pressed her face against Gar's shirtfront. "Take me home." The whisper was a poignant plea for privacy, and Gar responded with gentle care.

His arm around her waist, he walked with her, careful not to allow her to stumble, setting his pace to hers. On her other side, Eva Landers walked with Gar's suit coat over her arm, having taken it from the barber.

Gar supposed they made a strange trio: Leah, pale and drawn, her feet barely skimming the boards as he lifted her weight; Eva, smiling and nodding at those who watched with eager, avid faces; and himself, towering over the woman who had just borne a shock she could barely contain.

Just beyond the end of the sidewalk, where the road reached to touch the grass, he bent to slip his arms beneath her, lifting her against his chest. He felt no resistance from her, only a sigh that escaped her lips with a forlorn sound.

He was met by Sten, still adjusting the harness of the

black mare. The horse and buggy had just been put into the barn before they were once more called into service.

"Let me help you," Sten offered, and then stood aside as Gar lifted his wife onto the seat. Gar supported Leah until she regained her balance. Then he joined her upon the seat and put his arm around her waist.

"Here's your coat, Garlan." Eva handed it up to him and received a nod of thanks. She stepped back and watched Leah's lids close, her head leaning against Gar's shoulder, as if her neck had no strength of its own.

"May I come out to see her?" Eva asked.

Gar looked down at her. "Yes, of course. She will want to talk to you, I'm sure. Thank you, Mrs. Landers."

The black stallion had followed them all the way down the street to the blacksmith's shop, and now its rider watched as the buggy cut a sharp turn and headed out of town.

"Do you think it's true?" Leah's head rested against his shoulder, and Gar's arm tightened around her waist as she spoke. "How can such a thing be true?" she whispered, even before he had a chance to reply.

"Of course it can be true," he told her. "Whether it is or not may be another matter. But bear in mind, Leah, that Eric Magnor has no reason to lie. The man has never been known to be other than honest and aboveboard."

"Then why would he wait for three years to claim me? If he knew I was his daughter, why didn't he say so before this?"

That was a stumper, all right. Gar shook his head. "I don't know. But I do know he won't be satisfied until he talks to you.'' His grip on the reins tightened, and his hand protested the movement. In surprise he glanced down, noting the swollen line of his knuckles, the scraped skin that seeped blood.

Her mind seemed to work in tandem with his, and Leah reached to touch the angry flesh. ''You must have hit Brian awfully hard. Let me see your other hand.''

His fingers tightened against her waist and he shook his head. ''No, it's fine. You can kiss it and make it all better when we get home.''

His humor was wasted, for she subsided, leaning more heavily against him, and he bent to peer into her face. ''Leah, are you still feeling faint? Do you want to put your head into my lap?''

''No, of course not. I just can't make any sense of this whole thing. And now we've missed the train to Minneapolis, and we'll have to start out all over again tomorrow. If I thought everyone in town was having a heyday, watching me and wondering about me this morning, just imagine what tomorrow will be like.''

''I think Brian Havelock's tall tales have lost their clout. And being thought of as Eric Magnor's daughter is no bad thing, Leah. Maybe you should let the man have his say before you worry too much about what folks are thinking.''

''It just seems that I would remember him, if what he says is true.''

''How old were you when your mother took you away from here? Three or four, maybe?''

''Young enough that I don't remember anyone from town.'' She sat up straight in the seat, her mind intent on a new thought, it seemed. ''Why don't I bear his name, Gar? My mother was Minna Polk, not Minna Magnor.''

"You see, this is only one of the things you need to ask the man."

"I don't understand why my mother told me my father was dead. I always thought…" She lifted her face to look into his eyes. "I never told anyone in town that I was born here, and no one seemed to recognize my name. That's a strange one, isn't it?"

"Probably, Minna Polk was not known here by that name." It seemed logical to his mind, but if Leah needed to mull it over, he would give her time. It was better that she come to an understanding by herself.

The children were delighted to see the buggy's arrival, Kristofer running from the barn to greet them. "Didn't the train come, Pa?"

"Yah, it came, but we decided to go tomorrow, instead," he told the boy as he lifted Leah to the ground. "Come, help me put the horse in the pasture." His hands were firm on Leah's waist, as if he were hesitant to release her.

"Are you all right? Should I get you into the house first?"

She shook her head. "No. I was just so surprised that Eric Magnor should say such a thing that all the blood rushed out of my head." Her smile was crooked, and Gar was entranced by its vulnerability. He'd not seen this side of his woman before.

"Go on in the house, then. I'll be there in a few minutes."

He watched as she made her way to the porch, lifting her skirt to climb the steps. Ruth stood silently in the doorway, holding Karen, whose arms were reaching for her mother. And at that thought, Gar smiled.

Leah was the baby's mother. Of that there could no longer be a quibbling doubt. He'd not spend another minute thinking of Karen as Hulda's child. She'd been Leah's from birth, and that was his own doing. For weeks, he'd heard the mama sounds coming from the baby's mouth, learning to accept her preference for the woman who cared for her, even where he was concerned.

It was time to say farewell to the woman he'd wronged, time to forget the unhappy days he'd spent trying—and always failing—to be the husband Hulda deserved. It was past time to bury the guilt with the woman who'd so unwittingly caused it.

"Pa? Are you gonna put the mare away now?" Kristofer stood beside him, impatient with his dallying.

"I was just watching to see if Leah got into the house all right," he answered, and was amused at Kristofer's look of disbelief.

"She looks all right to me, Pa. Is something wrong with her?"

Gar shook his head. Not anything visible, anyway. The hurt she bore was bone deep, not appearing as a great wound to the eye. He, too, had borne such a wound for months. The ache where his heart beat in a steady pounding had kept him awake some nights.

And now, with Leah's presence in his home, that aching lump in his chest had begun to heal from its pain. In fact, if he wanted to be honest about it, there was no pain to be felt these days when he looked at the woman he had married.

For, if being unable to love one particular woman were a crime, then most of the men in the world were probably as guilty as he. And, if being entangled in the web of loving the woman he had chosen on his own bore consequences, he would be bound to face them.

His hands worked rapidly at the harness, undoing

buckles and loosening the mare from her bindings. He watched as Kristofer led her from the back door of the barn, following at a distance so as not to make the boy think he did not trust him to do the job.

The sun glittered on his golden hair as Kris watched the mare canter across the pasture. She tossed her mane and tail, as she joined the rest of the small herd beneath a grove of maple trees. Kris turned back to the barn, catching sight of his father, and his smile was brilliant, his white teeth flashing his delight.

"Pa! I'm glad you didn't go away. I was missing you already." His sturdy legs churned as he ran, and his arms were strong as they circled Gar's waist.

It was a blessing, indeed, this love that flowed from one person to another. From son to father it coursed, and then returned in full measure. His hand smoothed the straight hair that stubbornly fell across Kristofer's forehead, urging the locks to lie in place. Such a good lad. And then to his surprise, the words were uttered aloud.

"You're a good boy, Kris. I'm proud of you."

"Really, Pa?"

A pang of regret touched Gar's heart as he mourned all the days he had not given such faint praise to his son. "Yah, you are a fine lad."

He would need to come up with softer words to woo his wife, he thought, turning back to the house. Words that would better express the knowledge pressing against his mind this morning. He felt a great love for Leah, a need for her presence, an urgent craving for her body. That part he had already admitted to himself: her curves enticed him, her honey-streaked hair tempted his fingers to be buried in its depths.

But there was more. This urgency to possess her was

only a part of it. He craved her quick wit, her sharp mind, and the parts of the woman that drew men's eyes: the proud tilt of her head, the straight line of her spine when she walked, and the lush, rounding bosom he could not ignore.

He sighed. He was on the other end this time. For Hulda had loved him, a love he did not welcome but had instead taken advantage of, allowing her to care for his needs. He had gone to her at night when the urge of his body could not be stilled, and taken her without any depth of emotion.

For that, he mourned. The knowledge that he had not before now realized the pleasure that comes with the craving for one particular woman. The urgency of binding himself with this creature he had had the good sense to bring to his home.

He stepped into the kitchen and found Ruth at the stove. "Is dinner almost ready?"

She waved the big stirring spoon at him. "You're lucky I cooked extra, Mr. Lundstrom. There's enough for you."

"Where is my wife?" He glanced around the room, empty because Leah was not in it.

"She went upstairs to change her clothes. I'm sure she'll be back down in a minute. That was quite a time you had in town, I hear."

"Yah." He crossed the room, immune to Ruth's questioning look, intent only on finding Leah.

If she needed comfort, he would be there. If she allowed it, he would hold her...for just a few minutes, because it was daylight, and Ruth listened below.

And after all, it was not long until sunset. He could wait until then.

Chapter Fourteen

It was just at sunset when the knock came at the door. The kitchen was already shadowed, with the sun below the horizon on the other side of the house. Leah's hands were busy with lighting the lamp over the table when she heard the knock. She turned to the door, apprehension alive in her.

The thought of questioning looks directed at her was more than she wanted to handle at this time of day. Her stance was belligerent as she opened the door. A bulky form met her eye and she hesitated for a moment.

"Hello, there," she greeted, just now taking note of Gar coming from the barn.

"Mrs. Lundstrom?" It was a deep voice, with the trace of Swedish accent she had come to expect over the past years. "I have need of your help."

It was a plea she could not resist, no matter how weary she was. She opened the door to the caller. Gar followed on his heels, his words allaying her fears.

"Olaf, I have not seen you for a long time. What are you doing here?"

"I am come to persuade your wife's help," the farmer said. "My boys, both of them, are sick. Their mother says it is summer complaint, but all I know is that the fever and the vomiting, and then the runs, have worn them both to a frazzle.''

"It is late, Olaf," Gar said. "The sun is set already."

"I know that, and I would not ask if I didn't think—"

"I'll be ready in a few minutes," Leah said quickly. The thought of two small boys ailing through the night when she could be helping them would be enough to keep her awake. She'd just as well go with Olaf now and see what could be done.

"I will be so thankful," the farmer said, holding his hat in both hands as he delivered a smile of relief in Leah's direction. "It is cooling off, Mrs. Lundstrom. You had better bring a shawl."

"I'll get my bag," Leah said, turning toward the hall-way. She hurried up the stairs, pausing at Kristofer's bedroom door.

"What's wrong, Miss Leah?" He sat on the edge of his mattress, peeling off his stockings, readying himself for bed.

"I want you to wash up, Kris," she told him. "I'll be back in time to make breakfast. I have to go to a neighbor's to see if I can help some sick little boys."

"Yes, ma'am." His eyes wary, he stood by the bed. "You're gonna come back, aren't you? For sure?"

His doubting countenance was more than she could bear and she swiftly crossed to where he stood, bending to hug him tightly. "Of course I'm coming back, Kris. I love you too much to leave you, ever."

She dropped a kiss on his forehead and patted his shoulder. "Go to bed, now. Your sister is asleep al-ready."

Her bag was buried in the trunk, and she readied it

quickly, then snatched up her shawl as she left the room.

"Mr. Hanson will bring you back, Leah," Gar said as she came down the stairs. "I would go along, but I don't want to get Ruth out this time of night."

"Yes, that's fine." With barely a pause, she swept past Gar and left the house. Olaf Hanson waited to help her onto his wagon seat, and in moments they were rattling down the lane.

The Hanson place was several miles down the road, and Leah hunkered in the seat, thankful for the warmth of her shawl. She glanced at the worried man beside her, searching for words that might be consoling but could think of none. Summer complaint, if that were the reason for this sickness, was known to be devastating to the children. Babies were buried every year, their tiny bodies ravaged by the illness.

"They are sick, my boys. They throw up everything we try to give them, and then their stomachs hurt and they cramp up something terrible." Olaf turned to her. "Have you treated this before, Mrs. Lundstrom?"

"Yes, and it is always a problem keeping anything down. We'll see what we can do, Mr. Hanson. I have several things we can try." She stifled the urge to pat his hand. "How old are your boys?"

"Four and seven," he answered. "Just little tads."

"You only have two children?"

"No, there is a girl, less than a year old."

"Her mother is nursing her?" Leah asked, waiting for his nod. "That's good. We think this illness comes from cow's milk sometimes during the heat of summer."

"What can we do? Is the milk bad?"

Leah shook her head. "No. Just heat it almost to boiling for ten minutes or so, and it should be fine."

Olaf shook his head. "I never heard of this before. To think that my cows made my boys sick."

"This may not be that at all," Leah said quickly. "They may just have a stomach upset. We'll wait and see."

But her first glimpse of the ailing children was not what she had hoped for. Their eyes were dark circled, their skin dry, and they whimpered with pain, pulling their knees to their bellies.

Gerda Hanson bent over first one, then the other, cool cloths alternating with the fever-warmed towels she removed from their foreheads. "I am so glad you came," she said, her eyes filling with tears as Leah entered the room. "I have heard you are a healer, Mrs. Lundstrom. Even the people in town say you have magic in your hands."

Leah smiled, her hands lifting to deny that claim, and then, with rapid movements, she shed her shawl and opened her bag. The sour smell of soiled bedclothes piled next to the bed was evidence of recent purging. "Do you have hot water?" she asked.

"Yes, of course," Gerda answered. "How much do you need?"

"Enough to make tea from winterberry bark. I have some in my bag. It should stop the flux from their bowels and bring down the fever at the same time—if we can get them to keep it down."

And that would be the problem, she decided. With their stomachs so rent by vomiting already, they might not be able to retain anything. But even a few drops would help, and so they would try. She would have used the elderberry tea that had helped Eric Magnor in his illness, but these boys had already lost all their body moisture. They could not afford to sweat in copious amounts.

Gerda took the wrapped package of winterberry bark, and Leah was left with only the harried father by her side. "Perhaps we could remove the bedding and soak it outdoors," she said quietly, gesturing at the stained sheets on the floor. "We may need them clean in the morning."

"Yes, of course," Olaf said, hurrying to do her bidding.

"And I need a pan of cool water and a clean rag to cool their bodies and faces with," Leah said as Olaf left the room.

She took the towel from one child, swinging it through the air to cool its fibers, then replaced it gently. The red cheeks were hot to the touch, his lips dry and fever chapped. She repeated the procedure with the other boy, who watched her with listless eyes.

"Are you a lady doctor?" he asked in a weak whisper.

She shook her head. "No, just a lady who wants to help you feel better."

The night was long, with hours spent bathing and soothing, offering the cooling tea over and over again, then watching as fragile stomachs rejected it with little delay. And yet, before dawn, the terrible purging of their bowels ceased, and Leah leaned back in her chair beside the bed.

"I think they are holding down more than they are giving back," she said with a touch of humor. She closed her eyes for a moment. "You should go to bed for a while, Gerda. Your husband and I will watch."

Olaf stood and lifted his wife from the floor next to

the bed, where she had knelt for hours. "Come, let me help you," he said softly, his hands gentle as he led her to the door.

The woman looked back at Leah, a question alive in her eyes. "They will be all right now, I think," Leah said, only too aware of the worry that had kept Gerda awake for two days. "I'll stay for a while."

The room was quiet, the boys' breathing normal, their fevered flesh cool to the touch now. Leah swung a towel through the air again, cooling it, then washed both small faces, her hands passing over their skin tenderly.

The familiar draining of her strength was upon her, and she sat once more in the straight chair by the bed. Somehow, the hours spent with illness left her spent and weary, as if some part of herself was left behind when she walked from a sickroom.

Her mother had called it a healing touch that drew its strength from the healer. It bore a responsibility, this gift, she had told Leah. When God gives a talent, he expects it to be used. And on a night such as this one just past, she sometimes sensed the draining of her own strength in order to imbue another with her power, to mend their ills.

"I have coffee in the kitchen," Olaf Hanson offered from the doorway. "Would you like some, Mrs. Lundstrom?"

Leah shifted in the chair, nodding her head, and the man left quietly. It would refresh her, and if the boys continued to rest quietly, she would leave once the sun came up and Mr. Hanson had his chores done.

Gar would be waiting for her, his curiosity burgeoning after the words Eric had spoken with the whole town as his audience.

Such a statement for Eric to make. He'd obviously

wanted to protect the woman he had claimed as friend. But to tell such a tale was beyond belief. And yet...she yawned widely. It was more than she could comprehend right now. The questions pounding at her mind would have to wait.

"You need to sleep for a while," Gar said firmly, watching as Leah placed her bag back in the trunk where she stored it. "You haven't rested all night, have you?"

"No, I couldn't. They were so sick, Gar. And their poor mother was worn-out."

He watched her, feeling her weariness as his own. He had slept fitfully all night, reaching to touch her beside him in the bed, only to remain empty-handed. So used to having her beside him, he was aware of her absence in a way that frightened him. During the dark hours, he had come to realize how much this woman meant to him. Her very presence filled his home, her love overflowed on his children, and to him she gave the comfort of her body.

Perhaps the day would come when her eyes filled with love as she gazed upon him. Even now, as she rose from kneeling before her trunk, she looked at him with tenderness, her smile seeking his own. And he gave it, felt the corners of his mouth turn up as he lifted her to her feet before him.

"I would be in that bed with you, my wife, but the men would think I had taken leave of my senses if I lollygagged around instead of helped with the work."

"I'll dress Karen and feed her," Leah said. "Then maybe Ruth will come over and watch her for an hour or so while I catch up on my sleep." Her head found its place against the broad planes of his chest, and her sigh was deep.

"Are you so weary every time?" His arms enclosed her and he held her firmly, enfolding her with a gentle touch that yearned for more.

"When it happens this way, then I know what I have done has borne results. For some reason, my hands give comfort and healing, Gar. I cannot deny my help." She looked up at him. "I always fear the gift God gave might be taken from me if I do not use it well."

His mouth twisted in a stubborn moue. "I don't like to see you so weary, Leah. I will call Ruth over, of course. And I want you to stay in bed until dinnertime." His hands moved over her back, massaging and soothing. "I fear I must look forward to sharing my wife with others for all the years to come. You bring a high price."

Leah's eyelids were heavy as she attempted a smile. "Am I worth it, Gar Lundstrom? Do you gain enough for yourself from me?" Her arms slid up to circle his neck.

He was aroused, instantly, powerfully full and pulsing within the confines of his trousers, and he pressed the evidence of his need against the softness of her belly. "I will find some small amount of pleasure with you, I am sure," he whispered against the wisps of hair that fell against her forehead.

She swayed and he scooped her up, placing her on the bed, reaching to pull her boots from her feet. He tugged her stockings from their place and stripped them down her legs, then rubbed her feet, enclosing them within his big hands. She closed her eyes, a sigh expressing her pleasure at his touch, and he watched the

lines fade from her forehead as she relaxed against her
pillow.

His fingers were deft as he released the buttons of
her dress and he lifted her gently, removing the restric-
tive garment. "Now sleep. I will tend to Karen and walk
over to Ruth's with her. Kristofer will work with me."

Only the slight nod of her head told him she had
heard his words, and he bent to touch his lips against
hers, feeling the response she gave as her mouth moved
to accept his kiss.

"I love you, my wife." They were words he had not
spoken to Hulda, and yet they slipped with ease from
his mouth this morning as he gazed upon the weary
beauty of this woman he had taken into his home. She
had this way about her, he thought, straightening to
watch her for a moment.

She was kind and gentle with his children, making a
home for them and keeping them clean and well fed.
She was generous where it counted; for that, he was
thankful. And then there was the way she treated her
husband, with her sassy tongue and smart ways, giving
him no ease, always prodding him into line. A woman
who both intrigued and perplexed him yet added joy to
his home.

And now Eric Magnor had claimed her as his daughter.

The afternoon was short, it seemed to Leah. She'd
woken well after dinner at noon and found bits and
pieces to fill her stomach in the kitchen. Ruth had been
more than interested in the night's work, and Leah had
been patient with the questions that clamored for answers. It was difficult to relive such an ordeal, and she
became weary as she recalled the long midnight hours.

"I'm sorry I call upon you so often, Ruth," Leah said. "I told Gar you will tire of us and our claiming your time."

"No, I enjoy being here. Most of all, I appreciate the way this house has come to life since you came, Leah. Gar is a new man, and the children cleave to you, as if they had known you forever. I knew it would be so, when I sent the baby to town for you to keep."

Leah's brow raised in surprise. "You sent her? You told Gar to bring her to me?"

Ruth nodded. "I have feelings sometimes…about things that will happen. I don't talk about it much, but when it comes to be, I take a hand in things. As when Hulda died and you suffered such a harsh wounding for it."

"Does Gar know?"

Ruth shook her head. "Some things I do not tell everyone. But you understand. You have a gift also."

Leah settled back in the rocker and considered the woman who had become her friend over the past months. She had insisted that Leah only watch as supper was put together, and so she did.

Karen reached for her and snuggled close, as if she had missed her during the morning. It was good to be needed, in this way sometimes more than the other. Karen's need was so honest, so forthright, and Leah bowed to her small tantrums as the baby claimed her time.

Eric Magnor's buggy approached just before supper was ready to be put on the table, and Ruth met him on the porch. "Won't you come in? The men are still out back, but Leah is in the house."

His hat swept from his head in a polite gesture as Eric came in the door, his eyes seeking Leah with a swift glance. "I understand you have been up for many hours, tending the sick boys at Olaf Hanson's place. Are you well, Leah?"

She nodded, feeling her cheeks suffuse with color. "I am fine, Mr. Magnor. I dozed a little toward morning, then Ruth took over my chores here, and I slept for a while after I got home."

"And are the children recovering?" His gaze was shuttered as he spoke, his eyes touching her features, then finally meeting her own. "They did not carry a disease?"

She shook her head. "No, I doubt it. Just a touch of summer complaint, I think. Their mother will be more careful with the milk during the hot weather."

"Not the fever I suffered with, then?"

"No, theirs was a different complaint, Mr. Magnor."

"We need to speak of this, Leah. This 'Mr. Magnor' that you call me."

Her chin tilted, and she lifted her brow in silent query. "What would you have me call you? You told the whole town you are my father, but to me, you said nothing. If it were so, why didn't you mention it before?"

His face grew pale, and he lowered himself into a kitchen chair. "I have wanted to tell you for a long time, Leah."

"How long?"

"Longer than you can know, my child. Longer than all the years of my life, it seems sometimes. When you came back to town a couple of years ago, I watched you, and I wanted to go to you and let you know."

She felt her eyes dampen with tears, and she looked down at the child she held, unwilling to allow Eric to see such a sign of weakness. "Would it have been so hard? Didn't you think I'd want to know my father lived and breathed?''

He cleared his throat, and his voice caught, revealing the emotion he could not conceal. ''I didn't know where you were, for all those long years, Leah. I knew your mother bore me ill will, and I could not bring myself to cause her any more pain. I stayed out of your life, because it was her choice that I do so.''

''And it became your choice when I came back to Kirby Falls.'' Her whisper accused him and he bowed his head.

''I know...I know. I watched you, Leah. I told folks you were the daughter of a healer, and more than a few of them sought you out. I told the young men at my mill to give you their business when they needed their washing done.'' His words gained strength as he lifted his head and faced her.

''And then,'' he said firmly, ''I put my foolishness aside and determined to reveal myself to you. You were looking after Garlan's child, and I thought to relieve your shoulders of all they'd taken on. That was the day I heard you were to be married. So I watched and waited, and I knew Gar Lundstrom would be a fine husband for you.''

''Why didn't you tell me when I came to your home?'' The memory of that time was fresh in her mind, and she recalled all too vividly his words as he'd asked to be her friend. Her friend!

He waved his hand as if to dismiss her question. ''I was too ill at first, and then, when I spoke with you later and knew that you were a fine woman and a daughter to be proud of, I feared your contempt, because I had waited so long.''

Leah felt a presence behind her and glanced over her

shoulder. Gar stood just inches away and his big hands came down to rest against her shoulders. The warmth was welcome, and she attempted a smile. "I didn't hear you come in."

"I saw the buggy in the yard, and it was time for supper, anyway." He nodded to Eric. "I wondered when you would come."

Ruth stood by the stove, her hands deep in the pockets of her apron. "Would you like to stay for supper, Mr. Magnor? There is plenty. It is only the family for this meal."

"I'm not sure Leah considers me as such," Eric said with a meager smile.

"Of course you can eat with us," Leah said quickly. She rose from the chair and handed Karen to Gar. "I'll finish up, Ruth. You go now. Take enough for Benny's supper with you. It looks like you cooked plenty."

With a last wistful glance, as if she would rather stay than leave, Ruth pushed the screen door open, her hands full with two covered bowls. Kristofer held the door wide as she passed to the porch, and then made his way into the kitchen.

"I didn't hear the bell, Pa. Are we ready to eat?" His curious gaze touched upon Eric, then slid with apprehension over his father and Leah. "Are we having company?"

"Wash up, Kris," Leah said automatically, waving him toward the sink.

"I did already, at the pump." He sidled close to her. "Are you going away again, Miss Leah?"

His eyes met hers and she sensed his need. "Not today. Mr. Magnor just came out here to talk to me. He's going to eat with us. Now find another plate for him, and some silverware." Her hand touched his nape and she bent to whisper against his ear. "It's all right, Kris. Everything's fine."

He did as she bid, and in moments they were settled around the table, Karen on her father's lap. Gar spoke the words of thanksgiving over the meal, and for a few minutes, the three adults busied themselves with passing and serving the food.

"Your Ruth is a good cook," Eric said, admiring the ample fare. He took another bite of beef and tasted it with obvious relish. "If she uses your recipes, I must have them for my cook, Leah."

"I only fix what I learned from my mother," she said quietly. "You probably ate the same food when…" Her voice trailed off as Eric's fork clattered to his plate.

"I'm sorry." His eyes were pained as he met her gaze. "I didn't think of that. Of course. I didn't have a cook in those days, my dear."

"I think we need to speak of something else," Gar said quickly. "Leah, you and Eric might do better to spend some time alone after supper. Now, take the baby from me. She eats more willingly for you than her papa, I think."

Karen set up a clamor as Leah took her on her lap, apparently fearing that the steady stream of food from her father's fork was ceasing. Gar was capable of feeding the child, that was a fact. But giving Leah something to occupy her hands while he led the conversation onto a different track was Gar's aim, and for that she was thankful.

The talk was of the sawmill and the coming of new buildings in town. Eric spoke with respect to Gar, and Leah watched as her husband and father shared a conversation. Even that thought was difficult for her to fathom—her *father* was here in her home. He had claimed her as his child.

"Would you like to walk?" It seemed easier to stroll down the long lane than sit on the porch together. But even as they walked side by side beneath the tall maple trees, Leah felt distanced from the man who was her father.

"Why did my mother leave you?" It was what she had wanted to know for all her growing-up years, a question her mother had never answered, always sloughing off her need to know.

"She never told you?" Eric waited for her negative response, watching as her head shook once. "Then I must, I suppose. But, bear in mind, Leah, that I was a young man, and your mother was not always easy to live with." He looked at her quickly, coming to a halt beneath overhanging branches, where the twilight had already brought lengthening shadows.

"She had moods," Leah admitted. "She used to get angry easily, even with me. But…" Her mouth firmed as she tilted her chin and met his eyes with a challenging look. "I loved her, Mr. Magnor. She was good to me, and taught me all she knew, so that I would never be in need."

"She was a good mother," he admitted. "She did well with you, there's no denying that. But as a wife, she was not an easy woman."

"Gar says the same about me." Leah's laugh floated on the air as she recalled the words.

"You have an air of softness about you, daughter. Your mother—" He turned and walked on, and Leah kept pace. "She was more content away from me than in my company."

"So she left you?"

He shook his head. "She left because I made a terrible mistake, Leah. I have no excuse. I was wrong, and I knew it as soon as it happened. We had an argument and I stormed out of the house. And I met a woman."

The pause was long, Leah's mind rebelling at the thought she could not escape, until it was spoken, the words falling between them. "You were unfaithful."

He accepted her accusation with a nod. "Yes. Only the one time, but it was one too many. Or maybe she was looking for a reason to leave. I'll never know, will I?"

"Did you look for us?" Somehow, the idea that he had let them go, that he had washed his hands of wife and daughter and gone on with his life, was not to be borne.

"Yes, I knew that she took you to Minneapolis and you lived there for a couple of years with her sister. And then when I went there, prepared to beg for a chance to make things right, she was gone. Berta said your mother didn't want anything to do with me. She said Minna would never forgive me."

"I have an aunt Berta?" As she said the words, a picture of a fair, buxom woman came into Leah's mind. "Yes, I have. I remember a big house with a lot of men in it."

"She ran a boardinghouse in the city. Still does, I suppose."

"So you came back here and forgot about us," Leah said bluntly.

"I came back," he admitted. "But I never forgot. Yet, a man has pride, Leah, and I was blessed, or cursed, as the case may be, by more than my share."

He halted and turned to her, grasping her shoulders in his hands.

"I couldn't bring myself to come to you three years ago. But now, I want to help you, and I won't take no for an answer. What happened between your mother and me was another thing altogether. I can't change that, but I can do this for you."

"Help me?" For the long hours of this day, she had forgotten her situation, the sheriff and the detective from Chicago erased from her mind.

"I've already seen my lawyer, and he's made arrangements to check into the situation. We have a firm in Chicago investigating it for me." His touch was firm, lending her strength. It was a comfort, she found, and she allowed his hands to run the length of her arms, until their fingers clasped.

"I will accept your help," she told him. "For Gar, and for the children, if not for myself. I'm needed here, Mr. Magnor."

"Leah, Leah…" He shook his head. "Please can we find another name for you to use when you speak to me?"

"I don't know." There was too much to consider. She was weary beyond measure, her legs losing strength, her head drooping, so that she no longer looked at the man before her.

His sigh spoke of sadness, and she felt a pang that he should still suffer so for an indiscretion so many years past. "Come, I'll walk you back to the house," he said quietly, turning her around and releasing her hands.

They walked together, their steps in accord, and she

did not protest when he took her hand and tucked it inside his arm. It was good, she decided, to lean for just these few minutes. Good to feel the support of this man who had claimed her.

Chapter Fifteen

"We won't have to go to Minneapolis after all," Leah said, rising from the breakfast table and walking to the sink.

Gar grunted his disbelief at her announcement. "Come here. You cannot just tell me such a thing and then walk away." He pushed his plate aside and drank the last of his coffee, his eyes never leaving her. She had an uncanny way of provoking him with her remarks out of the blue. Like now, telling him that his plans for tomorrow were unnecessary. Especially when he had looked at the bedroom ceiling half the night, deciding how he could allot his workload for the men to accomplish during another two-day stretch.

She turned from the sink, wiping her hands on the front of her apron. "Eric Magnor says his lawyer has hired someone in Chicago to investigate." She had the grace to look abashed as he sucked in a great breath of air, and she plowed ahead before he could utter a word.

"I should have told you last night, but after I cleaned up the kitchen, it was late. And then when I put Karen to bed, I only meant to lie down for a few minutes."

He swallowed the ire he had been about to spew in

her direction. It stung that Eric Magnor should be the one to come to Leah's aid, and yet, the man had good reason. In any event, losing his temper would do no good, and so he summoned up a half smile.

"You didn't even wake up when I took your dress off. That's twice in one day I undressed you." He watched as a flush climbed her cheeks.

"I thought you might not mention it," she muttered.

"And why not? It was the most enjoyable thing I did yesterday."

She grimaced as she met his gaze. "It's been a hard time for you and the children, Gar. I'll be so glad when it's all over with. If everything goes well."

He tipped his chair back. "What did Eric say?"

"We talked about my mother, and about why she left here."

"Are you still angry with him?" Probably not, since the man seemed to do no wrong, Gar thought darkly.

Leah walked back to the table and leaned toward her husband, her hands fisted on either side of her empty plate. "I'm angry he waited for three years to claim me as his daughter. I'm angry he was able to sit back and watch me and never once offer me his friendship or his name in all that time."

Those words brought a moment of satisfaction to Gar's mind, much to his shame. So Eric Magnor would not get off scot-free, with Leah singing his praises.

"Why didn't you recognize his name right away? Did your mother not use her married name in Chicago?"

Leah shook her head. "She called herself Minna Polk, and I thought it was my father's name. But of course, it wasn't. And then when I began calling myself a widow, I took my mother's maiden name. I suppose that was how Mr. Magnor recognized me.''

There was deep sorrow in her look, as if she were wrapped in a blanket of misery, and Gar sighed for the pain she bore. ''I would make it right for you, wife, if I could. But only your father can take away the sadness you feel. You must find it in your heart to forgive him, or it will grow like a canker and poison your soul.''

''He didn't ask for my forgiveness, but I have given it already. I think,'' she said with a sigh, ''that, after all, I'm not so much angry as hurt.'' Her eyes filled with tears and she allowed them to fall unheeded. ''I have a father, Gar. I have an aunt in Minneapolis. There may be more family than that, for all I know. And here I've felt so alone all my life. Such a waste.''

She straightened and attempted a smile in his direction. ''Ah, well. There's no sense in mourning what might have been, is there? Now I have you, and the children, and a father who wants to help me.''

''I am more than willing to help you, too, Leah. But I'm smart enough to know that Eric has more influence than a farmer, and I care enough about you to let him take charge of this thing.''

He rose from the table and glanced out the door where his men were waiting for him. The horses were harnessed before the red wagon. ''I must tell Benny what has to be done today, Leah. Then I'm going to work with the three-year-olds for the next few hours.''

''Will the men be in for dinner?''

''I thought we could take it out to them,'' Gar said with a faint smile. ''The small sorrel is tame enough for you to ride, if you'd like to try her out.''

Her eyes lit up, and for a moment the pinched look she wore disappeared. ''I don't know if I can.'' She glanced out at the corral and then back at him. "But I'd like to try. If you think I can handle her."

He couldn't resist for another moment and his arms reached for her, his steps taking him to her side. She leaned against him and absorbed his warmth and the strength of his embrace. Her head tipped back and he took her mouth, his kiss a heated blend of lips and tongue.

"Just so, I would like to kiss you tonight, after dark, Leah. And much more." He swept one hand down her back and formed her to his body, taking ease in her soft curves. "I feel like a married man who has not yet had a honeymoon," he whispered, blending his breath with the puffs of air she expelled.

She attempted a laugh. "You are a married man who has had to take what he could get, piecemeal. I haven't been much of a wife to you, I'm afraid."

"You'll do, Leah mine. You'll do. What pleasure we have found together has only begun to whet my taste for you. Once our lives are sorted out and there is no more fear of your past in Chicago, we will settle down and be like old married folks."

Her smile was welcome, and he returned it as she swatted at his chest with the flat of her palm. "I'm an old lady already, Gar. Past my prime and long in the tooth."

"Ah, no," he whispered, bending to kiss her cheek. "You are a woman in the very prime of life, and your teeth are perfect."

She laughed aloud at his foolishness, and he was pleased. He'd banished the sadness she'd worn all morning and that was an accomplishment to be proud of.

"I'll be back in a couple of hours to get you. The

baby can ride in front of me on the horse and we'll carry the men's dinner in a couple of sacks behind your saddle.''

Her smile brightened even more. "It'll be like a picnic this time, Gar. I'll get out a quilt to take along. Will Kristofer ride with us?"

"No, he's with the men." Reminded of his duties, he released her and muttered beneath his breath. "You distract me, woman. I need to be about my work, and here I am smuckling in the kitchen with a beautiful woman."

She shooed him away, flapping her apron at him as he headed for the door. "Go on with you. I've got a mountain of work to do, Mr. Lundstrom."

"Papa!" Karen chortled from the high chair, waving a fistful of soggy bread in his direction.

He returned her wave and was gone, leaving the baby to turn her attention to Leah. "Mama!" she cried, holding up her arms to be taken.

"Yes, Mama, little girl. You are going down for a sleep, and I'm going to get busy. Your papa will be back in no time at all." Leah glanced out the door, her eyes fastened to the tall man who gave instructions with waves of his arms and pointing fingers as his men listened.

His shoulders were wide and his chest full and muscled. He was a man to be proud of, and he belonged to her, Leah Gunderson.

No, Leah Magnor. For the first time she tasted the sound of it on her tongue, and it was good. She belonged. Not only to the man she watched, the man who had made her Leah Lundstrom, but to the man who had sired her. She was the daughter of Eric Magnor, his flesh and blood.

If his influence proved to be as far-reaching as many suspected, her reputation might be restored. And if her story could somehow be proved to be the truth, Gar would harbor no doubts about her. And if wishes were horses...

The mare pranced nicely, tucking her chin against her chest, and Leah laughed aloud at her antics. She'd ridden her share of horses in Chicago, traveling to visit patients who lived outside the city. But nothing had been as much fun as this gleaming, sleek piece of horseflesh her husband had seated her upon today.

She rode astride, her skirts rucked up so that her ankles were well exposed, her dress catching the wind and blowing about as the mare broke into a canter. Gar's gaze settled on the length of limb beneath her billowing garment, and she laughed aloud. Her dignity was salvaged by the length of her drawers, and she felt warmed by his glances.

"You ride well," he said, coming alongside her. "It shows that you have done this before." Karen was tucked securely before him, his long arm clasping her firmly, and he slowed their pace as they spoke.

"But not with this much enjoyment," she told him. "I was always in a hurry, or all worn-out on my way home. This is like having a holiday, Gar. Thank you."

His smile widened into a grin, exposing his dimple, and she was gripped by an emotion foreign to her. Her regard for her husband went beyond admiration for his honesty and kindness, his stalwart strength and gentle demeanor.

This was different. As if a giant hand clasped her heart, as if her very being were held in limbo for these few seconds, she was enmeshed in the personhood of Garlan Lundstrom.

She held her breath. Indeed, she could have done nothing else, for her lungs seemed to be paralyzed. She blinked at his silhouette, that straight-nosed, firm-chinned image, his hair golden, falling almost to his shoulders.

Tears filled her eyes, not of sadness but of appreciation for this man. And more than that, she realized with a jolt. She loved him, with a depth of emotion she had never known before in any circumstance.

Not only because of his good looks or his kindness or the life he had offered her, but because of the spirit that dwelt within his magnificent frame. He represented all that was good and glorious in her life.

His touch contained magic, his hands bringing her pleasure untold. His eyes warmed her with their unspoken approval and his words multiplied that message as he whispered in the darkness of her beauty and womanly charms.

She was immersed in him, so closely drawn to his very being that surely he must sense the revelation she wallowed in. There were no words to describe it.

"There, see the men, just beyond that stand of trees?" Gar asked, pointing with the hand that held his reins.

Leah blinked at his words. So everyday, so mundane, so ordinary. She felt a smile move her lips, unbidden and unexpected, and then looked to where he directed. "Yes, I see them. Will we eat there with them?"

"Yah, but probably under the trees. The sun is hot today." He glanced at her and his eyes narrowed, as if he caught sight of something that held his attention.

"What? What is it?" she asked, looking down at herself, caught by the tension in his gaze.

He shook his head. "Nothing is wrong with you, just something I caught a glimpse of...." His lashes lowered as he turned to look down at Karen. "Perhaps I will have Benny take Karen back to Ruth after we eat. This has been a long ride for her, and she will need a nap."

"We won't be going back right away?"

"No. I thought we would ride to the end of my property, and I would show you all we own. There is a nice little stream, and we...well, I'll show you," he said, his smile secretive as he flashed it in her direction.

The little stream was indeed nice but not as little as Leah had expected. It gurgled over a bed of smooth pebbles, then formed a pool beneath the overhanging trees, finally washing over a tiny waterfall to continue on its way southward.

She was enchanted by the sheer beauty of the place. "Why haven't we come here before?" Her gaze took in the dappled sunlight on grass so lush and green it was almost too perfect to walk upon. The breeze carried the fragrance of wildflowers from the meadow beyond, and the rippling water offered a clean, fresh scent.

She bent to splash its cooling moisture against her face, her hands spread against her cheeks. On her knees, she glanced upward, where squirrels chattered in the limbs overhead.

"Listen to them." Her laughter was soft lest she disturb the tranquillity of this place, and Gar thought he had never seen such a lovely sight in his life.

He'd brought her here on a whim, a sudden vision filling his mind as they rode toward the men's workplace. She'd looked so gloriously alive in that moment, so concentrated on some wonderful thought that he'd wanted to be alone with her.

If he could only re-create that moment, surely she would tell him of her feelings. Certainly she would admit to him that he was important to her, that she yearned for him, at least a little.

"You are a beautiful woman." He dropped down to sit beside her and her eyes danced with delight, her smile flirting with him.

"Beautiful? I have hair of all different colors and my chin is stubborn, and my bosom is too big for the rest of me." Her eyes widened as she uttered the last of her denial, as if she had not meant to comment on the size of her figure.

"I think your bosom is just fine, my wife. The rest of your defects are bearable, even the feisty look you get when your chin pokes out at me."

"I didn't mean to say that," she whispered, and a rosy hue covered her cheeks.

"I'm glad you did. Now I can investigate the problem and see if our opinions are as different as I think."

"Investigate?"

"Yah. I brought the quilt along, Leah." As if he asked permission for what he had planned, he waited, watching as realization of his purpose dawned in her eyes.

"Out here?" Her gaze flitted about the glade.

"There is no one to see." His hand gestured at the pool, still and crystal clear, so that the sandy bottom seemed only inches away. "We could take off our clothes and swim a little."

She looked stricken. "I can't swim. I never learned." Peering at the water, she leaned closer. "It doesn't look deep enough to swim in, does it?"

"It's deeper than you think. But plenty shallow at the edge," he assured her quickly as she backed from the creek bank. He reached for her and drew her closer, his fingers moving to the buttons of her dress.

"I'll just help you a little, all right?" The buttons slid from their moorings readily, the dress being an old one, and he drew it from her body quickly, its folds settling around her hips. Beneath it her chemise was of finer stuff, a dainty batiste. His wife liked nice things next to her skin. And he could not help but admire the lush curves the garment covered.

"Will we go in the water with nothing on?" she asked, and he met her gaze.

His nod brought confusion to her features and he bent to brush his mouth against hers. "There will be only the two of us. You can pretend we are in the Garden of Eden. Before the fig leaves."

Her chuckle was contagious, and he laughed with her as she responded to his teasing. He eased her legs from beneath her and took her shoes and stockings off, his fingers deft but unhurried at their task. Not for the world would he put her off by rushing this thing.

She stood before him in moments, only her open chemise and her untied drawers covering her. Her fingers gripped the clothing that threatened to fall to the ground, and he allowed her their scant protection as he stripped quickly.

Beneath her round-eyed gaze, his manhood burgeoned, and lest he offend her, he turned, only to feel the touch of her hand on his arm.

"Don't hide yourself from me, my husband." She bathed him in her admiring gaze as he shifted his stance, and he felt his flesh respond as she moved her right hand, allowing her chemise to open wide. "I think you are wonderfully made, Mr. Lundstrom. Your body is a thing of beauty.''

It was too much, hearing her say such things to him, giving him such praise. He turned back to her and watched as the drawers she held as a shield dropped to the grass at her feet.

She shrugged her shoulders and the batiste garment fell from place, revealing the full curves of her breasts. Her arms were pale above the elbow, where she had rolled her sleeves while she worked in the garden. His gaze moved lower, skimming the rounding of her hips. Her hips…ah, such curving delights they promised. And beneath them, her legs beckoned, long and lithe, well muscled and rounded. And there, where they joined, honey-colored curls hid the treasure his body yearned to discover.

But it was not what he had planned. Not yet.

He took her hand and then watched as she stepped into the edge of the pool. She shivered and her smile was tentative. ''It's not as warm as I thought it would be.''

''It will seem warmer when you get into the water.'' Leading her with care to where the water deepened, he kept her close beside him, and then as they stepped past the shallow rim, he caught her by the waist and held her against himself. The bottom was smooth here, brushed clear of stones, and his feet were sure as he swirled her through the water.

Clinging to him, her eyes lit with pleasure as the current they created washed her body in small waves. He lowered her, dipping her almost to her neck and then bringing her once more against his chest. Her legs floated and she kicked them, wrapping them around his hips to anchor herself.

It was almost his undoing as his manhood surged against her, nudging the spot he yearned to occupy. "You will have me sooner than I had planned if you keep that up, sweetheart."

She stilled in his hands, blinking the water from her eyes. "You've never called me that before," she whispered.

"Haven't I? I should have. I've never had a sweetheart like you, Leah. You make my life so full, with every day a new beginning."

The words she had hoarded to herself over the past hour spilled from her lips, and her voice trembled as she spoke. "I love you, Gar. I didn't even realize it until earlier today, when we were riding out to meet the men. I almost told you then, but I wanted to wait until I could hold you and kiss you and let you know what I feel."

Tears moistened his eyes, and he was humbled by her admission. "You're my sweetheart, my love," he said, then managed to murmur the words he'd held inside, knowing he owed her this tribute. "You have become the woman of my heart, Leah."

His mouth curved in an embarrassed smile as he confessed his inadequacies. "I don't say these things well. Before this I've never told anyone that I love them. Not even the children. I always think they must know it. But for you, I must say the words aloud, so you know, so there will be no doubt in your mind that I love you."

Her arms circled his neck as she lifted her face for his kiss, and their mouths met in a gentle, pristine caress, brushing softly together as if for the first time.

"It is good," he whispered, "this being here, this telling of our love in this place."

"Will we come back?"

"Yah, we can do that. But it will never be as wonderful as it is today, sweetheart. This time is different, when we take new vows, when our marriage really begins."

"I think it needs to begin on the quilt, Gar, not in the water," she said, tilting her head to one side.

He nodded. "Maybe you are right. For this time, we will play the game your way."

"This time?"

"Yah, this time." His arms tightened around her and he stepped from the water, his great strength coming into play as they emerged dripping and shivering in the breeze.

"Come, I will warm you." The quilt was spread quickly and became a makeshift bed for their use.

She was more used to his love play now, and Gar felt her response as she moved against him, her arms eager, her legs twining with his. What he had planned was not to be, he soon discovered, for she nudged him to his back, and he acceded to her wishes, his curiosity piqued.

She rose over him, her breasts offered for his touch, and he accepted their bounty, his hands eager, his fingers agile. The warmth of her palms was against his sides, her eyes closing as she met his flesh with a firm grip. As if she measured him from armpits to thighs, she felt his muscles and the firm skin that covered them.

"You are so much a man," she said, her eyes opening as she whispered her praise. "I love to touch you, Gar."

Her body was slender atop him, her toes barely reaching his shinbones, and his hands were prisoners against her breasts as she lowered herself to kiss him. Lips damp and open, she captured him, tongue darting to meet his.

"Ah, Leah." It was a groan that carried her name, a sound of satisfaction he could not have contained had he wanted to. She gave him such pleasure, such joy, this woman he had married.

His hands crept from their hiding place and she lifted to allow it, watching him closely. His fingers slid along the backs of her thighs and between them, widening them until her knees pressed the quilt on either side of his body.

The gasp of delight she could not withhold brought a smile to his lips, and he tilted his hips upward until his manhood was nudging her tender flesh. "Let me in, sweetheart," he whispered, gritting his teeth against the pleasure of heat and the dampness of her desire.

She did as he asked, her movements eager, as if she were willing to learn all he might teach her. "I didn't know..." Her whisper broke off as he accomplished his goal, and he watched as she became one with him, as the enchantment of their joining added fresh, new beauty to the face above him.

His hands caressed her with care, bringing her to fulfillment, even as his body shifted beneath hers, seeking his own. And yet, it was not enough.

They entered the pool once more, silent in their joy, only their eyes communicating the pleasure they had found together. He bathed her with loving, gentle care, and she returned the favor, still endearingly awkward as she explored his body.

The sun moved in the afternoon sky, and the trees above dappled them with its filtered glow. "Let me teach you to swim," he told her, holding her on her stomach at the water's surface. Leah agreed, nodding dubiously. She kicked her legs and moved her arms as he instructed, then sank like a rock when he released her to paddle on her own and came up gasping.

"You did that on purpose!"

His laughter rang out as he wiped the hair from her face, bending to kiss her open mouth, because it was more than he could resist. "No, I thought you would be able to stay afloat, but I see you need more practice, little tadpole."

"You called me nicer names before," she said, her legs wrapping around his waist, her mouth pouting as she offered him her uptilted chin.

"Ah, let me see if I can remember any of them." His long legs carried them both toward the creek bank, and his muscles bunched and stretched as he carried her from the water.

"Now, if I put you here," he said, placing her in the center of the quilt. "And if I look you over real good, I may be able to come up with something better to call you."

His legs folded beneath him and he sat next to her, one long finger tracing the shape of her breast. "Let's see…I could say some words you might not understand." He grinned and nudged the crest of her breast, causing it to pucker even more.

"'Lovely' comes to mind, as does 'pretty,' my little dove." He enclosed the fullness of her in his palm and his eyes closed. "You are pretty, you know. Every part of you."

"I think you embarrass me."

"I don't want to do that, Leah. I just want to let you know all the things I think of when I look at you." His gaze traveled her length, and his heart wrenched within him. "You are a bride to be proud of. I am only sorry I waited so long to tell you that."

Her eyes caressed him, learning his body in another way. "I love you, Gar Lundstrom," she whispered, blinking rapidly so as not to allow her tears to overflow. "I'm so happy you brought me here today."

"You will be even happier by the time we leave," he promised. "I told you we would make good memories here. Now we will make you feel even more beautiful than before. I think it is time to work on 'wonderful.'"

It was as he had said it would be.

Wonderful.

Chapter Sixteen

"Sheriff Anderson says you're to come to town, Miss Leah." Lars Nielsen stood below the back porch and delivered his message through the screen door. "He waved me down and told me to let you know first thing when I got here."

Leah's mouth was dry as she responded to the broad-shouldered young man. Her nod acknowledged his words and she smiled at him through the wire mesh. "Thank you, Lars."

He eyed her soberly. "I'm sure things are going to work out just fine, ma'am. Sheriff didn't look down in the dumps or anything."

"Will you tell Gar to come to the house? He's in the corral by the stable." And probably already redolent with the scent of the three-year-olds. His first hour with them every morning was spent with a brush and currycomb, as he gained their affection.

"I'll tell him." Lars's smile was strained as he turned away, leading his horse to the stable.

Leah returned to her ironing board. The shirt she'd half finished ironing would do for Gar to wear on the trip to town. Swapping irons, she tested the sole plate with a damp finger and bent over the board.

In less time than it took to smooth the wrinkles from the second sleeve and the right front side, Gar was stomping his feet on the porch. She ran the point of the iron around each button and turned to hang the shirt over a chair back, lifting her eyes to meet his gaze. He dwarfed the doorway, one hand holding his boots.

"I must have picked up a bushel of dirt in the corral, and most of it is on the porch," he said with a grin.

"Better there than on the kitchen floor," she told him, aware that he deliberately lightened the mood with his levity. "I'll sweep the porch while you change your shirt and wash up."

"Lars is harnessing the mare to the buggy for me." Gar deposited his boots outside the open door. "I'll only be a minute, if you'll dip me some warm water in the basin."

Leah looked down at her dress, freshly donned this morning. It was clean and unwrinkled, and would do for this occasion. Certainly she was not setting out to impress anyone with fancy clothing. "I'll go as I am," she told Gar, opening the reservoir on the side of the cookstove to dip water. Her saucepan brimming, she walked to the sink and filled the basin, then found a clean cloth for him to use.

In minutes, she had hidden the ironing board behind the pantry door and swept off the back porch. The broom set aside, she watched as Gar ran long fingers through his dampened hair. He rubbed quickly with the towel, over his arms and shoulders, then approached her.

"I just ironed your blue shirt." She held it before her, almost as a shield, lest she cast it aside and claim him, holding his beautiful form against herself. "Turn around," she said, unwilling to meet his gaze, for surely her need of him was there to be seen. He did as she bade him, and she lifted the garment over his shoulders as he slid his arms into place. Her fingers smoothed the yoke seam in the back, and he stilled, his muscles tensing beneath her touch.

"Leah." Her name was soft on his lips as he turned to her, his arms enclosing her with a tenderness she had learned to anticipate. Her head leaned just above his heart and she closed her eyes. "I love you, my wife. All will be well."

"I am afraid." The words slipped out before she could swallow them and his arms tightened, as if he would take her fear and share it. She inhaled the fresh scent of his skin, and knew a moment's peace. Ah, yes. This, the warmth of his caring, was what she needed for now.

His voice rumbled against her ear. "Eric knows what he is doing, Leah. Do you think he has claimed his daughter, only to lose her so soon?"

"Mr. Taylor has money and influence also, Gar. And it is still only my word against his wife's."

"Ah, but you are the one telling the truth, and that is what will make the difference." His mouth touched her forehead, his head bending low, and she felt encompassed by his strength and the tenderness of his touch.

A surge of hope lightened her mood and she tilted her head, offering her lips for his taking. "Kiss me properly, Mr. Lundstrom." Her words teased him, and she met his smile with her own.

"Improperly is more like it, wife." He hesitated, then dropped a quick peck on her mouth and drew back. "I hear Karen clamoring for attention. Is she going with us?''

Leah nodded. ''I don't want to ask Ruth to watch her again so soon.''

He nodded his agreement. ''Benny will keep Kristofer here for us. Do you have dinner started?''

Leah motioned at the oven. ''I just put two chickens in to roast. Ruth will have to come and finish up.''

''I think she is coming now,'' Gar said, bending his head to look out the door. ''Go get the baby, and I'll tell Ruth what to do.''

But Ruth would not hear of it, and with her usual competence, she took command, and Leah was left empty-handed in the buggy. From the doorway, Karen was held high in the woman's arms to wave goodbye.

''I don't know what we'd do without her,'' Leah said, looking back until the hood of the buggy hid the baby from sight.

''Ruth cares for you, and she loves the children,'' Gar said, reaching to take Leah's hand. ''She thought you had enough on your plate this morning without tending to the baby, too. Now,'' he said, squeezing her fingers, ''tell me, what do you think of your new mare?''

''My new mare?'' She smiled at his attempt to distract her thoughts.

''Yah, the one you rode yesterday. Do you like her?''

''She's mine?'' He was serious. ''You're not going to sell her?''

Gar shook his head. ''Not if you promise to ride her at least once a week and take good care of her.''

''Can we afford not to sell her? I don't want to take from your income, Gar. But,'' she hastened to add, ''I haven't enjoyed anything so much in a long time, as I did the ride we took yesterday.''

"Was it the ride you enjoyed or the swimming lesson?" he asked with a teasing glance.

She felt a flush paint her cheeks, and she wiggled her fingers within his grip. "I think you enjoy poking fun at me."

His grin widened and he chuckled aloud. "There is that, too, sweetheart."

Her eyes widened as she caught his meaning and her free hand reached to swat at his shoulder. And then their eyes met and within the pale blue depths, she saw a deep welling of love emerge. It enveloped her, filling her with a sense of well-being she could barely contain.

"No matter what happens," she said softly, "I want you to know that you have given me happiness beyond my fondest hopes, Garlan Lundstrom." Her head pressed against his shoulder and his arm slipped behind her to circle her waist, enclosing her in the bittersweet silence of her thoughts.

The meeting was to be in the big house at the far end of town, according to Morgan Anderson. The sheriff rode his horse beside the Lundstroms' buggy, and Eric Magnor's stable man took charge with ease as the late arrivals joined the group already assembled.

Sarah Perkins opened the door as they climbed the front steps, her smile welcoming Leah. "Mr. Magnor is waiting in the parlor," she said formally.

"Thank you, Mrs. Perkins," Leah answered, her own smile trembling as she walked past the housekeeper toward the wide parlor doors. They opened as she approached, and Eric greeted her, both hands extended.

She could only offer her own, and was pleased by the warmth he lent to her chilly fingers. He smiled at her, a reassuring tilt of his lips that strengthened her own feeble attempt.

"Come in, Leah. You too, Garlan, and Sheriff Anderson. I'm not sure you know this gentleman, Leah," Eric said, leading her to a spare, well-dressed figure next to the fireplace. "Tobias Dunbar owns the newspaper, and hides in his office more often than not." The words were laced with humor and the newspaperman bowed his head, nodding his agreement.

"I fear Mr. Magnor is right. My hands are forever stained with ink and my shirts blackened with newsprint. My wife has given up on keeping them clean."

"Tobias is brother to Hobart Dunbar, Leah," Gar put in.

Leah offered a nod. "I am pleased to meet you, sir." Although what the man had to offer to this meeting was quite beyond her comprehension. Still Eric did nothing without a reason, of that she was certain.

He was in a good humor, she thought, and that in itself was enough to encourage her. Gar and the newspaperman were involved in a discussion regarding the new school to be built at the edge of town, and Leah lent her full regard to Eric.

"What is happening today, Mr. Magnor? Why did you send for me?" He still had a grip on her hand and it only increased as he frowned at her words.

"Leah, Leah. When will you bring yourself to forget this Mr. Magnor you seem determined to use when you speak to me? Can you say the word, *father?* Or is it too foreign to your tongue?"

"I've never called anyone by that name," she said haltingly. "But, I'd like to try…Father."

His eyes glistened, and he blinked, turning his head away for a moment, then cleared his throat. "I thank you for that, my daughter. It is something I have long waited to hear from your lips.'' He smiled fully then, his gaze fixed on her face. ''You called me Papa when you were a baby, but I suppose you are too old for that.''

''Leah?'' Gar called her name and she responded quickly, turning to him as he nodded his head at the doorway, then strode to her side.

''Ah...my visitor has joined us,'' Eric said, striding from Leah's side to offer his hand to the man who waited just inside the wide parlor doors. ''My lawyer's trip to Chicago was successful, Leah. Mr. Waterford, come in and greet my daughter, will you?''

A distinguished-looking gentleman entered, nodded a greeting at the men assembled there, then concentrated his attention on Leah. ''You are Leah Gunderson?'' he asked. ''I represent Sylvester Taylor.''

She had been caught in a trap of some sort. Leah felt the floor roll beneath her feet, saw flashes of light where none had been only seconds past, and in a daze, felt Gar's hands on her waist as he drew her to sit in a chair.

''That was badly done, Magnor,'' Gar said bluntly, an edge of anger tinging his words.

''Don't jump to conclusions, Garlan,'' Eric said quickly. ''Leah will understand in just a moment.''

Eric turned to the visitor. ''Let's not drag this out. Please take a chair and explain to Leah why you are here.''

Choosing a chair directly across from Leah, the gentleman met her gaze. ''My client has asked me to bring you a letter and to personally extend his apologies to you for the problems he has caused.''

''Your client? Mr. Taylor sent that to me?'' Leah

eyed the envelope Mr. Waterford extended in her direction as if it were a venomous snake.

Gar took it from Mr. Waterford's hand and opened it quickly. "May I read it to you, Leah?"

She nodded, aware that she could not have held the paper in her limp hands if she tried.

Gar began, a snort of disbelief marring the simple elegance of the greeting.

My dear lady,

My apologies cannot suffice for the problems I have caused you over the past weeks. I fear that I was swayed by the love I felt for my wife, a love that was sadly misplaced.

I have found that you were innocent of any wrongdoing on that night over four years ago. I should have recognized the truth then, but my grief overcame my good sense, I fear.

When I sent out in search of you earlier this year, it was at the insistence of my wife, Mabelle, who had become with child once more. She blamed you for the state of her nervous condition and I sought to pacify her.

However, when my lawyer contacted the physician who delivered her first infant, he found him to be reluctant to speak of that occasion, until it was explained that our second child had also died at birth, and that Mabelle was once again in the family way. At that time, the doctor signed an affidavit, swearing that he had suspected her of suffocating the infant he delivered, and was greatly concerned over her mental state.

Not wanting a repeat of such a sad occasion to mar his records, he then refused to attend her second delivery. Thus I sought out your services. It was his recommendation that I cease any pursuit of you, and concentrate instead on my wife's mental condition.

Mrs. Taylor has become totally overwrought by a state of nerves that caused a hysterical outbreak. She has since been committed to an institution here in Chicago, and is under constant watch, since she is threatening the life of the child she carries.

Although you behaved in a competent manner, and performed your services well, I can only blame my grief at my child's death for my treatment of you that night. I beg your forgiveness for the trouble I have caused, and ask your tolerance for my wife's state of mind.

Gar crumpled the letter in his hand, his oath loud in the silence that followed the reading of Sylvester Taylor's missive.

"Such a coward this man is! Why didn't he come himself and admit his wrongdoing to Leah? Instead he sends a messenger. At least he had the sense to keep his private detective in Chicago where he belongs."

Leah felt born anew and drew a deep breath, allowing only a small sound to escape her lips, when the urge to cry aloud was almost beyond her control. "It's all right, Gar. Cowardly or not, he told the truth, and that's what counts.

"I knew I had delivered a live boy to Mabelle Taylor that night. I knew he was healthy when I left the room. But the woman refused to touch the boy, and I feared she would not be a good mother."

Mr. Waterford nodded. "The woman is mad. Sylvester is beside himself."

"This is where Tobias comes in," Eric said, stepping forward to stand before Leah. "We have heard the letter and Mr. Waterford has told me all the facts. Now we will set about vindicating you in the eyes of the people here, Leah."

"Tobias? Mr. Dunbar will do that? What do you expect of him?" Leah asked.

"He runs the newspaper, Leah. He has influence, and an audience neither you nor I can match. He has agreed to run a front-page article that will clear your name and put to rest the gossip in town."

Leah was silent, considering the offer. "I don't know that I want to dredge it all up again." Her gaze sought Gar, and he moved from behind her chair to bend one knee to the floor before her.

His hands gripped hers and his lips curved with encouragement. "You must do as you see fit, sweetheart. Mr. Taylor has cleared you. Mr. Waterford is willing to swear to the truth of the matter. Now Tobias has offered to let the whole town know how it has come about, so you can be free."

"I'm really cleared of the charges?" Leah looked this time to the sheriff, and Morgan Anderson nodded emphatically.

"You betcha, ma'am. And for what it's worth, I'd take old Toby up on the offer. Clear the slate and start fresh."

"All right."

The room was silent for a moment, and then Eric slid his hands into his pockets and rocked back on his heels. "All right? Just like that?"

Leah nodded. "If it's the thing to do, then we'll do it. I need to get home and take care of my family and put this whole thing behind me." Her eyes met Gar's and she smiled widely, even though her lips quivered with the effort.

Tobias smoothed the brim of his hat and held it before him, his grin eager. "I'll need to have all the facts in order. This will be the biggest story of the year, doing an exposé on a big-city crime. Begging your pardon, sir," he added, nodding at Mr. Waterford.

The lawyer rose from his chair. "I'll do whatever I can to mend Mrs. Gunderson's reputation."

"Leah is Mrs. Lundstrom now," Eric said.

"I suppose I was not aware of that fact, sir," Mr. Waterford said.

"It has only recently come about," Eric answered.

Tobias appeared anxious to take his leave, shaking hands with Eric, as he escorted the lawyer to the door. His face was beaming as Gar handed him the crumpled letter, and his fingers carefully began smoothing the wrinkles from it. Probably pleased as punch as he considered the story he would be setting into print before the day was over, Leah thought.

As she would be when Brian Havelock's efforts to mar her good name were proved to be small potatoes.

"We must go home," Gar said, his fingers touching Leah's shoulder.

"Yes." She watched as the gentlemen left the room, Eric escorting his guests to the door. And then he returned and held out his arms in Leah's direction.

"Will you allow me to hug my daughter, Gar?" he asked.

With a nudge of his fingers, Gar gave his assent and Leah's feet fairly flew as she crossed the room. Her arms wrapped firmly about Eric's neck, and her face was buried against his shoulder.

"Thank you, Father. Thank you, Papa."

She lifted her head and touched her lips to his cheek, her mouth dampened by the glistening trail of tears he made no attempt to conceal.

"No, I actually did little, daughter. Circumstances worked out as they did without much effort on my part at the end." He cleared his throat, as if emotion surged within him. "I must thank you, Leah. For allowing me into your life. For forgiving my stiff-necked pride in waiting so long to make my peace with you. For giving me a fine son-in-law."

He looked at Gar over her shoulder. "Will we be friends, Lundstrom?"

Gar joined them and Leah stepped back, allowing him into the circle. "I have admired you for a long time, Eric. Now, it seems I must have you as part of my family. I suppose you will even want to be a grandfather to our children."

"Are there to be more than just the two?" Eric asked hopefully, his eyes falling to Leah's slender waist.

"One of these days, I hope," Gar answered.

"I wouldn't be a bit surprised," Leah said softly.

Two pair of masculine eyes met, bewilderment clashing with hope as Leah bit at her bottom lip and waited for their reaction.

"Are you telling us something, Leah?" Gar asked. His hands gripped her forearms and he turned her to face him.

"It cannot be," Eric put in. "Just look at her. Slim as a reed."

"I am looking." And he was, his gaze scanning her from head to toe, as if he searched out evidence that would be solid proof of her enigmatic claim.

"What do you mean, Leah? Are you in the family way? Are you sure?"

She nodded. "As sure as I can be, for now." Her gaze moved from one to the other of these men who had so rapidly become important in her life. Eric, her father, the man who had used his influence to clear her name, no matter the cost. And then Gar...husband and champion, so eager to defend her, so ready to give her all a woman could want in life.

"I'm so fortunate to have both of you," she whispered, looking from one to the other, as if her eyes could not take in the riches she beheld. "I can't believe that just a few months ago, I didn't know about any of this. I didn't know how happy I could be."

"Maybe she'd better sit down," Eric said over her head, seeking Gar's opinion.

"Yah, she's had quite a morning. She should probably put her feet up and rest awhile."

With one man on either side, Leah was led back to the sofa and settled with a footstool beneath her feet. In moments, Sarah Perkins had placed a cup of tea in her hands and was coaxing her with an assortment of muffins, fresh from the oven.

"If I'd known how lovely it would be to be pampered, I'd have told you about the baby yesterday, Gar," she said between bites.

"You knew yesterday?" She watched as his features took on a look of concentration, following his thoughts as he remembered the day just past, when they had spent the afternoon at the stream.

He frowned at her. "Maybe swimming was not a good idea."

"You went swimming?" Eric asked, his eyes lighting as he watched a flush climb Gar's cheeks.

"Yah, and she rode horseback, too."

"I'm healthy," Leah said sharply. "Being in the family way is not a disease, gentlemen."

Eric approached the sofa, then settled beside his daughter. "I can't tell you how happy you've made me, Leah. When I look at you, I can see the best of your mother shining from your eyes. You're not as sharp-tongued as she was—"

Gar hooted, almost choking on the mouthful of tea he had just sipped from his cup. "Just you wait, Eric Magnor, till you hear her in action."

"No, Leah is softer than Minna, more womanly perhaps. And yet, in some ways, in her looks, I think, she is much like her mother. She has the same honey-streaked hair, and her eyes are blue like the cornflowers in the spring."

Gar nodded his agreement. "Yah, she is womanly. And her hair is pretty enough."

Leah plopped her cup on the table beside her. "Well, if the two of you are done with dissecting me, I'm ready to call a halt to the pampering and head for home."

Eric laughed, the sound joyous, and Gar's chuckle blended in. "She is persnickety, this woman of mine," Gar said. "First she wants to be spoiled, then she tires of it. There is no pleasing her."

"I trust you with the job, nevertheless," Eric told him, his hand extended.

Gar met it with his own, and Leah watched as the two men shook solemnly, their faces working with emotion. "Go on with you now," Eric said after a moment. "I have work to do at the mill sometime today. Now that my personal affairs are in order, I can get back to business."

The buggy swept through town, curious eyes watching as Leah was drawn closely to her husband's side.

"By our next trip in, they will all know everything about me," she said. "I'm not sure I like the idea of my life being spread out on the front page."

"It will be well. And in another month or two, you'll be the talk of the town again, when you walk into the store with your dress too tight to fasten around your waist."

"My dresses have wide seams, Mr. Lundstrom, and I intend to let them out right away. I can wear a coat when I go to town, once the weather is colder. No one needs to know until it's time for the baby to come."

He was silent, and she looked up at him. "You're frowning. Don't you like my idea?"

He shook his head. "No, I can't say that I do. I think I want everyone to know. Right away, in fact. Maybe I'll just lean out of the buggy and tell people as we go."

Leah watched in horror as he tipped his hat to Lula Dunbar, who stood before the hotel doors, and her hand rose to cover his mouth.

"Don't you dare!"

He chuckled against her palm, and Leah nodded, smiling at Lula as the woman gaped at the couple who frolicked so foolishly right in the middle of main street.

"I was only going to wish the lady a good day," Gar said when Leah moved her hand.

She looked at him, doubt alive in her glance. "I somehow don't trust you, Mr. Lundstrom. You are not acting like yourself today."

"And is that so bad? That I should begin to be giddy in my old age?"

"How giddy are you planning on being?"

His eyes lit, and his mouth twitched with a mischievous grin. "I will let you know later on, wife. I have the rest of the day to plan for our celebration."

Chapter Seventeen

"I have asked Ruth to come and help you a few days a week." Gar made his announcement in his usual fashion, as a fact already in place.

Leah held her tongue, aware that he was ready for an argument from her. She was wrapped in his arms, resting against his warmth. Her nightgown was still on the floor where he had tossed it earlier, and she was contemplating sleeping without it.

"Do you think I need help?" she asked finally, conscious of his tension as he awaited her reply.

"Yah, you work too hard."

"Not any harder than any other farm wife," she said firmly.

"Well, I see you sewing at night, when you should be finished with your work for the day. And you've been looking tired in the afternoon lately." He caught his breath and rose above her, turning her to her back.

"Is that because of the baby? Are you feeling bad already? Are you sick in the mornings, and do not tell me?" His voice was beyond anxious, she thought. He was worried, and she would not have it be so.

Her fingers pressed against his lips and she shook her

head. "No, I'm fine, honestly. I haven't gotten sick at all, and I think it's the usual thing to be sleepy sometimes."

In the pale moonlight his face was drawn, his brow furrowed, a reminder to her of his worried look when first they had met. "I don't want you to overdo, like Hulda did," he said softly. "I fear for you, Leah. I could not bear to lose you."

Her hand slid to the back of his head, and the silken strands of gold covered her fingers. "I will not die. I am young and healthy."

"And that's another thing. You are thirty years old. Is that beyond the age to be bearing a first child? Should we go to Minneapolis to see a doctor and make sure you are all right?"

"I am sure," she told him, pulling his head to her, touching his lips in a tender joining of flesh. "I will have Ruth to help me if it'll make you feel better. And if I think there are any problems, I'll go to see a doctor. I want this baby probably more than you do, Gar. I want to give you a child."

"This is important to women, isn't it? This bearing a child."

"I have brought more babies into the world than you know. And each of them is a miracle, especially Karen, who struggled so hard to be born."

"I can only remember the blood and the terrible pain that Hulda went through," Gar said, bending his head to rest on her breast.

Her fingers remained tangled in his hair and she held him firmly in place. He would be secure only when the baby had arrived, when he had watched a child born without the agony of death to ruin the joy.

"Watch and see," she whispered, her fingers caressing his head. "Everything will be fine."

The year had been a good one, the wheat harvest being the talk of the town, and the final cutting of hay was in the barn. The last of autumn's color rustled underfoot before October was over, and the sky wore the gray of early winter.

As if a signal had been given by the powers that be, a wind from the north had brought a heavy frost during the night, and Gar stomped his feet at the door before coming into the kitchen.

"It looks like snow on my boots," he said, rubbing his hands together for warmth. "I'll be surprised if we don't get a good covering before the week is over, maybe today even. It is November, after all."

"Well, I'm glad you left your mess outside where it belongs," Leah told him, turning from the stove.

His grin was wide. "Yah, I learned my lesson good, wife." He wiped the soles again on the rug and then approached her. His hand covered the front of her apron, cupping the slight weight of her pregnancy, and his mouth nuzzled at the curve of her neck.

"How is my little one this morning?"

"Me?" she teased with a lifted brow. "Or the baby?" She turned her head, and his mouth brushed her cheek, his whisper for her ears alone.

"I know how you are, sweetheart. I found out all your secrets just an hour ago. It is the baby I ask after."

Her eyes closed and she leaned back against his solid frame. "Will I ever stop this blushing when you say such things to me?"

He wrapped both arms around her, his hands meeting

beneath the curve of her belly. "I hope not. It is a part of you I love, this womanly thing you do."

"Gar? When we go to town, how will I buy flannel from the store without someone knowing what I need it for?"

"You're not ready yet to tell the ladies? I am surprised you can keep a secret so well."

"I won't be able to much longer. I'm bigger already than I thought I would be. And I haven't even felt life yet."

"Life? When the baby moves?"

She nodded. "It should be soon, within a few weeks anyway. Maybe I'll be ready to tell my news then."

"Do you fear for the child, that you hesitate to speak of it with the ladies?"

She dropped her stirring spoon on the edge of the stove and turned in his arms, framing his face with her palms. "I have no fear for the baby, Gar. And yet, it's almost as if it's too good to be true, that I should be carrying a child. Maybe I'm afraid to speak of it until it moves inside of me and I can feel it."

He turned his face against her hand until his mouth touched the center of her palm. His lips brushed the sensitive flesh there and he closed his eyes, whispering his fear.

"I will not rest easy until the babe is in my hands, and I see you are well. I live with a dread in my soul, sweetheart, that something will happen to you."

She ached for his need, her heart yearning to comfort him but knowing her words would only fall on arid ground. What Gar needed, she could not provide, not yet anyway. Only when her own time had come would he realize the beauty of childbirth and the joy of pain that accomplishes a purpose.

"When the baby moves, perhaps then you will believe, Gar. When you see that I am healthy, even if I sleep sometimes when Karen naps. For now, I can only tell you that in all the babies I have seen born, Karen's birth was the most difficult."

"Be patient, my wife. Just love me and understand that I am a mere man." His attempt at humor brought a smile to her lips and she turned his face toward her.

"You did not seem so this morning, barely an hour ago," she said, repeating his words.

"I did not hurt you? I was not too hasty?" He sought reassurance and she gave it willingly.

"You have never hurt me, Gar. Not even the first time when you were more than hasty." Her smile was teasing, her words languid. "You are always what I need."

His body relaxed and she felt it mold more closely to hers as he grinned his pleasure at her words.

"Will we go to town then this morning? Perhaps, before we get there, you can think of a need for the flannel that does not involve diapers and baby things."

She shrugged. "If they begin to wonder, I won't mind I suppose. It's been awhile since we gave the town anything to talk about."

"Was the newspaper article so painful for you?"

She thought about the great to-do that had followed Tobias Dunbar's front-page rebuttal of the charges brought against her. He had quoted Sylvester Taylor's letter, the lawyer's statement, and even parts of the doctor's statement regarding Mabelle's babies and the deaths they suffered.

All in all, Leah had come out smelling like a rose, and the chilly atmosphere surrounding her presence had melted like the first snowfall when the sun comes out.

She was once more the obvious favorite of the ladies in town, only Eva Landers, Mrs. Thorwald and Bonnie Nielsen never wavering in their high regard of her.

"Folks are fickle creatures, Gar. They listen to gossip and tut-tut over the offender, and then when the truth is presented, they flow in the other direction. It is a rare person who can be a true friend even when things look bad."

"You saved the newspaper. I saw it on the closet shelf, Leah."

She nodded. "I thought I might need to get it out once in a while and read all the wonderful things Tobias wrote about me."

"I will tell you all the wonderful things you need to hear, sweetheart." He bent to kiss her and then peered over her shoulder at the stove. "I think the oatmeal is making bigger bubbles than it should. Do you suppose it is done?"

She pushed at his chest. "If you want breakfast before we get to town, you'd better go sit down at the table. And call Kristofer down from his room."

"Is Karen awake yet?" he asked, turning to the sink to wash his hands. "Should I go and get her?"

"No, just eat first and I'll tend to her. I want to leave early for town. I think you may be right. It looks like snow clouds coming in from the west."

"How many yards do you want, Leah?" Bonnie's eyes were shining with curiosity as she wielded her shears, cutting the brown paper that wrapped the bolt of cream-colored outing flannel.

"I think twenty will be fine," Leah told her, busying herself with cards of buttons and spools of thread.

"What will you do with so much?" Bonnie asked,

unrolling the soft fabric on the counter, then measuring it against a yardstick nailed to the edge.

"I have a lot of sewing to do," Leah said, smiling vaguely as she sorted out several cards of tiny pearl buttons.

"Seven…eight…I suppose Karen has outgrown all of her gowns. Nine…ten…" Bonnie counted beneath her breath as she measured, and Leah nodded her agreement.

Already her mind could envision small sacques and kimonos, and a pile of diapers, neatly hemmed.

"Will you need more later on? Perhaps some in colors? We are getting in a new shipment in a couple of weeks." Bonnie's queries were gathering interested looks from others in the store and Leah shrugged, hoping to avert questions she didn't want to answer.

"Maybe so, Bonnie. How about blue, for Kristofer's nightshirts?" And for gowns for the boy she fervently hoped even now was cradled within her body.

"Flannel, Leah?" Eva's voice was a whisper in her ear, and she turned her head to face her friend.

"I'd think you had more to worry about than my shopping list, Eva."

"You are all shiny around the edges, my friend. You may fool Bonnie, but I know the look you wear."

Leah's eyes filled and she felt tears balance precariously on her lashes then fall to her cheeks. "Does it really show?"

Eva's gaze scanned the length of Leah's coat. "Not so's you could notice, but I'll bet if you unbuttoned that thing, I'd have plenty to look at."

"I didn't want to tell yet," Leah whispered.

Eva hugged her briefly, whispering in her ear. "Then don't. No one needs to know. But I'm happy for you,

Leah. Gar is a good man, and a baby of your own is just what you need.''

Bonnie cleared her throat, her arms stretched wide to fold the voluminous length of flannel. "Will this be all, Leah? Do you want those buttons you set aside?''

"Yes." Leah turned back to the counter. "That and the list of groceries I gave you will do for today.''

From the front of the store, a bell rang as Gar pushed the door open. "Leah, it is snowing hard already. We need to load the wagon and head for home.''

His arms full with Karen, he headed for his wife, transferring the baby to her as he picked up bundles from the counter. "I'll come back for the rest of it,'' he told Bonnie, and then ushered Leah to the door.

It was snowing in earnest. She brushed it from the wagon seat and climbed up hurriedly, opening her coat to wrap its warmth around Karen during the ride home, watching as Gar came from the store with the rest of her groceries. Once beside her, he picked up the reins, flicking them in the air. The wagon lurched into motion as the team bent into their traces and set off for home.

"Did Bonnie pick and poke at you when you bought your flannel?'' Gar asked with a grin. "I'll bet you didn't get away with it, did you?''

Leah smiled smugly. "She thought it was for new sleeping gowns for Karen and I let her think so. But Eva knew. She said I was shiny around the edges, Gar. What do you suppose she meant?''

"You look like a happy woman, sweetheart. And your skin glows like there is a light inside of you shining through.'' He reached to tug her scarf over the front of her head, brushing the snow from her hair. "You are so pretty, with your bright blue eyes and that little straight nose of yours.''

"I'm glad you think so," she told him, sliding closer to him. Karen babbled, groping with one hand to snatch at the snow flakes that fell in profusion. She lifted her fist to her mouth to lick at the white crystals and laughed with delight.

"Her first snow," Gar said, enjoying his daughter's pleasure. His heart was warmed by the sight of Leah with his daughter. Even more so, it brought him joy to know that beneath the bulky coat, another child of his loins was sheltered from the storm, and Leah was more than able to love all of his children.

"We must hurry, Leah. Hold tight to the baby." So saying, he urged the team into a fast trot. The wagon lurched through the ruts in the road, heading into the increasingly heavy snowfall.

· They had come within a mile of the long lane that led to the farmhouse when Gar muttered beneath his breath and pointed ahead, toward the side of the road.

"What is it?" Leah leaned forward, the better to see, barely able to make out a wagon. It was pulled onto the grass, with a huddled figure on the seat.

Gar drew his team to a halt in the road and slid down quickly, his long strides carrying him to where the snow-covered woman sat. "Are you all right? Are you alone here?"

She lifted her head, a dazed expression on her features. "My husband has gone on ahead, trying to find help, sir. The harness has broken, and he rode the horse."

Gar's words were impatient as he reached up to help the woman down from the high seat. "Why didn't he take you along with him? This is no place for you to be, all alone, and in the snow yet."

And then he halted, aware for the first time that the

bulky coat the woman wore could not conceal the size of her abdomen. "You are going to have a child," he said, surprise coating his words. "Will it be soon?" His hands were gentle as he lifted her down, then held her before him as she winced and bent over.

"Very soon, I fear. Stephen wanted me to ride on the back of the horse with him, but I couldn't. I told him I'd be all right." She looked up apologetically. "I didn't let him know I was having pains already."

He led her carefully toward his wagon, pausing by the front wheel to look up at his wife. "Leah, shall I put this young lady in the back, or will she be all right on the seat with us? She is about to have a child, I think."

Leah turned toward the back, scrambling over the seat into the wagon bed, Karen clutched to her bosom. "Bring her back here, Gar. She may be better off where she can lean on the side boards." He did as he was told, more than willing to turn the responsibility over to Leah's capable hands.

Already the sweat was gathering on his back as he considered what the next hours might bring. Leah might need his help, and he shuddered at the picture his mind brought forth. Perhaps he would be in luck and Ruth could give a hand, and he could heat water and make tea and stay in the kitchen.

That thought cheered him.

The Warshems' house was dark, and Gar barely slowed the team as they passed the driveway. "It looks like Ruth is not home," he said over his shoulder.

"No," Leah answered. "She's gone to her sister's place to help out with the new baby."

"I'd hoped she could help out with this new baby,"

Gar muttered, slapping the reins against the broad backs of his team.

"We'll do just fine," Leah said soothingly, her voice taking on a new sound, as if she spoke a language only she and the young woman she tended could understand. As if she were readying herself for the task to come.

Just ahead was the lane and Gar turned the horses carefully, lest the wagon slide on the wet snow and land in the ditch. The lights from the barn shone like a beacon through the heavy snowfall, and he welcomed the signs of life there. Benny stood before the big doors, watching as the wagon drew up.

"Yah, Gar. It is good to see you here. Did you find a woman by the side of the road? Her husband just rode up, and we were getting ready to hitch up the buggy."

"I have her here," Gar said. "But I think we need to get her in the house right away, unless we want to have a baby born in the barn."

Knowing they were out of the storm, and shelter was nearby allowed him to breathe easier. The sight of a young man hurrying toward the wagon, anxious eyes searching the bed where the two women huddled together, cheered him even more. Leah could find her helper here, with the father of this baby-to-be.

"Is Kristofer with you?" Gar asked Benny.

"Yah, he is feeding the chickens. Maybe he is done already and gone to the house. I told him I would be right up to light a lamp for him."

Behind Gar, voices blended in a hushed garble of sound. Leah's calm words directed the young man, and within moments, he half carried his wife to the house, Leah holding Karen against her shoulder and bending into the wind.

"I'll go lend a hand, Benny, if you put the horse and wagon up for me."

At the other man's nod, Gar gathered up Leah's bundles from the back and headed for the house. He would tend to the children and find some supper for everyone, while Leah took care of everything else.

But it was not to be. Full darkness fell, and still the baby had not announced its arrival. From the bedroom at the top of the stairs, silence prevailed. Even when he took the children to their beds and tucked them in, the door remained closed. Only Leah's occasional forays for hot water and linens from the big closet broke the silence.

And then the laboring woman's husband, Stephen, stumbled down the stairway, making his way into the kitchen. "I can't stand to see her in pain," he moaned, slumping into a chair and bending his head. "Your wife said for you to come up and lend a hand."

"Me?" Gar rose swiftly, almost spilling the cup of coffee he had been nursing. "What can I do?"

Stephen's eyes were red rimmed as he met Gar's frantic gaze. "Probably more than me. Sharon is so young. I shouldn't have brought her to town today. We live almost ten miles farther north of here, on the old Burgess place, and I knew she was about ready to have the baby. But she wanted to see the doctor and make sure everything was all right, so I gave in and drove her to his house."

"You went to Dr. Swenson's place?" Gar asked with a frown. "He isn't fit to deliver a child."

Stephen shrugged dejectedly. "We didn't know that. We've lived here just a couple of months, and he was the only doctor we heard of."

Gar drew himself up and headed for the doorway.

"Well, you're in luck tonight. You ended up in the right place. My wife will take care of everything."

His courage lasted until he opened the bedroom door and stepped inside. This wasn't Hulda, he told himself sternly. And yet the woman who labored uttered the same low groans he had heard from Hulda's lips.

And like that last time, Leah was here, calm and sure in her movements. From the side of the bed, she bent low over the woman's side, her hands moving at some mysterious task. He heard soft murmurings that lent encouragement even as they seemed to soothe the young mother's fears.

"Gar, come and help me," Leah said, casting him a glance that moved him from the doorway. "Shut that door and come sit by Sharon's head. I need you to lift her up and let her rest against your chest while she pushes her baby into my hands."

Gar felt a wave of heat pass over his body, and he shook his head. "Maybe I'm not the one who should be doing this," he said bluntly. "Stephen…"

"I have no time to argue," Leah told him sharply. "Hold Sharon up and help her now."

There was nothing for it but to do as Leah said, and Gar inhaled deeply as he lifted the slender form, sliding behind her as he gathered her against himself. She was like a child herself, so small, so fragile feeling. And yet she was about to bear this babe that even now tore her body with the pain of its arrival.

"Take a deep breath, Sharon," Leah said, bending to reach beneath the sheet draped loosely over the girl's distended belly. "Push hard, now."

In his arms, Gar felt the young body tense as she strained, her head leaning back against his shoulder, her teeth gritted and hands clenching in the bedding. How could this thing be? How could Leah expect him to view such a sight, knowing how harsh his memories were?

"Again, Sharon. Another deep breath now, and push down hard."

As if she were in another world, Leah concentrated on the young mother. She bent low, her hands busy at the task of bringing life into the world, her words soothing and encouraging.

And then the air was split by a gurgling sound that escalated quickly into a shrill cry.

"Oh...oh...my baby!" Sharon's cry was triumphant as her body relaxed against Gar, her hands reaching toward the red, squalling child that Leah held in the air.

"Lay her down now, Gar, and come help me cut the cord," Leah told him.

He hesitated for a moment. Then, sparing a smile of encouragement at the young woman who watched while tears flowed silently down her face, he did as his wife asked.

"What do you need?"

"Take him from me," Leah instructed, her hands gentle as she placed the wiggling, slippery little bundle in his grasp. Like a greased pig at the fair, he thought, his smile widening as he gazed into the red, wrinkled face. And then the mouth closed, the crying ceasing for a moment, and blue eyes looked at him, blinking at the light and squinting a bit.

"It's a boy," Gar said, watching as a small stream of urine bathed the sleeve of his shirt. He laughed aloud. "Will you look at what this rascal's done to me?"

"Don't move now, just hold still!" Leah said, glancing up at him. In her hand was a small pair of scissors, just inches from the glistening creamy cord she was about to cut. The blades sliced the air halfway between two pieces of string she had tied in place. The cord fell victim to their sharp edges, and the babe was freed from his mother's body.

Miracle of miracles. The wonder of birth. His eyes misty, Gar turned to show the plump little fellow to his mother. "Look here what you have," he said, holding the baby close to her side, placing the tiny creature on the sheet.

"Oh, just look how beautiful he is!" Her words filled with wonder, the young woman adored her child, an inner glow lighting her countenance. It was there, that same look of beauty he'd seen earlier today when he'd looked upon Leah.

In the depths of his being his heart lifted with hope. A hope he had discovered here, in this room, as he had become a partner with the woman he had married. Here, where they had joined forces in a new, more glorious venture than any before.

Sharon seemed invigorated, even though her body was weary from the labor she'd expended on this birthing process. It was not always so, he remembered. Poor Hulda had always been so worn, so weary from her labors, that even after Kristofer was born, she lay in a stupor for days. His heart ached for the waste of it.

It would be different next spring, when Leah's time came to pass. Even as Sharon had strained and labored, so would Leah. And she had been right. It didn't have to be a time of horror, of death and defeat.

The sound of women's laughter rose to his ears. "What a beautiful child," Leah said softly.

"Let me have him," Sharon whispered, her eyes yearning as she held out her arms.

"I'll wipe him off first and wrap him so he won't

take a chill,'' Leah told her. In moments she had wrung out a cloth in warm water and tended the child, gently swaddling him in a flannel square before she placed him in his mother's arms.

Gar stood behind her and enclosed her in his embrace, his arms tender as he coaxed her to lean on him. ''Your back must be tired from bending,'' he said quietly.

''It doesn't matter,'' she said, dismissing his worry, her look joyous as she watched the scene before her. ''When a baby is born, nothing matters but the mother and child. I will take time to be tired tomorrow. Tonight, I am excited and happy.''

''And so am I,'' he said. ''So am I.''

The house was settled and quiet, Stephen sleeping on the floor beside the bed where Sharon's body sought a well-deserved rest. Leah had tried to persuade him to stretch out beside his wife, but he feared disturbing her sleep and was soon burrowed beneath a quilt, his weariness taking hold.

In the big room at the corner of the house, Leah stretched and yawned, then laughed aloud at the sheer joy of the evening's work.

''I can't sleep.''

''You should be worn-out, sweetheart. I think you labored almost as much as the mother.''

''Wasn't it wonderful?'' She leaned over him, and Gar captured her in his embrace.

''You were wonderful,'' he said firmly. ''You know so much, and you are so sure, so capable.''

''It doesn't always happen so quickly, so easily,'' she told him. ''But it's always a joy, watching new life, and seeing the mother greet her child.''

"You love what you do, don't you?"

She nodded. "Yes. It fills a need in me, as if it is something I was born to accomplish, Gar. I know you won't always appreciate it when I am called upon, but you will maybe understand better now."

"Yes, I think so," he agreed. "And we are going to talk to the men in town. Maybe we can find a doctor who is young enough to work hard and not expect to be rich overnight. The town needs a man who is dependable. Berg Swenson cannot be trusted."

"That would be good. With the mill running so well, more folks are moving here, Bonnie says." She rested her head on his chest and her fingers teased the soft curls there.

"I would not mind having a doctor come when I have our child, Gar."

He shuddered beneath her touch. "I should hope so. If you think I will do the honors, you are wrong, my little wife. I am good at heating water and making tea. In fact, I will even hold your hands and hold you up so you can push when the time comes. But don't expect me to be the one on the business end of things."

The winter was harsh, snow drifting against the house and covering the windows during February. Gar dug deep trenches through it to the barn and, for a week, they were snowed in.

Then the pale sunlight began its task of melting the piles of snow, and by March the ground appeared in patches. A late storm early in April provided a heavy blanket of white, and for a few days, Leah watched anxiously as she listened to the signs her body whispered.

Then, as if God had lifted his hands and taken from

the land its burden of winter, the sun rose high in the sky and the soft breezes dried the earth. Trilliums bloomed beneath the trees at the edge of the woods, and lily of the valley scented the air on the west side of the back porch.

It was like a gift from heaven, Leah thought, this perfect spring day that drew her from the house to pace from porch to barn. Benny listened as she told him what must be done, shaking his head at her foolishness, but to no avail.

This thing had nudged at her mind for weeks, and she had set it as a goal, planning for the first really warm, dry day, when the time would be right to accomplish it.

Kristofer lent a hand, carrying out the small valise she needed, opening it and exclaiming over the vari-colored small jars of paint and the assortment of brushes.

"I never knew you had paints, Mama," he said, his eyes wide with wonder. "Can I really help?"

She nodded, settling on a keg Benny had provided for her use. He'd wiped the wooden surface clean for her, muttering beneath his breath. Then he stood by to watch as the first flower took form against the red enamel paint.

In an hour, she had finished one side, her brush dabbing with freehand abandon, as she splashed color the entire length of the wagon. Kristofer moved along behind her, helping shove the keg to a new place each time she had reached as far as she could.

His brush was covered with green paint and he drew leaves such as had never graced a stem. But to Leah, they were beautiful, just the right size and shape for the tulips and daisies and nondescript blossoms she created with loving care.

She stood back a few steps, one hand at her back, the child she carried beneath her apron strangely quiet, and surveyed the panorama of spring she had brought into being.

"It's lovely," Ruth said from behind her. "But don't you think you'd better save the rest of it for another time? I have the bed ready for you, Leah."

Leah's smile flashed as her eyes met those of her friend. "I just needed to have it begun. One day in a week or so Kris and I will do the rest. When we take the baby to town for the first time, it will be in a splendid wagon with flowers telling of our celebration."

"Shall I call Garlan from the stable?" Benny asked, his gaze worried as he watched Leah's face tilt to the sky, her hands weighing the load of her pregnancy. She closed her eyes and drew deep breaths as the muscles tightened, their job well under way.

"Yes, it will be time soon, I think," she told him. "You will have to care for the new foal when it arrives, I fear, Benny. Gar will be tending a birth of his own doing."

And he did. Before the sun set, Garlan Lundstrom held his newborn son in his big farmer's hands, unashamed tears streaking his face as he examined the child he had helped to deliver.

"He will be called Eric," he said, turning to Leah.

"Ah, once again you are arrogant and bossy," she whispered, weary from her laboring.

"Will you agree that it is a fine name for our son?"

She nodded. "A wonderful name. Now, wrap him

well first, then go and show him to his grandpapa and his brother and sister.''

''I love you, Mrs. Lundstrom.'' The words came easily to him, it seemed, and they fell like a benediction on Leah's ears.

He held the child to his chest and bent over the bed, his mouth a tender caress against her forehead.

''I love you, my Leah. You are the woman of my heart.''

* * * * *

"Don't miss this, it's a keeper!"
—**Muriel Jensen**

"Entertaining, exciting and
utterly enticing!"
—**Susan Mallery**

"Engaging, sexy…a fun-filled romp."
—**Vicki Lewis Thompson**

See what all your favorite authors
are talking about.

Coming October 1999 to a retail store near you.

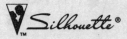

HARLEQUIN®
*M*akes any time special ™

WIN A DREAM

In celebration of Harlequin®'s golden anniversary

Enter to win a *dream!* You could win:

- A luxurious trip for two to **The Renaissance Cottonwoods Resort** in Scottsdale, Arizona, or

- A bouquet of flowers once a week for a year from **FTD**, or

- A $500 shopping spree, or

- A fabulous bath & body gift basket, including **K-tel**'s *Candlelight and Romance* 5-CD set.

Look for **WIN A DREAM** flash on specially marked Harlequin® titles by Penny Jordan, Dallas Schulze, Anne Stuart and Kristine Rolofson in October 1999*.

FTD · RENAISSANCE. COTTONWOODS RESORT · K·TEL
SCOTTSDALE, ARIZONA

COMING NEXT MONTH FROM

HARLEQUIN HISTORICALS